One Sister's Song

A Novel by Karen Carter

Pearl Street Publishing
Denver, CO

Library of Congress Cataloging-in-Publication Data

Carter, Karen, 1966
One sister's song

ISBN 0-9673867-3-X
LCCN 2002104090

Pearl Street Publishing, LLC, Denver, CO 80210
www.pearlstreetpublishing.com
10 9 8 7 6 5 4 3 2 1

To Mom and Dad, for their limitless faith and love,
and to Patrick, for every encouraging word.

Chapter One

A tangle of dead weeds smothered the ground in front of the aged gray farmhouse on Adams Street. Among them, overgrown shrubs stretched to scratch thick windows, brush against faded bricks, and caress a small stone slab near the porch, a slab which yielded the date 1848 upon close inspection.

Her sneakered feet planted in crimson leaves, gloved fists at her hips, Audrey Conarroe surveyed the scene.

"This is going to be hell on my manicure."

She gazed down the street, her eyes following the telephone lines that beckoned, as though tracing for her a certain escape. The autumnal sights and smells of her hometown failed to soothe her: the sweet scent of ripe leaves and grass mingled on the ground, the shocks of orange and red that graced sugar maples all around.

Audrey took in her familiar surroundings quickly and just as quickly dismissed them. She missed her old weekend rituals—her Saturday morning workout at a local health club, where she'd exercise early, in peace; her Sunday stroll to a coffee shop, where she'd read the paper outside in good weather and watch the world pass by.

Never had yard work been a part of her weekends, until now. She knelt to her task, pulling at plants in no special order, certain she appeared conspicuous as ever.

Audrey lived uneasily in her dead sister's house. She and her thirteen-year-old nephew, Julian, hardly belonged in this neighborhood of older—and white—families. In February, after she returned to western New York to live with Julian following his mother's death, Audrey was perturbed, but hardly surprised, when no neighbors stopped by to offer help, or sympathy.

She knew her sister, Laura, had been warned before buying the house that others considered it an eyesore and wanted it torn down. "You have to appreciate their frame of reference," her real estate agent had said, citing the effect the house had on neighborhood property values. "They hope no one buys it, so the lot can be cleared and a new house built there."

Laura told Audrey she'd described herself as a native who'd rather go into debt to own a piece of the town's history than stand by and see it destroyed. "I told him that was *my* frame of reference," she said, winking at her younger sister.

Despite this stance, Audrey had suspected Laura would still make friends with her neighbors, although most had probably never lived near a black family before. A charismatic young nurse, Laura had always drawn people to her easily with her broad, welcoming smile, her mahogany eyes, her soothing ways.

Audrey sat back on her heels, more memories of Laura threatening to overwhelm her. Laura, brown image of their white mother, favorite of their black father. As a girl, her auburn waves pulled back in a thick ponytail, her knee socks always neat, she'd represented an ideal her darker, clumsier little sister assumed would always lie out of reach.

How heavy that telephone receiver had weighed in Audrey's palm, a mere hour after her sister's death, as she'd fought encroaching images of Laura in a friend's crumpled car, a car that had slammed into a tree along an icy back road. Now, after eight months of mourning, she still found it difficult to think of her sister in the past tense, and almost expected to see Laura come out the front door of her house, beaming in her white uniform, ready for work.

Audrey raised her chin as though shaking hair from her face, an odd habit due to her closely cropped curls. As she squinted at a patch of peeling paint near a window, thin lines along her forehead, around her eyes, and at the corners of her mouth aged her for a moment well beyond her thirty-four years.

A cold breeze tossed leaves toward the house, carrying her gaze up to the darkening sky. Audrey reminded herself it was only October, yet feared the possibility of an early snow. She recalled a kitchen window view she'd had years ago after a bitter storm, when Laura's backyard had been transformed into a skating rink, the trees' iced limbs bent into low, frozen canopies. "It's always freezing here," she said, dreading another long winter's sure coming.

A car with a loud stereo rumbled by, slowed at the corner, then squealed its tires as it fishtailed toward town. Audrey thought of the New Bilford town center, where local kids hung out. Within those blocks of dilapidated diners and faded storefronts were three traffic circles designed to add novelty to the center. Instead, the circles forced drivers to pause and yield in an erratic, uncertain flow. When the flow accelerated, the circles swung cars in every direction, catapulting some people out of town while ensnaring others within.

She thought of Julian raking in the backyard. Her nephew liked to go to the town center and wanted to spend more time there, eating pizza with friends and watching girls. But Audrey rarely let him go out unsupervised and insisted he stay home after school, though she worried about the two hours he spent alone each weekday afternoon. At least her current temp assignment was in a nearby office park, so she was always home by five-fifteen.

Audrey continued to weed, a tight ache spreading from her lower back up her spine, toward her stiff shoulders. She rolled her head to stretch her neck, pausing to inspect the front of the house. Every aspect of the farmhouse seemed to be deteriorating, and all she saw when she looked at it was another expense she couldn't afford.

Eight months of searching for a hotel management position had yielded one promising interview, at the upscale Moon Resort east of Rochester, nearly an hour away. Audrey planned to wait one more week before calling to see if they'd made a decision, vowing if she didn't get this job, it was time to leave New Bilford. She could go anywhere, she reasoned. At least anywhere with a decent hotel.

The pain in her back worsened.

Of course, moving wouldn't be all that simple, not with Julian involved. Julian. He needed new winter clothes, as she did: sweaters, boots, a heavy coat. But Audrey hesitated to spend her savings on such items, especially with her sister's rusty car in need of more work, and the house's roof and furnace about to collapse. She'd considered wearing Laura's things, but could not.

Life had been so easy only a few months ago. She picked up a trowel and dug further into the dirt, daydreaming about her tidy apartment and easy commute on the D.C. Metro to her office in a four-star hotel. She had worked long hours to become a supervisor there, never regretting the time she put in, or her decision to move out of her dingy hometown and into a major city.

3

Moving back to Washington was not an option. She could afford to live there alone, but not with a teenager, not in a decent apartment near good schools. Nevertheless, for a few months she'd tried to keep in touch with former coworkers, people she'd considered friends, until her phone calls were no longer returned.

She stabbed at a long root.

Weeds. She'd read once that the mourning band in a man's hat or on a shirtsleeve was called a weed, and found that funny, for some reason. Weeds. Weeds for Laura, her dead sister. Weeds for Julian, her sister's orphaned son. Weeds for herself, for the person she used to be.

The sun ducked behind thickening clouds as another breeze chilled Audrey's bare neck. From across the street she heard a scraping that sent more shivers down her spine. An elderly neighbor sat in all types of weather on his squeaky front porch swing, piercing the street's relative quiet with unnerving screeches from the swing's rusted hinges. Audrey imagined the man, whom she knew only as Benton from the name on his curbside mailbox, peered all day from behind his heavy drapes. At any sign of activity, he ventured out to his swing, his worn face set in a disapproving frown.

Another scraping sound grew louder. Audrey glanced toward the corner of the house, listening for hints of her nephew's discontent as he pounded a metal rake along the side lawn.

"You're going to break it, Julian," she grumbled. She thought of Laura doing yard work, sinking her fingers deep in the soil. Laura joking with Julian, rather than nagging at him all the time. Laura urging Julian to walk, reading to Julian, consoling Julian. How can I do as well? Audrey wondered. Why in the world did she leave him with me?

She wiped the back of her wrist across her forehead and cursed Julian's absent father. "He deserves better," she told the weeds.

The scraping sounds—and the boy's silence—grated on her nerves. She picked up a hand rake and switched her weight onto her feet to relieve her aching knees, then attacked the weeds with new fervor.

"I hate this." She fell into a steady rhythm of scraping with the hand rake and plunging the trowel beneath plants to dislodge them. "I hate this town," scrape, scrape, "I hate this

4

house," plunge, plunge, "and I hate . . ." with both hands she yanked at a shock of crab grass, "these damn weeds!"

Audrey pulled, but lost her grip as well as her balance. She reached back to stop her fall—and spotted Julian at the corner of the house.

"Aunt Audrey!"

"What? What!" She jumped up, straining to see past the shadows that hid the boy's brown face.

"Mom's bulbs!" Julian stepped toward her, gesturing toward the ground. "You're digging up Mom's bulbs."

Audrey glanced from him to the weeds, then back. She'd noted many times the features her nephew had inherited from his mother: his high cheekbones and dimpled chin, his almond-shaped eyes with lush, curled lashes. Now Julian's eyes flashed with anger and the stern set of his mouth and jaw reminded her of someone else entirely: herself.

"What bulbs?" She brushed grass and leaves off her sweatpants. "There's nothing here but weeds."

Julian dropped the rake and scanned the ground, his forehead lined with concern. "I know she planted some out here—"

"Last fall?"

"Yeah, but they never came up."

Audrey shook her head. "This dirt is mostly clay, though. Nothing would grow here but weeds."

"Then why did she plant them?"

"Are you sure she did?"

Julian grimaced.

"Maybe she planted them somewhere else," Audrey suggested. "I'll be careful, okay? And we could always plant new ones. Spring flowers would be nice for the people who buy the house from us."

Julian moved away and picked up his rake while his aunt scrutinized the smoldering sky.

"I think we started a little late," she said, trying not to sound as weary as she felt. "Tell me when you're hungry and we'll finish up tomorrow."

Julian yanked the rake down the lawn.

"Take it easy, would you, muscle man?" Audrey called.

Her nephew continued his affront on the leaves as though determined to pound them into oblivion.

"If it'll make you feel better," she said, approaching him,

"we could buy some new bulbs tomorrow, or—"

"I don't care about the stupid bulbs," Julian snapped, still raking.

"Then what's the problem?" Audrey gritted her teeth, forcing herself to stay calm.

"You know," Julian mumbled.

"What?"

"You know!"

"No, I don't know!"

Julian looked up. "You didn't ask me if I wanted to move."

"What? We talked about this, don't you remember? We decided—"

"*You* decided."

Audrey groaned. "C'mon, you think this is easy? Selling your mother's house? This place is falling apart, and I don't know how to take care of it. I can't worry about roof repairs or the furnace blowing up, or—"

"Mom would know how to take care of everything."

"Yes." Audrey lowered her voice. "You're right. We were different in a lot of ways." She fidgeted with her gloves. "I think I've had enough for today," she said. "Let's take everything back to the shed."

Julian stood with both hands folded over the end of his rake handle. "I just don't understand why we have to move."

"Look." Audrey took a deep breath. "We need to sell, and if I can't find a job we'll have to move somewhere else, probably out of state, so—"

Her nephew groaned. "This is so lame. I never have a say in anything. Anything!" He slammed the rake's teeth into the leaves at his feet and dragged hard, pulling up grass as he scattered the pile.

Audrey cringed, wondering what their neighbor thought of this scene. When she noticed a white Crown Victoria had slowed in front of their house, she touched her nephew's arm. "Take it easy, would you?"

The huge car paused, then entered their gravel driveway. Audrey walked over and assessed the driver as he opened his window: a middle-aged man, gray at the temples, with a pink face and blue eyes, a cigar perched in the hand he held at the steering wheel.

She forced a smile.

6

"Hello," he said in a raspy voice. "Is the owner of this house in?"

"I'm the owner," Audrey said. "Can I help you?"

A woman passenger leaned to look past the driver, her face tanned and crinkled, her smile pursed and brief.

"Oh," the man said. "Yes. The McClatchy agency said this house will be on the market soon, and—"

"Excuse me?" Audrey heard Julian approach.

The stranger appeared confused. "They, uh, told me this house would be for sale soon. Is that correct?"

Julian stepped closer. "What!"

Audrey signaled him to be quiet. "I did speak with them," she said, "but we're still deciding whether to sell."

"Oh. They seemed pretty definite and—but, well, never mind. Sorry to bother you."

The woman leaned past him again. "We adore quaint old farmhouses," she said. "Don't you?"

Her husband chuckled. "My wife and I, we grew up in homes like this in Pennsylvania. This one sure is a beauty."

Audrey followed his gaze to the gray, wide front that loomed before them. She took in the cramped rickety porch, the dingy six-paned windows, the aged tin roof, wondering that this house appealed to anyone, or ever had.

Julian shifted beside her.

"Please," she said, "check back with us in a few weeks, maybe around the holidays."

The man laughed. "Hard to believe they'll be here soon, and the snow with 'em. Supposed to be another doozy of a winter, like last year, remember? When it snowed on Halloween? Or was that '92?"

Audrey tried to smile. "I just moved back to the area, so—"

"It was last year, dear," the woman said. "We had six-foot snow banks by Christmas. Taller than me, they were."

"I remember that," Julian said. "The furnace broke twice last winter. The house was freezing!"

"Julian," Audrey growled.

The man chuckled once more and put his car into reverse. "Well, old homes take a lot of special care, don't they?"

Julian shrugged. "I just hope the roof doesn't leak again if we get lots of snow."

"Julian!"

"Well, we'll be in touch." The stranger smiled, backed his car out of the driveway, and waved—abruptly—before heading down the street.

The sky had darkened further and the wind picked up, scattering leaves across the lawn while blowing bits of dirt through the air. Audrey removed her gloves to rub her eyes. "Real smooth, Nephew," she said, blinking to clear her vision. "Real smooth."

Julian stormed over to retrieve his rake. "All I know," he said, stomping toward the house, the wind whipping his words toward his aunt as he passed, "is I wish Grandma moved in with me, instead."

Audrey threw her gloves to the ground. "Fine, Julian!" she yelled. "Fine!"

Her nephew disappeared around the corner of the house, leaving Audrey alone in the front yard, her jaw clenched, the steady drone of her neighbor's porch swing ringing in her ears. Her pulse pounded at her temple, a sure sign of another headache. She picked up her gloves, cursing her sister's house as she glared up at it.

"Now I know," she said, "now I know I've had enough."

Chapter Two

That night in her room, the narrow guest room where she'd always slept while visiting, Audrey dreamed of a running figure—some sort of fugitive—who had haunted her dreams since Laura's death. Bent beneath a wide-brimmed straw hat, the fugitive appeared boyish and slight in baggy pants and a loose tunic. Bare ankles showed above makeshift shoes as the figure stumbled through ruts and rocky paths, under the protective cover of dense trees. Stooped shoulders and missed steps made it evident a long way had been traveled, and exhaustion was near.

The figure stalled, shoulders hunched to lend support as arms threatened to drop the tight bundle they carried. A glimpse below the hat's low brim revealed a dark, troubled face—young in years but aged by anguish, yet edged with beauty. As a corner of the bundle's fabric fell away to reveal an infant, the fugitive's form softened to a woman's, the tunic was raised, and the baby set to suckling. Within a heartbeat, wild eyes darted back toward shadows, the pace quickening once again.

Audrey woke shivering in her nightshirt, her own eyes darting toward the corners of her room until she remembered where she was, and realized she'd been dreaming. She fumbled for her robe and squinted at the clock: two-fifteen. Certain she'd have trouble falling back to sleep, she got out of bed, grateful the next day was a Sunday, a day of rest.

She padded down the long hall, which remained dim due to a broken overhead lamp. The line of windows along the back wall of the hallway also failed to aid her on such an overcast night.

She flicked on the bathroom light and peeked into Julian's room. The boy lay in his pajamas, sprawled across the bedspread on his stomach. His aunt pulled a blanket over him,

9

smiling when he moaned and rolled over, a perplexed frown on his sleeping face. She thought of their argument on the front lawn, certain Laura would have handled things much differently.

Audrey retreated down the back stairs to the kitchen, unwilling to risk an immediate return to bed after her intense nightmare. Her dreams of the fugitive were always intense. Who was this person and why was she running? she wondered once again.

Though cold, she refused to adjust the thermostat, determined as always to save a little money by leaving the heat down for the night. She switched on the kitchen light and sat at the table under its glow, resting her head on her crossed arms. The lingering image of the fugitive with her child reminded her of Laura with Julian when he was an infant. She recalled one early morning a few weeks after Julian was born. Laura had sat at that same table, nursing her son.

They'd made a stunning picture—the child wrapped in a quilt, his dark eyes closed while he suckled, the mother in a pink bathrobe, her hair pulled back to reveal the curves of her brown face. Laura soothed Julian with soft words, her free hand running over his hair, his cheek, his chest. Audrey had watched in silence, doubting she'd ever play the part of a loving parent as naturally as her sister.

"Better now, baby?" Laura cooed, still stroking her son. "Julian, my Jamaican jewel?" As her infant freed an arm from the quilt, she slipped her pinkie into his tiny fist.

Audrey pursed her lips. "Why do you call him that? Pritch was only part Jamaican," she complained, referring to the baby's father.

She had turned to the sink, then, to run water into a kettle. Icy rain pelted the window above the sink, prompting her to view her reflection in the dark pane. With her frumpy robe and mussed hair, she provided a sharp contrast to the nursing scene behind her.

She placed the kettle on the stove.

"He's got a little of everything in him, really," Laura had answered. "German, French, African, Jamaican." She glanced at her sister. "You talk as though his father's dead."

"He may as well be."

"He's a good man. Like Julian will be. A good man."

The kettle hummed as its water heated. Audrey jiggled it.

Laura cleared her throat. "Remember I mentioned I might go to night school, for premed?"

Audrey faced her sister.

"My offer still stands," Laura continued, "if you want to move in with us. No rent, just a lot of baby-sitting."

Audrey's expression remained blank. "I can't afford to quit my job, though."

Laura shrugged. "I'm sure you could find work here. Rochester's not that far."

"I don't know." Audrey jiggled the kettle again. "I want to help, but . . . I don't want to move back here, to New Bilford."

"It's not that bad. Better than being in some strange town, alone and miserable."

Audrey stared at her sister, incredulous. "I'm not miserable, Laura."

The kettle trembled.

"I thought it would do us all good—"

Audrey snorted. "So you'd be doing *me* a favor, letting me move back to this crummy town to live in your old farmhouse with you? Thanks so much, but I've got a great job in Washington, the weather's a hell of a lot better there, and I'm *not* miserable!"

The teakettle burst into a high-pitched whistle as the baby's suckling erupted into a series of loud, short coughs. Laura held him close, rubbing his back, cooing reassurances into his hair.

Audrey moved the kettle, switched off the stove, and sat beside her sister. "Is he okay?" she whispered.

Laura nodded as she maneuvered her son back to her breast. "He's still learning," she said, "that's all." The baby latched back on. "It's as natural as breathing, you know. But he had to learn to do that, too. We all did."

Audrey sighed. "I want to help."

"It's okay. I just worry about you, in such a big city, alone."

"I like being on my own. No ties, no hassles. What's wrong with that?"

"Nothing, I guess. If that's what you want." Laura raised the baby to her shoulder. He burped and gurgled.

Audrey rubbed her eyes, then smiled sheepishly. "Let me hold him a while?"

"Sure," Laura answered, moving Julian to his aunt's

open arms.

Audrey cradled her nephew, humming and rocking him, enjoying the pressure of his weight against her chest.

"You're a natural," Laura said.

Audrey inhaled, conscious of the room's warmth, her sister's strength, the baby's presence. Silence at the window signaled the sleet's end. She exhaled slowly, imagining a silent snowfall covering the iced streets of the small lakeshore town, her hometown, a town she remained compelled to escape.

Chapter Three

Audrey woke in the kitchen at dawn, her head throbbing, the sleeve of her robe damp with tears she barely remembered crying. She retreated to bed for a few more hours of sleep. At nine, she heard Julian slam the back door on his way out.

She returned to the kitchen a short while later for a quick breakfast and to wash some dishes. As she soaped and rinsed glasses and plates, she frowned at the dirty pots left from the spaghetti Julian had cooked the night before. While Laura had taught him to make some basic meals, Audrey knew she rarely had Julian do other chores besides occasional lawn work. The one time Audrey asked the boy to help her dry dishes, he complained so much she decided it was easier to do it herself.

At least he liked to cook a little. Audrey placed another clean glass in the drainer. She thought of her one close friend in town, Pam, who summed up her attitude toward cooking with the motto "If you've got a can opener, you've got a meal."

Audrey grinned, wondering if the arrival of Pam's first child would change her ways. Every conversation with Pam these days covered her favorite topics: her pregnancy, her new house, her husband, Frank, her annoying in-laws, and her pregnancy. An old friend from community college, Pam had been the first person Audrey called when she returned home in February. Regardless of the topics covered, talks with Pam always left her bent double with laughter, in the end exhausted but thoroughly relaxed.

She glanced out the window to see Julian race into the yard on his bike. With one swift movement, he swung his leg over his seat, jumped off, and set the bike against the rusted shed. With another, he bounded up the back patio's concrete steps. Then he entered through the back door, brushed past his aunt with a sullen "Hi," and stomped upstairs.

Audrey wrung the dishcloth until it chafed. The easy dishes done, she emptied the sink and dried her hands before removing a photo stuck to the refrigerator by a magnetic frame. She studied the familiar, though distant, faces of her mother, nephew, and late father. They were pleased yet reserved faces, all different shades, the boy resembling his grandparents not only in occasional features, but in his earnest, pensive pride. Laura had taken that photo a year before her accident, three weeks before their father suffered a fatal heart attack.

Audrey peered at her mother's slight smile and tried to remember if she'd ever seen her grin. Yvonne Duchek Conarroe had always been a striking beauty, and the most petite member of her family, she often reminded her daughters. The girls were forced to take her word for it, having never met their maternal relations. Yvonne neither dwelled on her past, nor invited questions about it from her curious children.

Returned to the dirty pots, Audrey refilled the sink with soapy water and considered the possibility of moving to Florida, to live with Julian and her mother there. She shook her head, determined to avoid that scenario, certain she and Yvonne would irritate each other as much as ever.

Pam had reacted emotionally when Audrey last mentioned she might move back out of state. "Audreee!" Her voice had wailed high and anxious. "You can't leave town again," she said, her brown eyes huge. "You'll still be my kid's godmother, right? You can't back out on me; there's a serious lack of women in our family. Ma says she'll have a fit if this one's another boy, but I tell her it doesn't matter, as long as the baby's healthy." Pam had then repeated a long list of risks associated with bearing children late in life, hinting Audrey should settle down soon if she ever planned to have a child of her own.

"No thanks, kiddo," Audrey had replied. "My life's complicated enough these days."

Pam had then launched into her plan to introduce Audrey to a friend, a corporate real estate agent, at her upcoming housewarming party. "If I can't convince you to stay in town, maybe he can," she had teased.

Audrey had laughed. "Or maybe I'll convince him to run away with me."

Later that morning, Audrey took inventory of her small

bedroom closet, in search of something to wear to Pam's party. She bypassed outfits one by one. "Too conservative, too dark, too summery, too expensive to clean."

Julian entered the room.

"Hi," she said, spinning toward him with a flourish. Neither had mentioned the argument from the day before. She planned to forget about it, and hoped he did, too. She posed with a navy pantsuit studded with gold stars along the shoulders. "What do you think of this?"

"For what?" He sat on her bed and leaned back on both forearms. "Joining the Army?"

"Funny," she said, replacing the suit. "I'm going to a party Friday night. Better stick to skirts."

"Why don't you wear something of Mom's? She wore pretty clothes."

Audrey realized her own shock at this suggestion only after Julian reflected it in his embarrassed shrug. She tried to act nonchalant and sound casual to avoid embarrassing him further. "That wouldn't bother you?" she finally asked. "My wearing her things? You don't even let me go into your mother's room."

He cocked his chin slightly. "You can go in her room, Aunt Audrey," he said. "Just don't mess things up."

"Heh, mess things up," she chuckled. "I'm good at that." She returned to the closet. "Is it supposed to get cold?"

"Maybe snow." Julian sat up and crossed his arms. "The toilet's running again."

"Again? How's this?" She held up a red leather outfit with padded shoulders and a short skirt.

"Kind of, um, racy."

"I don't know." She held the outfit in front of her and studied herself in a mirror. "I haven't worn it in ages," she said, pressing the skirt against her leg, "but it'll still fit. I used to look incredible in this."

"Um, don't you think—?"

"What, that I'm too old to wear leather? I'm only thirty-four!"

Her nephew grinned. "Why don't you just wear a sign saying 'I'm available' on it?"

"Julian!" She laid the outfit on the bed next to him and returned to the closet. "It is an expensive one to clean, though. Everything's so expensive, you know? The sitter asked me to bump her up another dollar an hour, believe that?"

15

"I don't need a sitter," Julian complained. "I'm almost fourteen."

"We've been through this before, kiddo. I'd worry about something happening if I left you alone at night. There are so many crazies walking the streets. And you can't count on our neighbors if you need them. Everyone's always out of town, or locked in their houses. Half of them wouldn't know you if you did knock on their door."

"You kidding? They'd freak. 'There's a black boy at my door! Help! Help!'"

Audrey frowned. "We don't exactly fit in around here, do we?"

Julian paused. "You really want to move, huh?"

She slipped two more suits over her arm. "We have to sell the house, but it needs tons of work before it can even go on the market. Then it could take months, even a year, to sell. We've got to decide soon."

Julian stood. "I know." He crossed the room to his aunt's dresser, where he lifted and replaced trinkets without looking at them. His shirt and jeans, though worn, hung loosely on his slight frame.

"I know this is hard," she said, dropping her outfits onto the bed, "the thought of leaving here, of not going to New Bilford High next year. Think about it for now, okay? And I'll decide if we need a sitter Friday night."

"Sure." Julian slipped out of the room, his eyes averted.

Audrey's smile vanished as soon as he left. She sat on the bed, fingering the velvet lining of a jacket Laura had given her. A moment later, she set that aside, lifted the red leather outfit onto her lap, and smoothed the skirt. She thought again about Pam's bachelor friend.

"Guess it's time to find a real estate agent," she said.

Audrey knew she'd picked the wrong outfit the moment she walked in Pam's front door Friday night. In addition to being the only dark-skinned guest, she was the only guest dressed in any type of party attire. Conservative brown and blond heads pivoted toward her with curious, primarily blue-eyed stares, while she stared back at the somber winter suits worn by Frank's office mates and the heavy sweaters, low shoes, and long skirts worn by Pam's faculty friends.

Pissed as hell, she opened her arms wide and announced,

"Pam darling, the party's here!" Then she dropped her coat and purse on a chair and strutted across the room, nodding and smiling to people, a benevolent queen in spiked heels and red leather.

By the time Audrey got to the makeshift bar—a card table stocked with plastic soda bottles, three jugs of wine, an assortment of liquor, and a bucket of bottled beer on ice—most of the guests had resumed their low-toned conversations. She knew some would glance her way throughout the evening, women as they sized up the competition and men as they tried to check her out without letting their dates notice. She hummed along with the Steely Dan tune playing on the stereo, opened a beer, and scanned the room.

She glanced at her watch. Barely eight. She decided to stay until ten so Julian, at home without a sitter, wouldn't think she'd worried about him all evening.

"Hey, girl!" A familiar voice startled Audrey back to the party buzzing around her. She focused on Pam's face as it beamed her way. With ten weeks to go, Pam had already gained enough weight for two pregnant women. She lumbered toward Audrey like a giant, grinning balloon in the Macy's parade.

"I thought I heard you come in," she said. "There's sandwiches and stuff in the dining room if you're hungry." She gestured toward the adjoining room. "Ma went nuts making all this stuff."

Audrey hugged her. "Happy housewarming. This place looks great."

"Thanks. I can't wait to get the nursery wallpapered, and curtains up in the kitchen, and—"

"Whoa, Laura Ashley, you're a bit pregnant, remember?"

"I know. Some of this stuff won't get done 'til after the bambino arrives. I only hope she's here by Christmas."

Pam's husband, a round, mustached man, approached from the kitchen. "Pammy, you should sit down," he said, smiling timidly from behind his huge wife. "Hi, Audrey. Nice outfit."

"Thanks, Frank." She pulled a folding chair over for her friend. "This reminds me, though, of the time I wore a dress to a pool party, when everyone else showed up in shorts and bathing suits."

"You look fine," Pam said, fanning herself with a limp napkin. "What I wouldn't give to be able to wear a dress like that."

17

Frank frowned at his wife, then left them to greet more guests at the front door.

"What's with Mr. Wonderful?" Audrey asked.

Pam shrugged. "Anxious, I guess." She patted her stomach. "We both are. How are you?"

"Me? Annoyed the Moon Resort still hasn't called, but fine, otherwise." She noticed her friend's concerned look. "What?"

"Nothing," Pam said. "You just sounded pretty down, the other day. And you said it yourself—you can't find a job, you're worried about Julian, you want to move. Maybe you need—"

"Sex," Audrey interrupted. "Sex is what I need. Remember Maggie in *Cat on a Hot Tin Roof*? That's me, all red hot and bothered and about to explode."

Pam grinned. "Which reminds me, bachelor number one should be here any minute. Be gentle with him, would you? He's still getting over that nasty breakup with his old girlfriend—"

Audrey flicked her wrist toward her. "You told me. The wonder model, right?"

"Ex-wonder model. Bridgit. They dated almost three years. She paraded him around to all her hotty totty parties, and as soon as he moved back home to take care of his mom—boom!—she dumped him. Broke his heart, I'm telling you. Not that he'd ever admit it. In fact," Pam raised her eyebrows and lowered her voice, "I heard from a friend of one of his sisters that he proposed, and Bridgit laughed in his face." She slapped her knee. "Just like that. Says I love you one minute, then take a hike, fella, the next."

"So you're telling me he's on a major rebound."

"No, no," Pam protested. "He's well beyond that stage, and more than ready to settle into somethin' sweet with someone new. Know what I mean? Oh, wait. There he is." She nodded toward a tall, red-haired man who stood inside the front door, talking with Frank.

Audrey assessed the man's broad shoulders and thick hair. "Hel-lo, bachelor number one," she said. "Mm, mm, mm."

"Don't I know it."

"Funny," Audrey added. "He looks familiar."

"Really?"

"What's his name?"

"James. James Sullivan."

Audrey saw Frank direct the newcomer toward them. "Jimmy Sullivan? Boy has he grown up."

"Care to clue me in here?"

"Ask him." Audrey put her beer down as James approached.

"Hey, little momma," he said, bending to kiss Pam on the cheek.

"Hey," she said. "Remember I told you about—?"

"Audrey Conarroe." James straightened. "This is incredible."

Audrey smiled. "Nice to see you, too, Jimmy." She took in his green eyes, wavy hair, slightly freckled complexion, and distinct jaw line, appreciating how his features had matured since high school, certain everyone in the room could hear her pounding heart.

Pam laughed. "I can't believe you two know each other."

"Knew each other," James said, "a long time ago."

Audrey's smile broadened as she remembered the boy she'd known in high school. Jimmy Sullivan had been a junior at a boys' school across town when she met him at a dance at the girls' school she attended. A confident athlete as likable as he was handsome, he spent hours talking with her that night, though she was only a sophomore. That summer, they arranged to meet a couple times, until their parents interceded. At sixteen, Audrey was deemed too young to date, while Jimmy's mother insisted he should see girls "his own age." Audrey still suspected Margaret Sullivan had been furious with her son for dating a black girl. She'd met Margaret only once, and very briefly. The way the woman's face hardened into a mask of self-control, however, made it clear she never wanted to see Jimmy with the likes of Audrey again.

"We met when we were kids," Audrey added. "In high school."

"Great," Pam said, "then I don't need to sweat through an awful introduction. Will you two behave if I leave you alone?" She braced a hand on the back of her chair, pushing herself up while James guided her by one arm. With a grin and a wink, she lumbered away.

"It was funny to hear her call you 'James,'" Audrey said, stepping back from him.

He turned toward the bar. "Only my mother and sisters still call me Jimmy," he said. "I think to them I'll always be eight."

"To me Jimmy Sullivan will always be seventeen."

He glanced at her.

"But I like James," she added. "It suits you, now."

Audrey checked him out while he opened a beer. Nice shoes, nice slacks, nice butt, sturdy back, strong arms under that tailored shirt. God, she wondered, could it really be him?

"How's your mother?" she asked.

He frowned. "Not well. Diabetes. I moved back to take care of things, since my dad died last year."

"Oh." Audrey realized leather itches when one sweats in it. "I'm so sorry. Your dad seemed sweet."

"He was. How about your family?"

She took a deep breath. "We've been through a lot." She told him about her father's and sister's deaths, and her orphaned nephew.

"Pam mentioned some of that," he said, stepping closer. "I had no idea it was *you*, though. I can't believe—"

She stood her ground. "Funny how things have dragged us both home again."

He peered at her and smiled. "I'm beginning to think back home may not be so bad."

Audrey returned a guarded smile, hesitant to reveal the effect his words, his gaze, his presence had on her. "So," she asked, forcing her voice to sound flippant, "where do you live now?"

"In my family's old place. How about you?" He wrapped a napkin around the base of his beer bottle.

"I'm just a short walk from here. A good thing since the car's in the shop again." She paused. "Does your mother live with you, then?"

He laughed. "No, thank goodness."

Audrey raised her eyebrows.

"Don't get me wrong, I love her and all that. But I'm the only one around, you know?"

"Aaah."

"I mean, I don't mind helping, I love to help. But she's determined to see me live my life the way she wants me to. I'm thirty-five, though, old enough to make sensible decisions, to know what I want."

"Do you?"

James laughed again, his ears and cheeks flushed red,

while a tense heat traveled from the roots of Audrey's hair to her suddenly sweaty palms. She justified her defensive mood, certain otherwise she'd appear an easy target for a rebound relationship.

"I mean," she continued, "I certainly don't know what I want, and it seems we're both in the same boat—back home to take care of family matters, when we'd rather be somewhere else."

"Not really. I always knew I'd settle down here. I just thought by now I'd have found Miss Perfect and have one or two kids. Now I'm not so sure I'll ever have that."

"Maybe not with Miss Perfect."

James chuckled, glanced at the floor, and shifted his weight, while Audrey waited for him to excuse himself to use the bathroom, or make a call. She knew he'd always tried to act as though her skin color didn't matter to him. His first steady look at her had belied none of the awkwardness most people reveal when they meet her, none of the shadows that hint their instant realization of her race, or their need to pretend it won't affect how she'll be treated.

He'd tried hard and nearly convinced her, until the last time they spoke, when he said maybe their parents were right and they should stop seeing each other.

Audrey asked the time, then realized she wore her watch. James didn't seem to notice.

"I need to call and check on my nephew," she said. "Be right back."

"Sure." He winked. "I'll be grazing in the dining room."

Audrey slipped away to the kitchen, relieved to find herself alone. She pulled a plastic cup off a stack near the sink, filled it with cold tap water, and took a long drink.

Pam entered the room, carrying an empty platter.

"Audrey?" She set the dish on a counter. "What are you doing in here?"

"Escaping." Audrey paced between the sink and the refrigerator. "For a minute. This is . . . I don't know . . . too weird."

"What?" Pam pushed her bangs from her forehead. "Is it hot in here?"

Audrey filled another cup with water and handed it to her friend. "You're pregnant," she said. "Drink this." She folded her arms across her chest. "I'm so vulnerable right now, so needy, you know? And suddenly there he is, after all these years, and I'm supposed to forget what happened and dive into a relationship that for him would probably be some short-term thing? I can't cope with all this right now. I just can't. There, I've made up my mind. Forget it."

Pam stared at her friend. "You're a lunatic, Audrey. A stark raving lunatic. This guy is perfect. You have some history with him, who cares what and when, and he's as needy as you, for lack of a better word. Each of you is exactly what the other needs right now."

Audrey wagged her head. "I'm just too—"

"Chicken."

"And he's too—"

"Sweet, successful, *gorgeous,* for crying out loud. Snap out of it!"

"This is too weird." Audrey checked the time again. "I guess I will call Julian. Mind if I—?"

Pam waved her toward the phone on the wall. Audrey dialed her number, listened to the connection click and the dull rings sound off, and took another sip of water. After four rings, she heard a familiar click and waited for Julian's hello. Then she realized the answering machine had picked up.

"Come on, Julian." When the recording finished, she waited for the beep. "Julian," she said. "Julian, it's me, Aunt Audrey. Come on, answer the phone. Jul-ian. Julian?" She stared at the receiver, listened again to make sure he hadn't picked up, and decided something was wrong.

"Julian, I'm on my way home. I'll be there in a few minutes." She hung up the phone.

Pam gaped at her. "What—?"

"I don't know." Audrey left the kitchen and crossed the living room to pick up her coat and purse while Pam followed as quickly as possible.

"Audrey," Pam said. "What happened? What's wrong?"

Once again, Audrey tried to ignore the other guests' stares. "Julian didn't answer. I need to make sure he's okay."

"Audrey, honey," Pam said, catching up. "You're upset and it's so dark out. Can't someone see you home?"

Audrey spun toward her, but found herself face-to-face with James, instead. "I've got to go," she said, breathless. Whether from her anxious desire to quit the room or the pleasure of being with Jimmy Sullivan again, of wondering, again, what might happen next with him, she remained unsure. "I—"

He touched her arm. "Let me give you a ride, Audrey. Maybe I can help."

Was he trying to make up to her, after all these years? "All I know is I've got to get home," she said. "I don't care how, I just need to get out of here."

With that, she walked out the door into the welcome coolness of the night, hoping Julian was safe, determined not to care whether James followed.

Chapter Four

Audrey heard Pam's front door open behind her but kept her pace steady, forcing herself to concentrate on her concern for Julian as she stepped down the driveway.

"Hey," James called.

Audrey turned as he put on a suit jacket. "You need a warmer coat," she called back. "It's freezing out here."

He crossed the lawn to his car at the curb. "I'd say it was pretty frigid in there, wouldn't you?" he asked, his smile illuminated by a nearby street light.

She approached him, her own face grim, while he held the car door open for her.

"Thank you," she said, avoiding eye contact as she slipped into the passenger seat. She noted the slick interior of his BMW and wondered if it was a company car.

James got in and started the engine. Suddenly alone with him, and in such close, quiet quarters, Audrey was tempted to look at him and laugh, as though sharing a private joke. How had they come to be together again, she wanted to ask, all grown up and both so available? His good looks unnerved her, though, and she knew one of his smiles—which she found wonderfully familiar and comforting—would disarm her completely. So she stared out the window during the short drive, speaking only to give directions, trying to focus again on her concern for Julian.

"A right at the stop sign," she said. "Then it's the third one on the left."

They pulled into the gravel driveway. Audrey searched for signs her nephew was still up, and still home, and was relieved to see a dim light in his bedroom window.

She began to get out of the car, then paused. She could dismiss James now, as easily as he'd dismissed her nearly twenty years ago, or she could take the gamble this chance meeting had occurred for a reason. She opted for the latter. "It looks like everything's all right," she said evenly, determined to remain calm despite her heart's shifting into turbo, "but would you come in for a minute, just in case?"

"Sure," James answered.

As they made their way up the driveway, Audrey tried to wish away all the oddities of the old farmhouse, beginning with the sagging front porch. Then there were cracks in the front hall's overhead light, gaps in the hardwood floors, water damage in the kitchen ceiling, rooms with faded paint and peeling wallpaper. Audrey fought the impulse to disassociate herself from Laura's house, to explain at length she had nothing to do with its dilapidated state, while she unlocked the door and invited James in.

She left him in the hall and went upstairs as quickly as her heels and tight skirt would allow. She knocked on her nephew's door, louder than intended. "Julian? Are you still up?"

"Yeah," came the answer. "Come on in."

Julian sat in bed, reading. His black curls were mussed, evidence he'd been running his fingers through them as he did when he was concentrating. Audrey realized he needed a haircut.

He pointed to his place on the page and smirked at her. "Another quick exit?" he asked. "What was this one, a bean counter or a computer geek?"

"Funny," she said, grateful to find him safe and in bed, but also to have a minute to regroup before returning to James. "Actually," she added, "he was neither, and he's downstairs right now. Why didn't you answer the phone when it rang a little while ago?"

Her nephew closed his book. "Who's downstairs? A guy?" He threw aside his NFL comforter and reached for his robe.

"Do me a favor and stay in bed, would you?" his aunt pleaded.

"I'm just going to get something to eat. I'll be nice and quiet. Promise."

Audrey frowned as she followed him down the back staircase and into the kitchen.

"Is everything okay?" James called.

Julian made a face, then opened the refrigerator.

"Everything's fine," Audrey answered, shaking her head at her nephew.

As she left the kitchen, Audrey caught her breath at the sight of James by the front door. For a reason she couldn't identify, his presence there pleased her. With the glow of his smile and his friendly, familiar face in view, the deep shadows and dingy details of the old house seemed to fade from sight. She smiled and signaled him to join her and her nephew.

Julian was still pulling milk and food out of the refrigerator. He turned with a grin that disappeared as soon as James entered the room.

"James," Audrey said, "this is Julian."

The boy deposited his food on a counter.

"Hey, Julian," James said, extending his hand. "Nice to meet you."

"Hi." Julian ignored the extended hand and returned to the counter to assemble a sandwich.

Audrey stared at her nephew's back in disbelief just as the ancient furnace downstairs coughed and clanked to life. Embarrassed by both, she glanced at James, who shrugged at her with a weak smile.

"Guess I'd better go," he said.

Audrey led him back to the front hall, then hesitated. "Listen," she said. "I'm sorry I snapped at you. And thanks for the ride home."

James waved his hand. "I was relieved to leave, really. Nothing worse than being alone in a crowd."

Audrey heard Julian stomp up the creaky back stairs and slam his bedroom door. She could tell by James's amused expression that he'd heard this, too.

"He only does that when he's upset," she said. "Could you stay a while longer? I should make sure he's okay."

"I lied." James smiled. "I'm in no rush."

Audrey gestured toward the living room. "Make yourself at home. I'll be right back."

Upstairs, she rapped on Julian's door again.

"Come in."

Julian sat on his bed, still in his robe, eating his sandwich. His glass of milk stood on the bedside table.

Audrey closed the door. "Want to tell me what that was all about?"

Her nephew gulped down some milk. "Want to tell me what *he's* all about?"

"His name's James, Julian. I knew him in high school,

and he's a really nice guy. You'd have realized that if you hadn't been so rude. He gave me a ride home because I got worried when you didn't answer the phone."

The boy took his time finishing his sandwich, then drank the last of his milk. "First of all," he said, brushing crumbs off his lap. "I was in the john when you called and you hung up before I could get to the phone. No wild party, no drugs, not even a sip of beer while you were out."

His aunt made a face. "I know." She sat on the bed. "I overreacted. I was worried."

"Second of all," he continued, "Ja-ames is whiter than a ghost. White white, with red hair even. Are you getting desperate or something?"

Audrey chuckled. "That bothers you? The idea of me with a white guy? I've dated white men before."

"I don't remember any."

"I don't plan to marry him, Julian. He just gave me a ride home." She paused. "But why shouldn't I date white men, anyway? There aren't a ton of black men walking around New Bilford, you know."

Her nephew's eyes widened. "You *are* getting desperate!"

"Julian! Get serious!" Audrey stood. "Just remember to be polite when you meet people, okay? You don't want everyone to think you're a juvenile delinquent, do you?" She picked up the dishes. "It's late, kiddo. Get some sleep."

Julian took off his robe and got into bed, then wagged a finger at his aunt. "I told you that outfit—"

"Good night, Julian." She opened the door to leave and switched off the light.

On her way down the front stairs, Audrey could see James in the living room, looking at framed photographs displayed on top of the television. She wondered what they revealed to him. In one, Audrey and Laura posed with a younger Julian at Disney World, all of them in Mickey Mouse hats. Then there were the two high school portraits of her and Laura, which contrasted her drastically with her sister. While Laura's showed her with a head of shimmering waves, distinct features, and red lipstick, Audrey's showed her with short hair, a pudgy face, and pimples.

James picked up a small, square snapshot of the sisters, aged fourteen and eleven, in frilly pink dresses and white gloves, their hair in braids and ribbons. While in that photo Laura smiled angelically, little Audrey scrunched up her face, crinkled her nose, and stuck out her tongue at the camera.

"That's my favorite." Audrey grinned as she walked past the living room. "It shows the true me."

She went into the kitchen, kicked off her shoes, and put Julian's dirty dishes on a counter. "I'm starving," she called. "Can I get you anything?"

James entered the kitchen as she pulled two beers from the refrigerator. She handed one to him, then rummaged in a cupboard for a box of microwave popcorn and read the package. "I always have to check the directions," she said. "I burn everything."

"There's always pizza and Chinese take-out." James leaned against the counter beside Audrey and looked down at her. The microwave whirred. "I knew you seemed taller at Pam's than I remembered," he said. "Those heels had me fooled."

She gave him a wry glance. "What, you mistook me for Whitney Houston?"

He laughed. "You're just as pretty, of course."

"Of course," she said. "But with short legs I've got another strike against me."

James ran a hand through his hair. "Another?"

"As far as your mother's concerned, I mean."

James swallowed a gulp of beer, then waved in disagreement. "If you're talking about your skin color, you've got my mother all wrong," he said, his hand now over his heart.

Audrey opened a cupboard to find a bowl, and to hide her flushed face for a moment. Though relieved to have confronted James with the issue, she was now anxious to get it over with, to see where it left them.

"Oh, please." Strengthened by her own audacity, and by the alcohol now fueling her emotions, she pursued the touchy topic. "Your mother made it very clear how she felt about me."

"Right." James pulled the popcorn bag from the microwave and shook it. "She felt you were too young, and I should date someone my own age." He poured the steaming popcorn into the bowl, then sat at the table.

Audrey took a swig of her beer and joined him. "You still believe that?"

"What about your parents?" He helped himself to a fistful of popcorn and slid the bowl toward her.

28

"My parents?"

"They said the same thing, that you were too young to date."

"So?" Audrey tossed a piece of popcorn into her mouth. "They told Laura that, too, when she was sixteen. I was trying to see what I could get away with."

James shook his head. "I couldn't even call you at home, remember? You said your dad had a fit the one time I called."

"Oh, sure, he was furious. When he said no dating until seventeen, he meant it. That rule drove me nuts, though. Talk about a lack of trust."

"I thought he was upset I wasn't . . . you know . . . black."

"You've got it backwards," Audrey said. "My father married a white woman. He was as far from being prejudiced as you can get." Your mother was the prejudiced one, she wanted to add.

"It's funny he was liberal about some things, but so strict about others. No wonder you complained about him so much."

"Me, complain?" Audrey frowned despite her attempt at levity. "I thought everyone complained about their parents. Everyone but my sister, that is." She shrugged. "Things began to get a little, I don't know . . . tense, with my dad, when I was thirteen or so. He hated that I talked back, maybe even resented me for being so difficult all the time. Laura was so well behaved, I must've seemed like a rebel in comparison, though I hardly caused any real trouble."

"Hardly?" James asked with a grin.

She returned a small, guilt-laced smile. "Maybe occasionally, but not all the time."

James laughed. "Julian seems to have a bit of both you and his mother in him," he said. "What'll you do when he comes home with a girl you don't approve of?"

"Please," Audrey answered. "I'm not going to worry about that until I have to. One thing I've learned this year is not to sweat the little things, because tomorrow may knock you for a loop."

James sat back. "You mean live for today, to hell with long-term plans?"

She shrugged again, then leaned toward him, realizing she was about to place her hand on his leg. Instead, she propped her elbow on the table and rested her chin in her palm. "No." She wondered if she should blame the alcohol for the sinking feeling that had settled in her belly. "I've got Julian, now, you know? I can't just live for today. Not if I want a clear conscience, anyway."

James pursed his lips. "Do you mind if I ask what happened to his father?"

Audrey scratched at the label of her beer bottle. "He skipped town a couple months before the wedding, right before Laura found out she was pregnant." She shivered and wrapped her arms around herself, wishing she wore sweats rather than a short dress. She listened to make sure the furnace still rumbled downstairs.

"Sometimes I wonder if Julian should have gone to live with my mom," she continued, "but I'm not so sure that would've worked. It was hard on all of us, losing my dad and Laura so suddenly."

Audrey glanced up in surprise as James stood, took off his suit jacket, and handed it to her.

"You look cold," he said.

She slipped the jacket on, appreciating its weight and the way it wrapped her not only in fabric, but in his warmth. She was shocked to find her eyes had filled with tears.

"Why the hell am I crying?"

"I'd say you have good reason."

He smiled, and Audrey wanted to lose herself in that smile, in his green eyes flecked with specks of brown, in his gold-etched waves of red and orange hair, in him.

She stood and turned to the sink to compose herself. A memory flashed, and once again she heard the sickening sound of her sister's ring as it clattered down the drain.

Audrey had been given Laura's engagement ring after the funeral. Though it was loose on her own hand, she wore it a few weeks, only to see it fall down that drain one morning. She had stood paralyzed, then grabbed for the phone. Two hours later, a plumber removed the trap of the pipe beneath the sink and retrieved the ring. Since then, it had remained locked in her sister's small jewelry box upstairs.

Audrey glanced at the dark window, encouraged by the reflection of herself draped in a suit jacket and of James behind her, seated at the kitchen table.

"It's warmer in the living room," she said. "Not so drafty." She smoothed her hand along the sleeve of his jacket as she led him back to the living room, where she switched on a floor lamp.

James stood in front of two framed landscapes illuminated by the lamp's glow.

"My dad painted those," she explained, "of the hills outside his hometown."

James nodded. "In Tennessee, right?"

"You remember that?"

"Of course," he answered. "I remember everything about you."

She sat on the couch. "I could never understand why you wasted any time with me back then. I was hardly a beauty queen."

He remained standing. "I loved to talk to you, for starters. You were different, not like other girls I knew."

Audrey stared at him, wondering if he had any idea what the simple word "different" could mean to a person who'd been labeled that all her life. She let a slow smile cross her face, choosing—as she had so many times before—to ignore an unintended slight.

"So the truth comes out," she said.

"What?"

"You had absolutely no romantic delusions about me back then, did you?"

James smiled. "Delusions? No. Fantasies, though . . ."

"Excuse me?" Audrey gasped, her mouth open in mock astonishment. "Stop! You're making me blush."

He shrugged. "C'mon, I was seventeen, and you'd wear those tight jeans, with the flared legs and the flower embroidered on the thigh—"

"Oh, Lord," she moaned. "My father hated those jeans."

"He should've burned them. They made you look very . . . mature, for your age."

"So you didn't know you were robbing the cradle?"

James flashed a smug grin. "I knew exactly what I was doing. Like I said, I was seventeen. I had all sorts of ulterior motives."

"Listen to you!" Audrey teased. "Sounds like you had *lots* more on your mind than just talking, Mr. Sullivan."

James chuckled and joined her on the couch. "Lots more on my mind, but too scared to do anything." He gave her a sheepish glance. "You weren't exactly easy to read. And I wasn't exactly experienced."

Audrey tucked her feet up under her. "Just curious."

He watched her for a moment. "Intrigued," he corrected her. "And still very much so."

She met his gaze straight on, but said nothing, letting him decide what to say next, where to go from here.

James looked around the room. "Is it true you're thinking of selling this place?"

Ah, she mused. Back to safe ground. "How'd you know?"

"Pam mentioned it," he said, "when she briefed me on the mystery woman she wanted me to meet."

She nodded. "I hope to sell, if I can. After we get it fixed up."

"Maybe I can direct a few buyers your way. People love old houses like this."

"I guess that's why Laura bought it." Audrey frowned at the room's dark corners, from the huge, boarded-up fireplace to the heavy drapes that hid any view out the front of the house. She yearned to be rid of the place, of the worries inherent in owning a decrepit house she couldn't afford to maintain, much less improve. Audrey had no idea when a water pipe might rupture, the furnace expire, the roof cave in, so it made perfect sense she should sell her sister's house. The illogical, emotional sense that spoke to her from her heart, however, cried foul with every step she took toward that end.

"I could help you find a new place, too," James added. "If you decide to stay in town, I mean."

She studied his expression, now, searching for signs of deception. All she saw, though, was a very handsome man offering help to a friend. Audrey knew already she wanted to be more—much more—than a friend to James. Still, she warned herself to take care.

"It's funny," she said, "but when I was little I always wanted an old house. It was going to be huge, though, like my father's family's homes outside Nashville. Big old farmhouses. I'll always remember how they smelled, like heaven, from the foods the families cooked and the oils they used. The rooms were infused with this incredible incense. I loved visiting there."

"Sounds like you belonged there," James said, peering at her.

Audrey blinked, surprised.

32

"Sorry."

She waved away his apology. "I don't mind."

"It's just, what I do, you know?"

"What you do?"

"In my job. Try to figure out what people are looking for, what they want."

"Mmmm." Audrey tried desperately to ignore her desire to lean on him and fall asleep, her cheek pressed against his collar, her hand on his chest, inhaling his musky cologne in deep, drowsy breaths.

"Back then," she said, her words slow, careful, "I wanted more than anything to belong there. We only visited a few times, but every time I'd wish my dad would pack us all up and move us down there, to live in my grandmother's house. I was so sure that, after a while, I'd fit right in."

"Fit right in?"

She shrugged. "I was different from everyone, you know? Even though I resembled my cousins, I was still different."

"Did your sister feel the same way?"

"Laura?" Audrey smiled dreamily. "No, she never felt out of place anywhere. She liked all the kids in Tennessee, but she loved our grandmother best. I remember Grandma Rose as this tall, kind of stern lady, but Laura told me she was graceful as a lily and she always smelled sweet, like lavender. She said her smile aimed at you made your heart race, and the feel of her hand on your forehead at night was soft and smooth as a rose petal."

She'd almost forgotten James was there.

"I wish I had a picture of her," she added, "but at least I had Laura."

The light kiss James placed on her cheek surprised and pleased Audrey. It wasn't a kiss of passion or desire, but a gentle reaction to her confession of loss. Tears once again filled her eyes, this time spilling onto her cheeks. He moved closer, taking her face in his hands, smoothing her tears away.

"If you kiss me again, I'll really fall apart," she whispered.

He lifted her chin and kissed her again, this time on her forehead, then on her temple, and once more on her cheek. Audrey laughed and sniffed as she pulled back. James stayed close and laughed with her. "I've never had that effect on anyone before," he said, taking her hand.

"You've never made anyone cry?" She forced herself to face him with clear eyes.

He looked down, and she followed his gaze to their clasped hands. She watched as he traced the polished oval of her thumbnail, trying to ignore the sensation of his touch, trying to decide what to say, or do, next. He spoke first, saying her name as she hadn't heard it said for so long, in a tone filled with sincerity as well as hope, and desire. "Audrey."

She remained silent, waiting, wondering, relieved he did not confuse her with more kisses. Then she smiled, took her hand from his, and stood, slipping off his jacket.

James accepted it and put it on as he stood. "Too late?" he asked.

Audrey studied his fine face and sighed. "For tonight, Jimmy." She smoothed his lapel, then dropped her hands from him. "Just too late for tonight."

Chapter Five

Audrey smacked her buzzing alarm clock. She knew she should get up. Pam had offered to take her to get Laura's car at the shop that morning, and Audrey knew she'd arrive within the hour, eager to hear every detail of the previous evening. But the gray shadows of her small room enticed Audrey to remain in bed just a few more minutes, to review what had occurred between her and James less than eight hours before.

And though enticed, she worried about Julian, instead. She'd found her nephew's reaction regarding James disturbing, and his incredulous tone with her painfully familiar. For years, especially through high school, Audrey had endured varied levels of disapproval laced with doubt from her parents. She'd alluded to this when James asked about her father, but had been hesitant to reveal how little faith both her parents had always had in her judgment—and how much that lack of faith still undermined her ability to trust herself.

Audrey blinked against the room's slow brightening as more details of the bed in which she slept, the old dresser that housed her clothes, came into focus. Rather than dwell on discouraging memories, she decided to get in the shower.

The memories would remain, however, just off stage, close enough to edge her to mild irritation throughout the morning. The shower's steam and steady pulse upon her failed to soothe away her doubts and frustrations, and she suspected even Pam's insistent, jovial monologues wouldn't help. Audrey clenched her jaw, determined now to simply make it through the day.

Eighteen years had passed since Audrey, at sixteen, first realized her parents were truly impossible to please. The summer of 1976 was supposed to be one of freedom for her. Or so she'd assumed. Though she argued against her father's demand she find a summer job, and fought for her right to drive the family car all she wanted, she lost on both counts. Her father, of course, won. Audrey was allowed to drive alone only after she'd found a summer job, and then only to and from work when the family car wasn't needed by her mother.

Laura, nineteen and home for her summer break from nursing college in Syracuse, had her own car. She'd saved through high school to buy it, and found a bargain in a used Buick with low miles and little rust. Audrey and her sister would spend the summer coming and going, passing each other in the kitchen, in the hall between their rooms, in and out the front door. They had little in common and even less to say to each other.

Dr. Benjamin Conarroe, a sociology professor at the University of Rochester, had no need for the car during the week since he rode public transportation to and from work. As a girl, Audrey had often watched her father approach from the bus stop down the street, his long strides carrying him home so efficiently. On cold days, he appeared to be a brown overcoat and fedora in motion, his face and hands tucked away against the wind, his briefcase hugged tight to his side in the crook of his arm. Sometimes she'd be unaware of the temperature outside until, from an upstairs window, she'd see her father's confined form approach. Then, she'd realize, yes, of course, yes, it's a bitter day.

The summer of '76, however, sweltered and stalked while Audrey endured her sentence working the counter of a pretzel shop in her hometown's first mall. She remained as unimpressed as her mother with the mall's collection of stores and restaurants squeezed between Sears at one end and Penney's at the other. Yvonne had taken her daughters to the mall when it opened, surveyed it, and announced she'd never return, preferring to shop in downtown Rochester, where she could get some fresh air between purchases.

A family of five invaded the pretzel store one afternoon, young parents with a wailing toddler, a drooling baby in a stroller, and a school-age boy who begged to have a Coke, not a lemonade, this time. Audrey didn't notice the two girls from her school who'd slipped in behind the family, and only spotted them while she filled the boy's lemonade.

The family hustled away, the children momentarily hushed as they sucked on their pretzels, while the two girls,

Marie and Terry, debated the caloric content of pretzels with salt versus those without.

"Hi, Audrey," they each said.

"Hey." She noted their halter-tops and lipstick, two things her father had forbidden her to wear. These were brainy girls with glasses, but they still made themselves up. They wore eye shadow behind their thick lenses, combed their feathered hair in mirrors taped in their lockers, rushed to and from honors classes all day. Marie and Terry were friendly enough, but distant. Maybe even shy, Audrey thought. They knew her simply due to the small size of the girls' school they attended. Everyone knew each other at St. Therese's, knew their families and older sisters, knew what had become of past graduates, what was expected of current students. These two would head to major universities in New England on scholarship, while Audrey might get a business degree at a local school. By the time St. Therese girls reached the end of their sophomore year, such things had already been determined.

"I'll have one without salt, and a Dr Pepper," Marie said. She took two bills from the pocket of her shorts while Terry ordered the same. Audrey served them and watched them go, huddled together, their bony shoulders hunched as though against a draft. She supposed they must be cold in the air-conditioned mall, but knew they'd never bring along sweaters, smart girls though they were.

Audrey's hours at the pretzel shop were filled with such encounters. At least they helped time pass. Plenty of other kids also worked in the mall and stopped in now and then for a pretzel, but rarely just to talk. Most went to New Bilford High and didn't know Audrey. Rainy days kept her busiest, when kids who'd planned to spend the day at the lake headed for the mall, instead. They filled the arcade and played putt-putt at the course upstairs, flirting with each other, or moved in packs from one shop to another, the boys eating everything they could afford, the girls spending their baby-sitting dollars on cheap blouses and drugstore makeup. Audrey watched them come and go, counting down the minutes to her escape on a clock shaped like a pretzel.

Her mother preferred that Audrey drive herself to work, so the car usually sat out in the back parking lot, waiting. After her shift, she drove with the windows down, welcoming the waves of warm, humid air that enveloped her as she wove through her town's back streets, through secret ways she was just now discovering. One day after a sudden rain, she found a lake-side lane that wound through an overhang of willows. The trees waved soaked branches at her as she passed, pelting the car's hood and roof with heavy drops. Audrey laughed at the irony as Billie Holiday's throaty "Pennies from Heaven" played on the tinny radio. Her father had found a station that featured the classic jazz and blues artists he favored: Billie Holiday, Louis Armstrong, Ella Fitzgerald.

Audrey drove through time warps in music: from Top 40 hits like "Silly Love Songs" and "Oh, What a Night," to her favorite "oldies" of Smokey Robinson, The Beatles, Simon & Garfunkel. Usually, though, she'd bop to Ella's scats or cruise with Billie. She knew these songs by heart, after all, from hours of listening to them on her father's ancient phonograph, usually on Saturdays while her parents ran errands. On those afternoons, she'd belt out Billie's "No Regrets" in the living room while her sister read their father's books in the adjoining study.

Audrey had new respect for Laura, these days. Her sister had decided to attend nursing school in Syracuse rather than at the University of Rochester, where tuition would have been waived due to their father's position. Laura had argued it would do her good to live on her own, and the scholarship she received, plus the lower cost of the state university program in Syracuse, made it financially feasible. While Dr. Conarroe hadn't been thrilled with his daughter's decision, he'd agreed to give Laura time to try it out, as long as she promised to eventually consider transferring.

Audrey had heard Laura confess over the phone to a friend that she'd been homesick her first semester away, and couldn't wait to get back to sleep in her own room and see all her friends. Audrey wondered if Laura ever missed her. She hated the suffocating silence of the house—and her parents' full attention—without her busy sister home, and had looked forward to Laura's return for the summer.

Neither sister knew what she was searching for, those long afternoons while their parents were out, though each suspected the other was doing more than simply pass the time. Audrey would lie across her mother's love seat, imitating Billie Holiday draped across a piano singing "My Man" in a smoky bar, the blues and her tumultuous lifestyle having drained every ounce of everything from her. She'd stare at the ceiling, the music swirled around her, and wonder what her sister was reading, this time.

Their father's well-stocked bookshelves offered a variety of choices. Squeezed between standard sociology texts with titles like *Democracy and Education* and *Pedagogy of the Oppressed* were dozens of novels the girls knew their father would never expect, or want, them to read: Wolfe's *Look Homeward, Angel;* Wright's *Native Son;* Maugham's *Of Human Bondage.* Even a few works by women such as Harper Lee and Zora Neale Hurston sported dog-eared pages and margin notes in Benjamin Conarroe's distinct, stilted, script.

Her father's private interests intrigued Audrey, as they hinted at his earlier, more daring, days. Southern-born and bred, he'd headed north for his degrees at a young age, attaining his doctorate from the University of Pennsylvania by the time he turned thirty. Then he'd gone to work for the University of Rochester, in yet another strange state. Audrey suspected such accomplishments were highly unusual for a black man in the 1950s, and wondered what had driven him to them, and so far from his home in Nashville. Her father maintained a quiet affinity for things Southern. She'd seen him get misty-eyed over corn bread, and his study walls featured his two paintings of Tennessee. He'd done them from photographs as a grad student, when, he once explained, he'd had "time to waste on such trivial pursuits."

Audrey frowned as she turned the car out of the lakeside lane, toward home, wondering when her father had become such a bore. She remembered him playing with her and Laura when they were little, splashing at the beach with them, tossing leaves in the air over their heads, building snowmen. As they'd aged, though, he seemed to decide distance was more conducive to discipline.

While "Pennies from Heaven" melted away, Audrey decided this was heaven, for her: freedom to roam through the dense summer, to discover new avenues, new directions, on her own. Certain her father would consider such pursuits trivial, she harbored a keen, forlorn understanding that, at this point in her life, they were all she had.

Jimmy Sullivan called that night. They'd met two weeks earlier at an end-of-year dance their schools held together, and Audrey had assumed she'd never hear from him again. She'd been silly, wound up, at that dance, goofing off in front of classmates, there simply because everyone was expected to attend.

She'd slipped one of her mother's lipsticks into her pocket and sneaked into the girl's bathroom as soon as Yvonne dropped her off. Angry her father wouldn't let her drive herself to the dance, she pushed her way through the crowded bathroom to a mirror and painted her lips bright red. Amy-something from English class offered to line Audrey's eyes with a charcoal pencil, but Audrey refused. She wanted to concentrate on the feel of that lipstick on her mouth. Jimmy Sullivan was the only thing that night that took her mind off her determined rebellion. Or, she would later muse, maybe he contributed a great deal to it.

She stayed off the dance floor, putting on a show for the "bad" girls in the back corner of the gym, the girls who skipped Geometry and smoked after school near the woods. One pointed out Jimmy Sullivan as he watched them from a small group of boys a few feet away. The other boys gawked at the bad girls in their tight sweaters, ribbed each other, laughed at their own jokes. Jimmy Sullivan, though, stepped away from the group and toward the girls, toward Audrey, with a curious smile.

"Hey, looker," one of the bad girls cooed.

"Hey," Jimmy replied, otherwise ignoring her. "Do you want to dance?" he asked Audrey. The bad girls "oohed" in a chorus.

"I am dancing," Audrey answered. She continued to move her shoulders and hips and snap in time to "Joy to the World," wondering why she felt so wound up, so high.

Jimmy Sullivan grinned, then fell into step with her, much to the enjoyment of their audience.

"Ooh, he's determined, huh?"

"Watch out there, girlie, he's got his eye on you."

Puzzled, Audrey spun away, then faced him with a sly smile of her own. "I'm Audrey."

He nodded. "Jim."

What next? she wondered. Had his friends dared him into this? Would he draw her into a lame conversation, pretend to be nice, then walk away, laughing?

"You're not much of a dancer," she announced. The bad girls guffawed. She stepped closer to Jimmy Sullivan, realizing a sudden desire to leave the bad girls behind.

He stepped closer, too. "But you are," he said. "Why aren't you on the dance floor?"

She shrugged. "I'm having more fun back here, where it's dark."

He nodded.

"And not so crowded," she added.

Three Dog Night faded away to Captain & Tennille's "Love Will Keep Us Together."

"It's a lot less crowded outside."

Audrey raised her eyebrows. "Outside? You think I'm crazy?"

He shrugged. "In the hall, then. I hate this song."

"In the hall." She stood still long enough to fully assess his pressed jeans, tucked-in striped shirt, red hair trimmed close, his even smile. Momma's boy, she decided. "All right."

She led him to a water fountain near the bathrooms, where she knew there'd be plenty of traffic, in case he tried anything. With the dance music subdued to a rhythmic hum inside the gym, they talked and joked until ten. No decent girl, Audrey's father insisted, stayed out past ten. Before going to meet her mother outside, Audrey slipped into the bathroom once again to remove what remained of her lipstick. Wanda, one of the bad girls, sidled up to her. "You think he's gonna ask you out?"

"Huh?" Audrey hadn't even considered the possibility. She shrugged. "Won't matter, anyway."

Wanda patted her perm into place. "You mean it wouldn't last long, huh? With the racial thing, and all." The bathroom's fluorescent lights made her look washed out, like a bitter housewife. "If," she cocked a finger knowingly, "his parents let him date you to begin with."

Audrey blinked. "No," she choked. "I'm not allowed to go out with anyone for another year, that's what I mean. If it's any of your business, anyway." She glared at her own reflection, noted a faint shadow of lipstick she hoped her mother wouldn't notice, and realized her eyes were about to spill over with tears. She banged her way out of the bathroom, ready to go home.

When Jimmy Sullivan called two weeks later, he reminded Audrey he'd been away with his family. "Remember I told you about my grandparents' summer house, on Lake Erie? How we go every year and open it for them?"

"Right. Shouldn't you get a Scout badge or something, for that sort of thing?" Audrey ignored her family's frowns from around the kitchen table. The telephone cord kept her from moving out of earshot, and Jimmy Sullivan had called right at the end of dinner. Her father had answered the phone, as usual. He'd asked who was calling, then handed the receiver to his daughter with a stern stare that suggested she keep it short.

Jimmy Sullivan laughed. "Really, I should. What are you doing over the summer?"

"Working. At the mall."

"I'll stop by to see you. Which store?"

She turned her back on her family. "Perfect Pretzels. I'll be there tomorrow, ten to four." She didn't have to see her father to know he was angry. She could picture his broad forehead creased with his anger, his eyes red, his fists clenched. Her mother's kitchen was large and open in the back of their two-story Colonial. Still, the silence that filled the kitchen at that moment made the room feel cramped and close. She shut her eyes, the receiver pressed to her ear, wishing for a way to climb through the phone and out of the house, away to anywhere, as long as it was far from her father. She knew what was coming.

Her mother cleared the table while Audrey finished her call. Laura excused herself and left the room. Audrey hadn't expected her to stay. While calm and confident, Laura did not like to watch another person suffer when she knew she couldn't help. Audrey assumed Laura had heard enough of her fights with their father to know this one would be loud, brief, and somehow detrimental to Audrey's pride. No need for her to endure it, too.

"Who was that?" Dr. Conarroe snapped as his daughter hung up the phone.

"Jimmy Sullivan."

"I heard the boy's name, Audrey Elizabeth. Now please explain what business he has calling you."

Audrey slumped into a chair. "We met at the dance. We talked, he called me."

Her father leaned close. "I'd watch your tone if I were you." He sat back and tapped the table. "Of course you know better than to date a boy before you're seventeen."

"Of course."

"Do I need to repeat the reasons?"

Audrey shook her head.

"Talking on the phone is one thing, but planning to take time from your job to flirt with a boy is another."

Audrey sucked at her teeth, her mouth shut.

"Be sure to notify Mr. Sullivan of the rules of this household, so he'll know he may ask you out next year, but not before then."

Audrey rose to leave. "May as well ship me off to a convent," she muttered.

Yvonne turned water on at the sink full blast, but was too late.

"Are you sassing me?" Dr. Conarroe slammed his open palm onto the kitchen table, making silverware, his wife, and his daughter jump. "Young lady," he railed, "would you like all driving privileges revoked, effective immediately?"

Audrey spun to face him again, her own fists now clenched. "What difference would it make!" She'd known it would come to this, she and her father taking jabs here, pushing buttons there, trapped in an angry dance they knew so well. Her mother had finally turned from the damn dishes, finally approached to play the mediator, once again. Audrey glared at her, furious with her refusal to ever take sides, to stand up for her.

Dr. Conarroe passed his daughter with a weary wave. "You know the conversation's over when you screech at me, young lady. Tell that boy to keep to himself, or I'll stop by his home to insist he does. End of story."

Chapter Six

Julian woke to the sound of a car door slamming. He blinked, then rolled over to study the slits of sunlight that edged his window shade. As the echo of the door faded with that of the soft grinding of gears, Julian remembered his aunt had planned to go to the garage with Pam early that morning to pick up the Buick, his mother's car.

He rolled onto his stomach, pressing his face into his pillow, his arms pulled tight against his chest. He'd stopped crying about his mother weeks ago, forcing himself to face pangs of pain by inhaling sharply and holding his breath until the urge to cry, or moan, passed.

He exhaled into his pillow and shifted to focus on a framed picture that hung near his bed. In it, a young couple dressed in semi-formal attire—his mother and father—posed at the foot of a spiral staircase. His mother had described that night to Julian many times, usually while tucking him in. He closed his eyes and searched his memory for her words, the tone of her voice, the lilt of her laughter.

"Your father," she'd always start. "Your father was so handsome in that new suit, and so nervous!" She'd smooth the sheet at Julian's chest. "But when he stood in that hotel restaurant and asked for everyone's attention, all those strangers stopped, dead silent, and stared at him. And, mind you, every single face in that room was white as paper, but those people were fine, and very kind, and they didn't hesitate to comply."

Julian had always loved to watch his mother's face when she spoke to him that way. Now he tried to remember the lines of her high forehead and cheekbones and her delicate, dimpled chin.

"Then," she'd continue, "he knelt on one knee and asked

44

me to marry him. And when I said yes so loudly folks out on the street probably heard, everyone at the restaurant cheered."

The vision of his mother faded from view and Julian opened his eyes. He studied the photograph again, relieved to see her smile. Still, he ached to feel her embrace, the same way he'd always felt it on nights when she'd talk about the engagement, when she'd describe his father, Harrison Pritchard, Jr.

Julian listened to the muffled sounds of another Saturday morning—cars rolling toward town, a lawn mower grumbling to life down the street, the stiff scratching of a rake next door. He wished he could place neighbors' names with the sounds and wondered what it would be like to have friends his age a house or two away. He urged his mind, now fully awake and restless, to settle on a plan to get him through the day. His stomach growled, prompting him to swing his legs over the edge of the bed, get up, and put on his robe.

The house remained dark and chilly despite the sunshine outside and the heat clanking from the furnace. Julian went to the bathroom and downstairs to the kitchen, taking comfort in the silence of the old house, pulling his robe around him as he plodded through the close, familiar rooms.

His aunt had left the morning paper out with a note: "Gone to get car, back soon." Julian knew she'd return as quickly as she could, and suspected she'd even considered waking him to go with her. He understood how much his aunt worried about him, how cautious she was about him, but wished she'd trust him to take care of himself, sometimes. He fixed a bowl of Wheaties and read an article in the paper on the baseball strike, still shocked players and owners would deprive fans of a World Series, certain his beloved Yankees were pressured into the deal.

After breakfast, he took a quick shower, the radio on the corner of the bathroom sink tuned to his favorite station. The shower done, he wrapped a damp towel around his thin waist, wiped steam off the mirrored medicine cabinet, and studied his upper lip for a sign of whiskers. "Still nothing," he grumbled, lifting his chin to check his jaw.

He hummed to a Hootie & The Blowfish song and tugged a comb through his hair, patting curls into place. Julian imagined the surprised looks he'd get at school, especially from Tina Alani, the hottest girl in the eighth grade, if he were to get his hair cut with a funky fade or a design etched along the side. But he knew he'd have to go to the Blues Brothers barbershop downtown to get that done, and he also knew his aunt would howl with laughter if he even suggested the idea. He mimicked Audrey in the mirror, waving a finger at his reflection. "When you're eighteen, sir, and not a day before," he said in a high-pitched voice. "Then you'll be your own problem. For now, you're mine!"

Julian grinned, his almond-shaped eyes nearly closed as his cheeks rounded. Baby cheeks, his aunt called them, usually with a pat. Baby cheeks for a baby face. Julian smoothed his hairless jaw, then opened the medicine cabinet to make sure his supplies—a can of Edge shaving gel and a twin-blade razor—were still there.

From downstairs came sounds of Audrey's arrival as she moved from the front hall to the kitchen, dropping her purse and keys noisily on a table. He knew she'd pick up the paper and retreat to the back patio with a cup of coffee, and within moments he heard the kitchen door open and slam shut.

"And she says I'm loud." He pulled on the jeans and T-shirt he'd brought from his room and thought of his aunt's week-end clothes: loose striped pants, a snug sweater, thick-heeled shoes. He'd seen men follow her with their eyes and knew she was attractive. Still, he was sure she'd be more beautiful, like his mother, if she'd grow out and straighten her hair and wear long flowing skirts, not outfits made for teenage girls.

Julian smiled and thought of Tina again. He opened the linen closet in the narrow bathroom, knelt on the cold floor, and pried open a door that had been cut into the floor for an old laundry chute. He reached inside the closed space for the manila envelope he'd hidden there.

Julian was glad his aunt didn't know, or care, about the house's nooks and crannies. He enjoyed having secret spots to hide his favorite things. He checked in the envelope for the note he'd written to Tina, a note he doubted he'd ever deliver, and for his Yankees trading cards, which he doubted he'd ever trade.

The doorbell rang. Julian replaced everything, closed the closet door, and ran out of the bathroom and downstairs. "I'll get it!" he yelled to the empty house, wondering if Audrey realized anyone was there.

He opened the front door to a black man, immediately wished his aunt were with him, then wondered at his own reaction.

Dressed in new jeans and loafers, with a green turtleneck

under a cabled sweater, the stranger hardly appeared threatening. He stood with his feet apart, his hands folded, and bent toward Julian, speaking in a round, accented voice. "Hello, there. I'm looking for an old friend whom I believe may live here." He squinted at Julian curiously, then happily, as though he'd realized something. "Are you related to Laura Conarroe?"

Julian nodded, and the man's face brightened.

"You look just like her."

Julian inhaled, forcing the words out as quickly as possible. "My mom died in February."

For a moment, Julian forgot to worry about how he looked as he spoke, how clearly his face revealed the instant rush of blood to his heart, the dizziness, the sudden feeling that another word would knock him over. Instead, he watched the stranger's face age as his reply registered. Then Julian caught his breath.

"You're, you're Harrison Pritchard, aren't you?"

The man blinked. "Heard of me, then?" he asked, his words now fast and clipped. "Good things, I hope?"

The urge to laugh out loud rushed over Julian, as did the urge to cry, to scream, to pummel Harrison Pritchard's chest. He swallowed, struggling for control. Why couldn't this have happened a long time ago? He stared into the stranger's likable face. Everything could have been perfect—he could have had a normal family, with a father. This man could have given him that, but instead he showed up too late. His father was someone with lousy timing, someone who had left his mother when she was pregnant, who had abandoned his family, who now would expect Julian to be the understanding, forgiving son. Julian knew what had happened between this stranger and his mother and how he had left anyway, after loving his mother, and with his mother still in love with him, for years still in love with him.

He thought of the picture upstairs and the other photos his mother had shown him, and tried to imagine this man with her, smiling, laughing, his arms around her, hers around him. And he hated him, hated him for bringing her so much happiness, then taking so much happiness away.

Julian glared at Harrison Pritchard. "What do you want?"

Pritch stepped back, an odd smile playing across his face. "I'd hoped to see your mother. I'm an old friend."

"I know," Julian said. "You're my father."

Pritch's smile widened. "Excuse me?" He blinked, one hand pressed to his chest. "You misunderstand, son. I was a friend of your mother, but I moved long ago, long before you were born."

Julian wasn't sure what to think. Could his mother have lied to him? Was the man in all those photos—this man—his father, or not?

"Don't you live with your daddy?"

The stranger's words rang in Julian's head. His throat tightened, cutting off any words he might speak. All he could do was stare at his bare feet beneath the cuffs of his jeans. He shook his head, struggling to overcome his desire to cry, furious for being such a baby. Then he felt the man's hand on his shoulder.

"Excuse me!"

Audrey's exclamation made them both jump as she appeared in the doorway. Julian moved aside, relieved by her presence.

"Pritch?" She peered at the stranger's face.

"My, my," Harrison Pritchard replied. "If it isn't Miss Audrey."

The man's voice remained friendly and his expression cordial enough, but Julian wondered at the unusual way his aunt had been addressed.

Pritch continued. "I was just telling the boy I was passing through. I realize it's been a long while."

"It certainly has."

Julian wondered if Audrey was going to ask him inside. He usually found her easy to read, but at that moment her face revealed only that now she, too, struggled to remain calm.

"Come on in," she finally said, leading Pritch to the living room and waving him toward the couch.

Julian sat in a chair next to the television.

"I had no idea," Audrey said, pacing, "whether you stayed in New York, or moved to Canada, or what."

Julian continued to watch her, observing only that her voice remained low and steady. He knew this sign of apparent calm could be deceiving, knew her voice could drop to a whisper and then suddenly crescendo to a high-pitched, furious scolding. He'd been the object of such a scolding only once, when he'd stayed at a party way past curfew, coming home to find her dead tired and fuming. Now, he heard no whisper and no crescendo, only a steady, serious tone. Still, her taut face made it clear she was just as upset as she'd been that night.

She settled in an old chair by the fireplace. "Laura wondered where you went, too."

Pritch smoothed his pant legs to his knees, then leaned forward, folding his hands. "The boy told me she died in February." He squinted at Audrey, his expression as tight as his clasped hands. "How?"

"A car accident," Audrey answered.

Pritch stared into his lap. "I wish I'd known." He glanced at Julian. "How hard for you, to lose your mother at such a young age. You're how old, eleven?"

Audrey straightened. "Julian's thirteen, Pritch."

"Oh," he said, "so sorry. I—" He shifted to face her. "Thirteen?"

"Yes, sir," Julian said.

"But—"

Julian's stomach tightened. He noticed his aunt had perched at her chair's edge, and knew she was trying to decide how to explain things in front of him. He took a deep breath and spoke quickly, staring again at his bare feet. "I think Mom was pregnant with me when you left town."

He glanced from Audrey's shocked face to the stranger, who grimaced, his eyes shut tight.

Pritch's mouth moved, but no words came out. He lowered his forehead to meet his open palms and emitted a low moan. "Laura. Oh, Laura."

Julian watched him, memorizing every word, every motion, every sign.

"She had no way, no way to tell me."

"She didn't know she was pregnant until a couple weeks after you left," Audrey said.

"She was pregnant," Pritch echoed. "Oh, but this means . . ." He stared at Julian. "My God," he said, one hand to his temple, the other motioning toward the boy. "My God, I have a son."

Julian would long puzzle over his reaction to these words. As soon as his "father" said this and stood, Julian stood, too, deathly afraid the man was about to embrace him, and bolted out of the living room and upstairs to his room. He tugged on a pair of socks and his sneakers and considered escaping down the back stairs and out the kitchen door. He scowled at the photo of his parents and decided he couldn't give his mysterious father reason to think he was nothing but a stupid kid, even if he never did see him again. He grabbed his jacket, ran down to the front hall, and stopped at the entrance to the living room, trying to appear as tall, mature, and calm as physically possible. "I have to go practice," he announced, cringing as his voice cracked. He avoided both adults' eyes.

"Soccer?" Pritch asked.

"Julian . . ." His aunt came toward him and placed her hand on his shoulder.

"Tryouts for basketball are next week," he mumbled, hoping she wouldn't force him to stay.

"Back before dark, okay?" she said, smoothing his arm.

Julian nodded, then slipped out the front door.

Her fists and teeth clenched, Audrey turned back to Pritch, who remained by the couch where James had stood the night before. She wondered at the strange turn her weekend had suddenly taken. "I need some answers," she said.

He shrugged. "I'm shocked as you."

"This isn't good," Audrey grumbled. She resumed her pacing, then gestured toward the hall. "Do you have any idea how confused Julian is right now, any idea at all? Why the hell didn't you call first? We're in the book, for God's sake. Did you really think you were going to be welcome? Even if Laura were here? *Especially* if Laura were here?"

Pritch cleared his throat. "I know you're in the book, Miss Audrey. That's how I found you." His words vibrated in a low register, every syllable clear. "Now when you have calmed—"

"Don't patronize me, Pritch," she sputtered. "I'm not your girlfriend's kid sister anymore."

He paused, then spoke with even more care. "I understand you're upset, so I'll make this quick, then be on my way."

Audrey crossed her arms, waiting.

"I decided only this morning I was coming." He stepped toward the collection of family photos on the television, staring at Laura's high school portrait. "I had to, before leaving the state, in case Laura would see me, in case she would listen to my pathetic apology."

Audrey watched him, her head throbbing. Certain Laura would have seen him and listened to him, forgiven him and still loved him, she cursed the irony of Pritch's arrival, eight months late.

He moved away from the photos. "I was fired last week," he said, "for no good reason, after nine years with a Buffalo construction firm. I left right off, something I should have done ages ago, and was headed to Philadelphia, to see an old friend there. He says there's no work for average Joes, but he swears by me, knows I'm worth the trouble, so there I go. Or was going, at any rate.

"I had to stop here first, though," he continued. "Had to. But instead of finding Laura happily married with a house full of family, I find her sister in her empty house—with my son. Julian."

Audrey marveled at the beauty of her nephew's name as his father rolled it off his tongue, as he tested its weight, its tone, its sound, realizing its full significance.

Pritch stared at her, his eyes bright with unshed tears. "And now," he said, his voice still low and steady, but his expression defeated, "now I don't know what in God's name I'm to do."

Audrey rubbed her aching temple. "Neither do I," she said, her shoulders round, her face slack. "Neither do I."

Chapter Seven

Harrison Pritchard, Jr., first drove into New Bilford in March of 1979. It reminded him of a dozen other towns he'd worked in over the previous six years, but he viewed the aged storefronts and weary homes of this one with a bit more interest than usual. Laura had invited him to visit her parents' house while she was home on spring break. Pritch remained anxious about the prospect of meeting his girlfriend's family, but knew it was the expected thing to do, after so many months of dating.

Laura had seen Pritch through a difficult winter. Though younger by two years and still a student, she'd exhibited considerable compassion and patience as he'd grappled with his mother's passing after a long illness. The funeral back home in Buffalo had taxed him financially as well as emotionally; he'd been forced to go into debt to cover its costs. Laura had suffered through his tormented tirades over his father's long absence, and provided the sounding board he needed despite the many demands of her courses. She would graduate in May with her nursing degree, and Pritch intended to be there to cheer her on.

Meeting her parents now might be the right thing to do, but Pritch remained leery. He'd had previous girlfriends, even biracial girls like Laura, whose protective, paranoid parents had extinguished any hope of a continued relationship. Pritch knew what people saw when they met him: a dark, stocky man, a handyman without a degree, a man with an odd accent they couldn't peg but found difficult to trust. He knew Laura's father was an intellectual, a black college professor, but remained unsure that an educated man would consider him any differently than others had. Pritch was, after all, dating his daughter.

At the white Colonial bearing Laura's address, Pritch strode to the front door and rang the bell. "No time for weak knees, now, Harry," he muttered to himself, his hands clasped in front of him. When Laura opened the door, though, her smile wide, her hair in those waves past her shoulders, her brown eyes pleased, excited, thrilled to see him on her front step, all the doubts in the world crashed down on Pritch. God, to lose this, to lose her, over things as base as his job, or his skin! He could not let that happen, he decided. He simply could not.

"Harry," Laura said. She held her hand out to him, and drew him inside.

Laura had never seen Harry so nervous. She'd intended to embrace and kiss him as soon as he arrived, but thought better of it when she opened the door to his forlorn face. So she took his hand, then took his coat, then led him to the kitchen where her parents were having coffee. Laura had arrived home the day before and baked cookies that morning. A plate of them sat in the middle of the table. Only a few had been eaten, Laura noticed, probably by Audrey, who was upstairs studying for an exam.

Laura would fondly remember the pleasant welcome her parents extended to Harry that day. Her father stood to shake the young man's hand, and her mother immediately offered Harry a cup of coffee, something she'd never offered any of Laura's friends before.

"Have a seat," Dr. Conarroe exclaimed. "We've heard so much about you."

Laura blinked. While her father had exhibited some interest in her boyfriend, he'd hardly seemed thrilled by the prospect of meeting him. She'd described Harry only briefly, leaving out many details of his past. Harry was a very private person, and she thought he should decide how much of his personal life her parents needed to know.

"We were so sorry to hear about your mother, dear," Yvonne suddenly announced, her hand on Pritch's arm. "Do you take cream and sugar?"

Pritch gave her a quizzical look, but thanked her for her concern. "Black is fine," he answered, nodding toward his cup.

Laura suppressed a grin, certain she'd never seen Harry drink coffee. She watched her boyfriend, an endearing, bold twenty-four-year-old who'd endured so much heartache in his family life, as he sat through a suffocating display of attention from her parents. She'd brought a few boyfriends home from high school, but they'd been the typical New Bilford types:

small-town boys whose dads ran local stores, or whose mothers taught at one of the elementary schools. They'd all been white, and none had had much ambition. Certainly none of them had generated so much interest from Yvonne and Benjamin Conarroe.

Laura heard her sister come downstairs, and wondered what Harry would think of Audrey. She'd warned him she could be a bit outspoken, even rude, at times, depending on her mood. She glanced at her boyfriend as Audrey entered the kitchen.

"This is my sister, Harry, the loud one I warned you about?"

Audrey made a face at Laura. "Loud? Am I carrying on down here while another family member is trying to study?"

Yvonne stood to rinse the empty coffeepot. "Shush, now, girls. Let's at least give Harry the impression we're a big, happy family."

Audrey picked a few cookies off the plate. "I think he'd find us lacking in both departments, Mom. Two kids don't exactly make a big family, and I'm counting the days 'til I move out of this loony bin."

"You're counting," Dr. Conarroe chided his daughter. "What is it, fourteen months to your graduation?"

"If I'm lucky," Audrey said. "Or if I find someone to take my exams. You know anything about economics, Pritch? You prefer to be called Pritch, don't you?"

Laura frowned at her sister.

Pritch shrugged. "Either Harry or Pritch is fine, thank you. As for economics, I know enough to balance my checkbook, but hardly a thing beyond that."

"A lot of good you'll do me." Audrey took one last cookie and headed back upstairs.

"Charm school's next, for that one," Dr. Conarroe said, his tone apologetic. "Laura tells us you work for a construction company in Syracuse."

Pritch nodded. "For the moment."

Laura's parents waited, their eyebrows raised.

"I mean," Pritch stammered, "it's a seasonal kind of business. I take jobs as they're available, move on when work gets slow. It allows a great deal of flexibility."

Dr. Conarroe nodded. "I see."

Laura noted Harry's anxious frown and tried to encourage him with a smile.

54

"I already plan to return to the Rochester area this summer," Pritch continued, "to a firm that's employed me before."

"Just for the summer, dear?" Yvonne sat back down at the table, next to her husband.

Pritch shrugged, staring now at his full coffee cup. "We'll see, I suppose."

His somber answer convinced Laura that Harry wished he had more definite career plans to share with her parents. She reached for his hand. "We hope for much longer than the summer," she said. "But we'll see."

With only two months left of college, Laura had already accepted a nursing job with the New Bilford Medical Center. She'd admitted being incurably homesick, told her parents she would move back to town after graduation, and planned to find an apartment while on spring break. After an hour in the Conarroes' kitchen, Pritch was relieved when she asked him to go visit a few apartment buildings with her.

"I'll be back later, after dinner some time," Laura told her mother and father, who had walked her and Harry to the front door. She handed her boyfriend his coat and put on her own.

Pritch shook hands with her parents. "It's been a pleasure to meet you, Dr. and Mrs. Conarroe."

"Please," Yvonne gushed, "call us Yvonne and Benjamin."

Dr. Conarroe cleared his throat. "We'll see you at Laura's graduation, then."

Pritch ventured a small smile. "I look forward to it."

"Don't worry if I'm late, tonight," Laura added.

Pritch grimaced.

"We might go to a movie, or something," she said.

Dr. Conarroe coughed. "All right, then. 'Bye, now."

Pritch led Laura to his old pickup, exhausted. "Did you have to say that?"

Laura giggled. "Sorry, I didn't—"

He gritted his teeth, but resumed the conversation as they drove away from the house. "They're sure to think we're going to some motel, after that comment."

"A motel? Harry, they were young once. They know dating couples aren't obsessed with having sex all the time. Why in the world—?"

"It was the way you worded it. It sounded so . . . suggestive."

Laura patted his arm. "Let me worry about my parents, and what they think, Harry, okay? There's no need for you to—"

Pritch gripped the steering wheel. "Yes, there is a need for me to worry. Don't you see? Don't you understand what they think of me right now?"

"What? That you're a sex-crazed maniac who's just abducted their daughter? Harry, we've been dating for six months. They'd be surprised if we *weren't* having sex by now."

Pritch shook his head.

"My parents loved you," Laura continued. "They treated you like the son they never had, for goodness' sake. I wish I could make *you* understand *that.*"

Pritch and Laura had time to visit two apartment buildings before offices closed for the day. They stopped by Laura's first choice, a two-story building with balconies and air conditioning less than five miles from the New Bilford Medical Center.

"A fine location, eh?" Pritch said, trying to change the tone their afternoon had taken.

Laura squeezed his hand as they walked inside. "It's not the cheapest one around, but I think I'd love it here."

In the rental office, an elderly clerk fiddled with some keys, then showed them to a unit down the hall. "There's an exercise room in the building," he said, eyeing Pritch while opening the door for Laura. "If you think you'd need that sort of thing."

"Sure." Laura passed him and walked through the apartment. Pritch did not follow. "Lots of closet space," she called. "Big bathroom. This would be terrific." She returned to the two men. "You'll have a few available in May?" she asked the clerk.

He nodded. "One on this floor, two on the second. Take your pick."

Laura grinned. "I'll let you know. I've got a few more places to check, but this would be perfect. Don't you think, Harry?"

Pritch noted the clerk's grim face. "It's going to be your apartment, Laura."

A few moments later, he and Laura got back into his pickup. "Perhaps you should visit the next apartment without me," he suggested.

"What?"

Pritch let out a curt sigh. "You didn't notice the way that man glared at me?"

Laura shook her head, incredulous. "Is that why you didn't walk through the apartment?"

Pritch exhaled, wondering when they might get some dinner, and if he'd have the energy for the drive back to Syracuse that night. Maybe he'd stay in a motel, after all. "He thought I was moving in with you, Laura, and he wasn't very pleased with the idea. You really need to pay attention to these things. They're important."

"No, they're not, Harry. Not to me, anyway. Why should I care what other people think? And why does it matter so much to you?"

He'd upset her, now, but reasoned it was unavoidable. Surely she recognized that others suspect people of color, people like them, of everyday deceits, of constant cycles of deception. How could she ignore that, how could she insist such treatment didn't matter, or make a difference, in their lives? And if they were to continue seeing each other, if they planned to eventually make a life together in her hometown, wasn't it critical she learn to see things the way he did, to open her eyes to these issues? He puzzled over the fact she'd remained blind to them for so long.

"You assume too much," he said, turning the key in the ignition, "if you think everyone accepts you for who you are, regardless of your skin color. You need to realize how dangerous such naiveté can be."

He checked over his shoulder before backing out, fully expecting Laura to respond in an anxious, perhaps even angry, manner. Instead, she beamed at him.

"I don't worry about a thing when I'm with you, Harry," she announced. "You worry more than enough for both of us."

For a moment, Pritch forgot what he'd been about to do. Laura's smile dazzled him, but he could see in her eyes the hint of irritation that belied her attempt at levity, and her slow realization that her teasing had irritated him. Pritch fumbled with the gearshift, jamming it back to park, then abruptly turned off the engine.

He crossed his arms. "I worry for a reason," he growled.

Laura kept her gaze focused on him, her smile gone, her brown eyes now intent on understanding. "Do you really mistrust the world, Harry?" she asked. "Did your father treat you so badly?"

Pritch glared at her. "What in God's name does my father have to do with this?" he demanded.

Laura leaned forward, her wide eyes and silken hair, her mouth, her sweater, her pearl-drop earrings mere inches from him. "I don't know, Harry," she said, each word deliberate. "Isn't that the problem? That I don't understand?"

Yes, yes! he wanted to yell. Yes, you need to understand, you need to hear, and see, and know, finally, that the world is not a perfect, fairy-tale place. He clenched his jaw, determined to enlighten her. "Fine," he announced. "Where shall I start? The first time my old man beat me? No, much too far back. How about the twenty-fifth, or the ninety-ninth?" He kept his gaze steady, his fists clenched in his lap.

Laura sat back, her lips set in a perfect, level line paralleled by her even brows.

"Some day," Pritch continued, spitting out the words, "I suppose I should try to understand my dear father, to consider his motives for abusing his only son. Did he endure trauma as a child? Ever have a belt taken to him?" He glanced at her, expecting some sign of shock and repulsion, but found none. "I imagine so," he said, "since in his youth beatings were very likely common occurrences, as he made sure they were in mine."

He searched for something more horrific, intent now to reveal all, to drive her away for good, if that's where all this was leading.

"I had a wonderful, liberating hobby as a young man," he sneered. "I'd pummel an old shed behind the house in which we rented a few rooms. Whenever my father smacked me around, I'd go out and beat up the shed, and bloody my meager fists." He surveyed his scarred knuckles for a moment, lost now in his acknowledgment of what he'd endured so long ago, what he'd locked away for such a long time. He lowered his voice as he went on. "The landlady caught me once and complained, and of course my father beat me for that, and I went right back out and beat upon the shed. What did it matter if she complained again?" He focused on Laura with his question, puzzled for a moment by her sad stare. "He had plenty other sorry excuses for taking his miseries out on me."

Pritch took a deep breath, on the verge of crying, on the verge of begging Laura to redeem him, to convince him of his goodness despite his miserable past. He pounded the steering wheel, trying to drive back the tears. "Thank God," he wailed. "Thank God he finally left!"

She was in his arms, now, placing fervent kisses on his neck, his mouth, his temple, his closed eyelids and wet lashes. She kissed him through his sobs, her tears mingled with his, then rocked him while he buried his hands and face in her hair. She smelled of such promise, as always; of joyous bouquets, of rain-washed lilacs and newly bloomed azaleas, of the blossoms that had filled his mother's small garden. His mother had gone to her garden often, to escape, he'd assumed, but never to simply put-ter in the dirt. No, she surrounded herself in beauty out there, drawing from the earth an urgent display, determined proof that pleasure remained despite pain, that life went on, that past tragedy could not derail the drive to pursue tranquility, to culti-vate peace.

"Thank God he left," he repeated when they'd both calmed and quieted. He realized the windows of his truck had steamed suggestively but tried not to care, certain Laura would laugh at them in another moment. He combed her hair with ten-der fingers, and sighed. "Mother knew little English," he went on. "I had no choice but to take care of her, and was lucky to have no choice. Caring for her saved me, literally. Saved me from the varied ways I otherwise would've destroyed myself."

Chapter Eight

Audrey hoped Julian had found somewhere to calm down after coming face to face with his father for the first time. She'd recognized his excuse to go practice basketball for what it was, but hardly blamed him for making it up.

Pritch remained at the house most of the afternoon discussing his options, including the possibility of staying in town a while. Audrey, though skeptical, provided the morning paper when asked for it so he could check classifieds for a month-to-month lease on a room or studio apartment.

"The boy may not think much of me now," Pritch said, "but we both deserve a chance to get to know each other, don't you think?" Armed with a few leads and promising to stay in touch regarding his plans, he left around four.

Julian had not returned. Nor had he returned by dinner, or by dark as promised. Dusk advanced to night, and Audrey realized with growing concern that she had no phone numbers to call if she hoped to track him down at a friend's house. She knew only his friends' first names—Steve and Joe, Eddie and Jay—and had dropped Julian at their homes only once or twice, so she had no recollection of their addresses. She paced, cordless phone in hand, praying Julian would call.

"He's fine, he's fine, he's fine," she whispered, trying not to imagine him stranded on the side of a dark road, his bike tire flat, or lying in a ditch, his head bleeding. "I bet he didn't wear his helmet, he never wears his damn helmet. I bet he took off down some road he's never been on and now he's lost, cold, hungry, crying." She shook her head. "No, he's with one of his friends, screwing around, not even thinking. . . ."

She glared at the kitchen clock, which read twenty past eight, then slammed the phone onto a counter. "Ring, would you?" she yelled, her hands open and pleading, her tired eyes filled with hot tears. Blood pounded in her head as the empty house echoed her pathetic plea. She was sick of praying for phone calls—from the Moon Resort, which still hadn't reported the results of her interview, and now from Julian or someone who could explain why he hadn't come home. She grabbed for the phone, fumbled and dropped it, then retrieved it just as it rang. Eddie's mother's voice so relieved Audrey that for a moment she failed to understand what the woman was saying. Then she learned Julian was at his friend's house, and Eddie had asked if he could spend the night. Audrey agreed, vowing to give Julian hell the next day.

Sunday morning, Audrey woke early and waited. She sat at the kitchen table and scribbled frustrated notes on a yellow legal pad. Convinced she would not be offered the Moon Resort position, she had decided to write a series of follow-up letters and mail them through the end of the year. Maybe then they'd offer her a job, she reasoned—any job, just to get her to leave them alone.

She heard her nephew's bike rattle into the backyard and listened for Julian's quick steps. Instead, she heard him slowly make his way to the back door.

The boy walked into the kitchen and frowned at her. Audrey frowned back.

"Do you want to talk about it?"

"What?" Julian passed her and opened the refrigerator. He stared into it, his back to his aunt.

"Your father, Julian. He plans to stay in town a while, to look for work. We should talk about this."

Audrey willed herself to remain calm, to keep from pushing her nephew further into silence. She waited for a sign of any kind from him as he closed the refrigerator and turned toward her. At the sight of his weary, annoyed expression, she wondered if all parents—and guardians—eventually find themselves shut out of a child's world. For the first time, she felt painfully uneasy with Julian—anxious about his troubles, yet so far from understanding them, so far from knowing how she might help.

The boy glowered, but remained silent while Audrey told him his father was recently fired after an employee in his department stole company funds.

"He was fired for that?"

"They said he was an ineffective supervisor, but Pritch says they used that as an excuse to let him go."

Julian crossed his arms. "Is he going to sue?"

Audrey glanced at him. "It's not that easy. There are lots of . . . issues . . . involved."

He shrugged. "You mean discrimination. So, he should sue."

"Maybe he will, I don't know." Audrey wondered that her nephew assumed discrimination was an easy thing to prove, a petty crime for which victims commonly were compensated. "Still," she continued, "he needs a job. He's got a lead in Philadelphia, but he plans to look here, too, now that he knows about you." She watched her nephew. "He used to work construction in town, and he's offered to help us out."

"By fixing up the house."

Audrey nodded.

"So you can sell it even if I don't want to move."

"Julian—"

The boy raised both hands, palms outward. "I know, I have no say in all this, but you still think I should know what's going on, right?"

"Don't test me, Julian. You were very close to being grounded last night."

"So ground me! My life already stinks; what difference would it make?"

Audrey slapped her legal pad onto the table as she stood. "Spare me, would you? You have no idea how worried I was last night, how—"

"And *you* have no idea—"

"Would you let me finish?" Audrey stepped toward her nephew, realizing her anger just as it overwhelmed her. "Would you just let me speak, for God's sake?"

Julian's eyes darkened in an unimpressed glare. "Go ahead. Talk all you want."

Audrey saw in his cocky expression that he had no intention of listening to another word. She grabbed his shoulders and shook him. "What do you want from me!"

The boy and his aunt stared into each other's familiar face, shocked by the altered features they glimpsed, features they knew revealed pain they had caused.

Audrey let go.

"I want you to leave me alone," Julian growled. "You're

making me miserable because you hate being here, hate having to take care of me." He turned away. "It's not my fault my mother died."

Audrey followed him, now longing to reassure him. "I'm sorry," she called to her nephew as he ran up the back stairs to his room. She heard his door slam. "For everything, Julian," she added, her arms at her sides, her hands empty and useless. "I'm sorry."

James arrived at Audrey's office late Monday morning. They stood in her company's foyer, Audrey in a business suit, James in a suit and raincoat, a dripping umbrella at his side. He quickly asked her to lunch.

Audrey stepped back, her thumb to her chin, while James waited for her answer.

"Audrey?" The receptionist stood at her desk. "Could you mind the door for me? I'll be right back."

"Sure, Angie." Audrey told James she and Angie worked for the same temp agency. "She got the receptionist position when I moved to Customer Service."

James raised his eyebrows. "Pam said you've only been here a few months."

"Right."

"You work fast."

Her smile broadened.

"What?"

"Nothing."

"When you smile like that—I don't know, I get the feeling I'm missing something."

She shrugged. "I'm glad you stopped by, that's all."

"Sorry I didn't call over the weekend," he said. "Mom kept me busy at her place, moving furniture, then moving it back again, that kind of thing."

"Hm."

Audrey's frown made James realize how little she liked to hear about his mother. He reasoned she probably still harbored some resentment toward Margaret, and couldn't blame her. He recalled his mother's reaction when he was in high school, when she found him strolling around the mall with Audrey during one of her breaks from the pretzel shop. He'd been so absorbed in this new girl he'd met, in his enjoyment of her dry humor, his attempts to get her to crack one of her terrific smiles, that he hadn't noticed Margaret as she'd advanced down the hall toward them, a large shopping bag from Sears gripped in her fist. He'd failed to notice her until she was almost upon them. "Who's this, Jimmy?" Margaret had demanded. He had stammered through the introduction, unable to face Audrey, already certain of the meeting's outcome. His mother wasted no time insisting "Miss Conarroe" return to her job and he head home at once. "I'll meet you there," she'd hissed as Audrey walked away. "We have some talking to do, young man."

James blinked away the bothersome memory, determined to ignore the frustrating effect of his mother's domineering ways. He took Audrey's hand. "Listen," he said. "I feel like I've been given a second chance with you, and this time—"

Audrey gave his hand a squeeze. "This time, we'll both be up front . . . about everything."

He nodded as the receptionist returned. "Fair enough." James realized he was grinning, pleased with her answer, imagining the attractive—if unusual—couple they made.

A few moments later, they stepped through the misting rain to his car. Audrey directed him through narrow back streets of crowded brick homes and neglected yards to a busy street close to the town's center. At an intersection, James pointed out two empty storefronts. "So much has changed here since we grew up." He nodded across the street. "I remember when Fred's Ice Cream Shop served the best sundaes in town. Now it's a sad little Super Drug." They drove down the block to a diner, passing another group of run-down buildings. "They look as though they're about to collapse," he said.

"Like everything else in this town," Audrey murmured.

He glanced at her and found her staring out the window. She frowned. "Including my sister's house."

"My offer still stands." He pulled into the diner's lot. "To help find a buyer, I mean."

"I know."

Inside, they sat at a table away from the drafty door. A waitress filled their coffee cups while they studied laminated menus. After ordering lunch, they cupped their hands around their mugs of coffee, waiting for the steam to carry some of the heat away. James watched Audrey's face, noting her smooth, cocoa-brown complexion, the arch of her eyebrows, the curve of her mouth. She smiled and looked away. He followed the line of her jaw up past her temple to her forehead, pleased her close hairstyle provided such a clear profile. She turned to him, then, meeting his gaze with laughing eyes the color of a perfect hazelnut.

"You think I'm funny." He forced his voice to sound light, raising his cup to test his coffee.

"I've never been so studied," she replied. "It feels as though you're memorizing me."

"I wish I could. I can't get over how different you look, from when we were kids."

Audrey laughed. "Thank goodness."

The waitress arrived a short while later to deposit plates of food in front of them. "Anything else?" she demanded.

Surprised by her tone, James glanced up, his stomach growling in response to the smell of his hamburger. He noticed her odd frown, and the way it made her look much older than she'd originally appeared. "No, thanks," he answered. "We're fine."

After the waitress left, James leaned across the table. "Someone's having a bad day," he said, directing his forehead toward their moody server.

Audrey brandished a French fry. "New Bilford angst, I've always called it." She acted offended, her shoulders back, and glared down her nose. "What, you expect me to be polite? To smile at you? Why the hell should I?" She flicked her wrist toward him. "Please," she said, "I've seen it a million times."

James paused, amused by her imitation but wondering that she characterized people from her hometown as so uncaring.

Audrey gave him a quizzical glance, then put her sandwich down. "You've never been subjected to that before, have you?"

"Sure." He glanced away, embarrassed by the teasing look on her face. "Just—"

"Just not a million times," she finished for him.

James stopped eating. "Was it hard," he began, "growing up here?"

"The only blacks in town?" Audrey asked. "Not really. No burned crosses on the lawn or anything extreme, just the subtle kid stuff, the best friends who suddenly avoid you at school, that kind of thing. You get used to it." She paused. "Of course, Laura wasn't bothered by any of that. I could never pull that off, the way she did. I felt out of place in Nashville, where all our relatives were black, and out of place here, where everyone was white." She shrugged. "Only Washington felt like home to me, I think because it was so mixed. Like me, I guess. Or maybe mixed up is the right term."

James was relieved to see her face relax into a slow smile.

"You know," she continued, "that night we met, at the dance?"

He nodded, remembering the sassy girl in the corner of the gym, clowning with her classmates. She'd stood out, in those jeans of hers, dancing as though she were in front of her bedroom mirror, oblivious to the effect of her body's new curves on the boys who'd gravitated her way. He marveled still that he'd found her dancing alone, though he suspected the reason. It had taken every ounce of courage to approach her.

"You were so sweet," she said, "and kind, really, the first boy to dance with me, much less talk with me all night."

James wondered that he'd made such an impression. He sat back and watched her, relishing this chance to learn more about her. As they enjoyed their lunch and continued talking, he remained amazed at how different she was from the girl he'd known in high school. While her dry sense of humor was still evident, she'd acquired a thoughtful, reserved air that appealed to him.

As soon as they finished eating, a sullen busboy whisked away their plates and the waitress reappeared to drop the bill on the table.

James grinned and picked up the check. "Guess we'll try dessert next time."

Audrey slipped a few bills from her purse as they stood. "For the tip," she said.

"Not that it's deserved."

"C'mon," she teased. "It's not her fault she's stuck in this place."

They drove a few blocks to a small park, where wet benches along a duck pond remained deserted despite the lunch hour. James left the engine and the heat running. He gazed at Audrey, who watched ducks on the bank ruffle their feathers against the light rain, and noted her furrowed brow. "Is everything okay with Julian?"

She nodded. "I always worry about him—and wonder if I'm doing anything right."

Let me help, James wanted to say. He'd thought all

weekend about the opportunity this chance reunion with Audrey had presented. Pam had been right when she'd described her friend as lonely but fiercely independent. She'd also suggested, slyly, that James would make a terrific knight in shining armor. He'd gone a few steps further, over the weekend, reasoning he could help Audrey in many ways: with the house, with Julian, perhaps even by providing a stable family life for her and her nephew as her husband. He and Audrey could then plan to add to that family with children of their own. He'd chuckled to himself at such thoughts, certain he was jumping ahead, but reasoned it would be so easy, with Audrey.

It would be so easy to marry her, to finally escape the doldrums in which he'd wallowed for so long, to move on to the next stage of his life, a stage he'd always assumed he'd have reached by now. All he wanted was a family of his own, and if Audrey proved to be a willing partner, could anyone blame him for jumping ahead a bit, for hoping to pursue his dream with such an intriguing woman?

"My dad was on the road a lot," he offered, "so my mom was on her own, most the time. She did a good job of it, though. I'm sure you are, too."

Audrey sighed. "His father's in town."

"Julian's father?"

She nodded. "He came by Saturday."

James frowned, not entirely sure why this news worried him. "Do you think he'll cause trouble?"

This time Audrey frowned as she glared back out the window.

"Something wrong?" James asked.

She shook her head and James grew certain something was wrong. "Did he already do something? Audrey, what happened?"

"Nothing *happened,*" she scoffed. "You don't realize—never mind."

"What? What don't I realize?"

She faced him. "How prejudiced you just sounded, assuming Julian's father, who of course is black, would probably 'cause trouble' or that something already 'happened.'"

"Wait. I didn't mean any—"

"People assume a black man who's made one mistake is doomed to become a loser. Julian's dad is a regular guy who's been given the shaft and right now he's a bit in shock at discovering he has a son. So no, I don't think he's going to cause any trouble, but I do know Julian is confused as hell and suddenly I'm even more unsure about everything, which is why I'm yelling at you right now. Okay?"

"Audrey, I'm sorry. I didn't mean—"

"No, I'm sorry for jumping down your throat for assuming what nearly every white person in this damn country assumes about a strange black man—that he's something to fear, rather than someone to trust."

She stared outside again. "He's a good guy," she continued, "but a little overwhelmed, I think. So is Julian."

"I'm sure," James said, not at all sure what to say.

The car's engine shifted as it idled, and the heater hummed.

"It's so difficult to explain," she added, "and so frustrating to face, all the time."

"Audrey, I—"

"I know you didn't mean anything by it. Most people don't, these days. But things are still thought, still said, you know?"

James nodded.

"Sounds like Pritch will be around for a while," she said. "A few months, at least."

James wondered what effect this would have on her, and her nephew. "You don't sound thrilled."

"I think it'll be good for Julian, but I don't want him to get hurt, either. Pritch has offered to inspect and fix up the house a bit, which will be a big help. It's going to be hard to sell an old place in such poor shape, especially in such a weak market."

James hesitated, not wanting to sound anxious by repeating his offer to help find a buyer. "People love old houses," he said. "I'll let you know if I hear of anyone who might be interested." He glanced at her. "I want to help, any way I can."

Audrey laid her hand on his. "You already have," she said, "by listening to me rant and rave and not leaving me on the sidewalk for it."

He smiled. "You're just being up front." He paused, then took her hand. "I know this sounds like I'm rushing things, but I'm going to a wedding in two weeks—"

"And you're hard up for a date?"

James laughed. "I want to bring someone special."

Audrey's face harbored a hesitant smile.

68

"There's a catch, though," he said.

"A catch?"

"You'll have to put up with me for at least twenty-four hours. The wedding's at a hotel on one of the Finger Lakes. I figured things would run late, so I reserved a room months ago."

He held his breath as she hesitated.

"I'd love to go," she said.

He slowly exhaled.

"But . . . it's, well, Julian. After this weekend, I don't want to leave him alone, or with a sitter, even for a night out. I should stay close to home, I think, see how things go."

James nodded. "We could always go out somewhere with Julian. Is he into video games?"

"I guess so."

"There's a huge arcade opening at the mall Saturday. How about we take him there, go shopping, make a day of it?"

"Sure," she said. "I think he'd like that."

James grinned, pleased with his spur-of-the-moment idea. "Great. I've got meetings in Rochester the rest of the week, but I'll be in touch, okay?"

Audrey smiled. "I certainly hope so."

She dreamed of the fugitive almost nightly that week. In one dream, the woman huddled in the barn of a small dairy farm, comforted by the closeness of the cows that shared her quarters. As always, even in hiding, her face remained veiled in the shadows of her hat's wide brim.

Her baby slept beside her while she gulped milk from a forgotten pail, grateful for it and for the shelter she'd found for the coming night. A storm was on its way, of this she was certain. She'd learned to track everything on her journey, including the sky. Nothing escaped her anxious attention.

The baby began to wail. Recently fed, he pushed away all his mother's attempts to shush him. She cooed and cajoled and pressed him tight to her chest, eyes fastened on the barn door, mind reeling in vain search of a weapon in case anyone came upon her. She'd just wrapped her screaming child in a sack from the floor, prepared to bolt rather than risk discovery, when the door opened and a young miss entered, disheveled and dressed in boy's pants, but a young miss, nonetheless.

The fugitive froze. The girl, pale and wide-eyed, ran to her, no pause in her step, and presented a biscuit, its edge soaked in milk. The baby sucked on it with vigor while the girl held it for him and beamed at his mother.

"You're a runaway," she whispered. "I heard his cry from the house. The wind carried it to me, called me to help. Here," she shoved a bag into the fugitive's startled hand. "More provisions, for you both. You're safe, for the time being. Pa's drunk and dead gone already." She shrugged off her coat and dropped it in a heap. "He'll whip me good to find that gone, but take it, and this blanket for the little 'un." She pulled things from hidden pockets, from thin air.

She caressed the baby's cheek. "What's his name?" The fugitive said nothing, and the girl barely paused for breath before answering herself. "He looks like a Daniel," she announced, startled at the volume of her voice. She shushed herself. "You'll be coziest in the loft, I nap there all the time. But long 'fore sunrise, head off, 'hear? Pa'd be the first to haul you to a bounty hunter and holler for his reward." The girl considered the baby for a long moment, pressing his fist with her own fragile fingers. "He's golden, a golden child," she murmured.

Stunned by the stranger's tender ways, the fugitive battled competing urges to pull the child close, or to transfer him wholly to the girl's eager arms. What a relief it would be to give him over! Surely the little miss, frail though she was, would conduct him to safety. The fugitive stole a glimpse of the girl's eyes, the first eyes of a white person she'd ever considered, and found them kindly but shallow, empty of the depth of emotion she harbored. She suspected, down deep, all white people might actually have no emotions at all, they were such capable agents of misery and pain. She held her baby even tighter, shocked now at her impulse to forsake her son.

"I read, you know," the girl announced, her thin chest inflated with pride. "Taught myself. So I've read about people who help runaways—abolishers, I think they're called. Guess I'm one of them, now, 'cause my heart's fairly pounding out of its cage!" She grinned, but shushed herself again. "I know a farm what harbors runaways, or at least its farmer's partial to the cause. I'll draw you a map. It's a long way off yet, but my map'll get you there . . . with little Daniel here . . . all right."

She faded from view, and Audrey woke, hardly comforted by her words. How these dreams disturbed her! She tried to think of other things each day, to preoccupy her subconscious in hopes of avoiding further dreams, but they returned, over and over. At least this most recent one provided some clues. Audrey understood now that the fugitive was an escaped slave. How terrified women like her must have been, she mused, as they traveled unknown roads desperate for freedom, dependent on strangers—black and white—who could betray them in a heartbeat.

On successive nights, Audrey dreamed this same dream, with minor variations, three times. The Saturday morning she and James were to take Julian to the mall, she shattered a juice glass in her sister's scarred kitchen sink, recalling what she'd once overheard, or read, or been told directly: A dream dreamed three times was bound to come true. She wondered if a dream dreamed three times might also be based in truth, fueled by the past.

Chapter Nine

After closing on her home in October 1980, Laura stood with Audrey on the front lawn, amazed the house belonged to her. The sisters shielded their eyes from the afternoon sun as they looked around. The neighborhood was full of mature trees, and Laura relished the thought of viewing their colorful display every fall. Each time a breeze rustled the sugar maples in her own yard, falling leaves traced silent, undulate paths around her and Audrey on the way down to rest at their feet.

The house appeared regal in its sunlit orange and red frame. Laura recalled the first time she'd seen the farmhouse, how drawn she'd been to it. She'd loved its straight lines, the simplicity of its ordered windows, its solid, traditional bearing. Inside, she'd smoothed the ridges worn into the built-in shelves on both sides of the grand fireplace, marveled at the floorboards cut of so many different lengths, probably from a pine off the premises. The home's evident history enthralled her.

"It's the kind of house old people haunt," Audrey said.

The young women stood side by side, like two soldiers saluting a looming sergeant. From another angle, they might have been mistaken for mother and daughter, with Laura in low heels and a maternity dress while Audrey sported jeans and a short sweater. Sunlight sparkled off their gold earrings, and off the small diamond ring on Laura's left hand.

"It may very well be haunted," Laura said.

Audrey squinted at her sister. "I meant by live people, not dead."

Laura brushed away her sarcasm, determined to savor the view for a few more minutes. She realized Audrey's comments were laced with concern over her purchase of the house, and about the old home's condition, which Laura admitted was poor. She'd bought the farmhouse for next to nothing, though, a fact she'd made clear to her sister many times. More importantly, she loved the old place, and knew this was her best chance to ever own a home like it. "The real estate agent told me there are stories behind it," Laura said. "He said it may have been a site on the Underground Railroad."

"I say that guy saw you coming from a mile away," Audrey replied.

Laura smiled, then crossed the yard and ascended the porch stairs, brandishing her new key. Audrey watched, unmoving, as her sister opened the front door, entered her house, and was swallowed whole by its shadows.

Audrey had insisted on taking a few days off to fly home and help Laura move in, though her sister told her she'd have plenty of help from friends at work. Laura was six months' pregnant, now. Pritch had been gone just as long. Their parents, who'd been planning for over a year to move to Florida, had left just a few weeks before. Audrey continued to complain about their timing.

"How could they?"

Laura shrugged every time her sister brought it up. "It's not their fault I'm pregnant, Audrey."

"But how could they still move?"

"You know how sick Dad's been the past few winters. His doctor was right, he needs to be in a warmer climate. They'll visit in the spring, to see the baby."

"But Mom. At least she—"

"She'd never leave Dad alone. I'm a nurse. I'll be fine."

"Well, I'll come for Christmas, then for a couple weeks in January, to help or . . . whatever."

Laura laughed. "Don't worry, I won't ask you to be my labor coach."

But Audrey did worry, a habit she'd taken on quite seriously since learning of her sister's predicament in the spring. She and Laura had gotten into the habit of calling each other every other weekend, so Audrey knew something was wrong when Laura called her a second time in the same week.

"I'm pregnant."

"What?" Audrey dropped into her office chair, wishing her sister had called her later, at her apartment. Her cubicle hardly allowed for privacy. Their last conversation had involved a lengthy discussion of Pritch, who'd broken off his short engage-ment with Laura in early May and promptly left town. While Audrey had ranted and raved over his many faults and idiosyn-crasies, Laura had insisted it was best he left now, if he had mis-givings, rather than later. Audrey had finally stopped fuming when her sister confessed she'd been bawling non-stop for three days, and had to tell patients she was having problems with her contact lenses, her eyes were so red and swollen. "One lady thought I was contagious," she'd joked, her weak attempt at laughter giving way to a fresh wave of tears.

When she spoke of her pregnancy, though, Laura said nothing of crying herself hoarse every day. "I've known so many women, friends and patients, who desperately want children, and can't have any," she told her sister. "I'm not a scared little schoolgirl. I can handle this. I just wish I could reach Harry, to let him know."

Her sister's forgiving attitude toward her ex-fiancé astounded Audrey. Though certain Pritch had suspected Laura was pregnant and skipped town as quickly as his cold feet could carry him, Audrey forced herself to keep such opinions to her-self, to avoid upsetting her sister. Laura had always been the practical one, the levelheaded one, but Audrey suspected she'd recently succumbed to some sort of hormonal imbalance that affected her common sense. For the first time, Audrey felt pro-tective of her sister. And she grew increasingly angry with her parents for moving away when Laura needed them most.

Audrey spent the rest of the weekend insisting Laura not lift anything. Various friends from the medical center did stop by to help—men who moved furniture, women who unpacked boxes and asked Laura where she'd like which dishes put. Laura joked and laughed with everyone, showing signs of close attach-ment to each coworker. Audrey teasingly inquired about a cou-ple of the male nurses who appeared to be about their age, but Laura brushed away her suggestive comments.

"They're all married, gay, or otherwise unavailable," she said. "Trust me, no one's interested when you've got a tenant the size of a soccer ball." She rubbed her stomach. "Plus, I'm exhausted by the time I even get to work. I've got sciatica, which sends lovely shots of pain down my leg every once in a while, and I forget where I've put my keys when they're still in my hand. I'm no one's dream date, these days."

If Laura had known that Sunday in mid-April was the last happy, carefree day she'd have with Harry, she'd have forced it to slow to a crawling pace so she could memorize every detail: the wrap of his arm at her waist; the heat of his breath on her neck; the pressure of his hands; his laughter; his teasing. He revealed his Jamaican heritage, on days like that, saying Laura looked "pretty like-a money," slipping into a patois that lit his face as he spoke it.

"Not patois," he'd insist. "Real English, real English." He'd then strike a disapproving pose. "Why ya tek so long, dawta? Cum ya, yuh ina big choble. Dem boys is a no good bunch. Dey a-go up inna Miss Macey's mango tree. Mi see dem. Mek dem go weh."

Laura loved these performances, confident they helped Harry cope with his emotions regarding the loss of his mother, his only tie to this unique part of him. She knew he regretted having been away from her when she died, and remained bitterly angry with his father for all the pain he'd caused her. She'd hoped Harry would find comfort in her family, and consider himself a welcome member of it. But he seemed convinced her parents disliked him, despite their constant attempts to make him feel at ease in their home. Laura recalled the past Easter, which had turned out to be a tense, troublesome reunion.

Dr. Benjamin Conarroe, while only fifty-nine, had retired early from the University of Rochester. Recurrent bouts of the flu during winter had kept him home for weeks at a time, and his blood pressure had become difficult to manage. His first semester away from work was a miserable one. Yvonne confessed to Laura she was tempted to run out of the house, screaming, some days. Dr. Conarroe refused to exercise, as his doctor recommended, and either shuffled papers in his study or moped about the house all day. Yvonne said she felt as though she'd adopted a moody, six-foot child.

In January, Audrey and Laura learned of their parents' plan to move to Florida at the end of the summer. By April, the family's house was up for sale, so their mother had insisted on having everyone there for Easter dinner.

Laura knew Harry preferred to spend Sunday afternoons alone. Saturdays were spent running necessary errands, but Sunday was for relaxing, he'd say, for resting up for the week's work ahead.

"But it's Easter," Laura insisted, for once frustrated he

refused to make her family a priority. "And my parents will be gone in a few months. This will be the last holiday we have together in their house." Laura knew she was whining, but couldn't help it. Something was wrong, with Harry, or perhaps with her. She'd noticed gray circles under her eyes that morning, and had felt light-headed, and a little disoriented, lately. She suspected she was coming down with a cold. Winter had hung on longer than usual.

She took Harry's hand. "Please," she said. "This means a lot to me." Was she begging? She didn't care. In the few months since he'd proposed, Harry had grown more distant from her parents, more reserved around them. Laura knew her parents were hurt by this, and by the fact she and Harry rarely stopped by to visit. She'd hoped the Easter dinner, especially with Audrey there for comic relief, would be a good thing, for all of them.

"Of course we'll go," Harry had answered, not at all enthusiastic. "Perhaps we should bring flowers."

Laura and Harry arrived at the Conarroes' house an hour later, a potted mum and an Easter card in hand. Audrey greeted them just inside the front door. "Know any good restaurants?"

Laura gave her sister a weary look. "What?" She inhaled the aromas of roasting turkey and baked pies, and knew Yvonne was working wonders in the kitchen, as usual. She soon grew queasy from the familiar smells, though.

"The turkey's taking forever," Audrey confided. "Mom's about to throw it out the window."

Laura wondered if her father might have a beer for Harry. "Does she need any help?"

Audrey laughed. "I wouldn't go near the kitchen, if I were you."

Laura sighed. "Well, Harry. Let me know if you'd rather just go. I could drop you off, and—"

"Go?" Audrey took them both by their elbows and steered them into the living room. "I'm not here to hang out with the folks, Laura. Mom's fuming and Dad's wandering around like a lost puppy." She took their coats, put the mum on the coffee table, and positioned her sister and future brother-in-law on the love seat. "There. Now stay put and behave. That means you too, Mr. Pritchard."

Pritch bowed his head. "Your demand is my command, Miss Audrey." He winked at Laura. "She tells it like it is, eh?"

Laura shrugged. "Always has."

By the time dinner was finally ready, Pritch had drunk two of Dr. Conarroe's Bud Lights and poured himself a generous glass of Beaujolais. Determined to endure the event for Laura's sake, he'd decided to indulge as much as necessary.

He sat at his place, staring at his empty plate. He'd recently begun to suffer from anxious misgivings over the prospect of joining this family, and suddenly was overwhelmed by them. When he'd proposed to Laura, he'd thought only of spending the rest of his life with her. And though her parents planned to soon move out of state, he knew Laura would always remain under their influence, and his own judgment of himself, his career choices, even decisions regarding home and family, would be subject to the Conarroes' constant scrutiny.

Laura drank only water, and rarely spoke. He squeezed her hand while her mother bustled about the table, filling plates. "Feeling all right?" he asked.

His fiancée nodded and gave him a weak smile.

"So," Dr. Conarroe announced from the head of the table. "What's new in the construction business these days, Harrison?"

Pritch gritted his teeth. He hated being addressed by his father's name. "Nothing new, sir," he replied. "Business remains steady, despite the miserable weather." Pritch chose not to mention he'd been overlooked for a promotion to foreman. He knew he had the experience to do the job, but was told he was too young, and too new to the company. Even Laura remained ignorant of his struggles at work. He certainly had no intention of broadcasting them to her quirky parents.

Yvonne asked what else was needed, sat for a second, then shot up to run to the kitchen for salt and pepper. Pritch remained baffled by her overanxious attention to trivial details. He'd long suspected she insisted on such performances not for his or any other guest's sake, but because she considered it her duty as a professor's wife, hostess of her flawless home. He could hear her pretentious bracelets jangling from behind him as she returned to the dining room.

"So," Dr. Conarroe began again. "We're getting ready for our trip to St. Lucie to find a townhouse we can move into in September. Assuming we sell this old place by then."

"We should have no trouble with that, dear," Yvonne

said, sitting again.

"Yes, well, wish I could be so sure. I still think it would make perfectly good sense for Harrison and Laura to—"

"Daddy."

Pritch cringed to hear Laura address her father in such a manner. "We'd be honored to move into your lovely home, Dr. Conarroe," he said, noting Audrey's amused smirk from across the table. "But I'm sure you're aware the price is beyond our reach."

Benjamin Conarroe put down his fork. "And I'm sure you're aware we'd do whatever we could to—"

"I'm no charity case, sir."

"Harry, please."

"Perhaps," Pritch continued, "we ought to change the subject."

"Agreed," Yvonne said, glaring at her husband.

Dr. Conarroe opened his palms toward the ceiling, an innocent bystander. "I just thought—"

"Well, stop thinking, Benjamin," Yvonne snapped. "There's no need for Laura and Harry to worry about buying a house at this point. They have a wedding to plan. July will be here before they know it."

Pritch realized Laura had put her hand on his. He stared at the simple engagement ring she wore and decided, with gut-wrenching despair, that he'd made a terrible mistake. Certainly she deserved better. A better ring than he could afford, a better home than what he could buy her. She worked full-time, yes, but even with both their salaries . . . Taxes were so high. Then there were insurance and heating bills . . . So many expenses built into a house, a family, a future. So many demands, such expectations. And what would he do when the walls came tumbling down? Follow in his father's footsteps? Surely he'd set himself up to fail. Surely Laura would be better off without him.

Pritch slipped his hand out of Laura's grasp and glanced at Benjamin Conarroe, convinced on this point, the old man would agree.

Chapter Ten

Audrey heard Julian sigh a deliberate teenage sigh in the back seat while James, driving beside her, told endless stories of high school pranks as they passed their town's bars and restaurants on the way to the mall. Audrey wondered if James always babbled when he was nervous, and why Julian's presence affected him so. She found his tales of teenage high-jinx more annoying than entertaining, and suspected Julian found them patronizing.

"See the Big Boy outside TJ's?" James pointed to a small diner with a plump statue out front. "We stole that senior year and hid it in the gym the night before the last assembly. You should've seen Coach Martin's face the next morning." He shook his head. "After that, they riveted the thing down in a block of cement."

Audrey stared out her window, irritated by everything—and everyone. She'd suffered through a restless night, thanks to her recurring dream, and begun the day already tired and frustrated. All she wanted to do was sleep.

The phone call yesterday from the Moon Resort hadn't helped her mood any. After learning the open position had gone to someone else, Audrey was told the personnel department wanted to send her résumé—and a glowing review of her interview—to hotels throughout the Moon chain. These included locations in Europe, Canada, the Caribbean, and in U.S. cities as far-flung as San Diego, Minneapolis, Tucson, New York . . . and Washington, D.C. The possibility she might be offered a job she couldn't refuse in any of these places worried Audrey as much as it excited her. The fact that an appropriate opening could arise any time—or never at all—pushed her into an unnerving state of limbo.

At a stoplight, her eyes were drawn to a sudden shower of yellow-brown leaves from an old oak at the corner. That morning, she'd wakened to see everything coated in an early snow. She imagined how Laura would have exclaimed at the beauty of her powdered trees, especially when sunlight sparkled off the glazed crimson and orange foliage, perfecting the scene.

Audrey had viewed the season's first snow with weighted, numbed dread. She was relieved to see it melt away in watery streams, dragging more leaves to the ground.

Leaded leaves, she thought, wondering why she, too, felt so heavy, so hollow, wondering why she found comfort in watching dead leaves fall to their fates. She shrugged as the oak surrendered its last. At such depths, it seemed, she craved mutually miserable company.

James babbled on. "No, sir," he said, "Big Boy's never going anywhere again until they tear that place down. Here we are." They swung into the mall parking lot, then parked in front of a department store. "The new arcade is at the other end of the mall," James said, "but I thought we could walk through this store first, if you guys don't mind. I've got a wedding gift to buy."

"Sure." Audrey tried to ignore the reference to the wedding he'd asked her to attend. As they walked to the store's entrance, she decided James must have been either a very cute or a very goofy-looking child, with such a broad grin and ears that reddened so easily. In high school, of course, she'd considered his looks beyond reproach. Now, though, she couldn't determine whether he still hoped to impress Julian, or was honestly excited about visiting a video arcade. She knew he'd be disappointed if he hoped to see signs of Julian's excitement. At thirteen, Julian had perfected the unimpressed expression that made adults feel like fools for trying to entertain a teenager, or assuming a teen might be interested in anything. Her nephew followed a few steps behind them, with the deliberate gait of the self-confident.

James held the door open as Audrey stifled a yawn. "Tired?" he asked.

"Didn't sleep well. Had the strangest dreams, one about flying, and being back in Washington." She wondered what he'd think of her fugitive dreams, but doubted her ability—or desire—to describe them to him.

"Washington?" He fell into step beside her.

Julian slipped by them and headed toward the Young

Men's department.

She nodded. "In the summer. It was hot and I was sweating like crazy but I loved it, loved being there in my old apartment. It was strange I was so hot, though, since I always had air conditioning. I remember thinking that in my dream. Then I woke up, dying of heat under an old comforter, and looked outside to see snow all over the place."

James grinned. "Wasn't that great? Too bad it melted so fast. You ski?"

She raised her eyebrows. "Me? No way."

"C'mon." He took her hand. "You'd love it. I could be your personal instructor."

"No, thanks. Really."

"It's no fun living in the Northeast if you don't play in the snow."

"Tell me." She slowed as they neared the escalator. "The gift section's over here. Do you see Julian?"

James continued toward the escalator. "He was near the jackets. We'll be right back. I want to go downstairs for a minute."

"What's down there?"

He grinned. "You'll see."

They descended to the lower floor, which housed women's clothing. Audrey followed James to the party dress section, where racks displayed an array of sequined gowns and dresses.

James stood beside her in the main aisle. "I wish you'd reconsider going to the wedding next weekend," he said. "You'd look amazing in any of these dresses."

She shook her head. "I can't afford any of them."

"Let me buy you one. Even if you don't go to the wedding, you can save it for the holidays, for the New Year's Eve party I'll be asking you to." He winked, and Audrey smiled.

"I can't let you spend that much money on me," she said. "I've got plenty of nice outfits to wear to parties—and weddings."

He blinked. "You'll go?"

"I'll think about it."

"Fair enough."

Audrey led him back to the escalator, anxious to return to the Young Men's department to find Julian. Back upstairs, she navigated the aisles of denim and sweaters, searching for her nephew among the racks. She glanced around, then followed the sound of voices to the back of the department, where she finally found Julian—with a security guard and two female store employees.

A middle-aged, plump saleslady glared at Audrey and James as they approached. Audrey tried to make eye contact with Julian, but failed. She glanced from one adult to another, trying to glean hints as to what had happened.

"Are you with this boy?" the saleslady demanded.

"Yes," Audrey answered. "He's my nephew."

"You're his aunt?" The woman's voice pinched high as she squinted from James back to Audrey. "We just paged you. I caught your nephew here trying to steal a leather jacket, a very expensive leather jacket."

"What?"

The other woman, a brunette with a name tag identifying her as the store manager, intervened. "He was caught walking out of the store with this." She touched a leather-trimmed New York Knicks jacket lying next to the cash register.

Julian remained silent.

"Is that true?" Audrey asked.

Her nephew shook his head.

She addressed the manager. "Is it possible he was trying it on and some kind of mistake was made?"

"No," the saleslady interjected. "I keep an eye on kids when they're in my department without an adult, and he was clearly leaving the store with that on." She stabbed a forefinger toward the jacket. "That costs $150! You can't tell me he was planning to buy that now, can you?"

Why not, Audrey thought, because he's a black boy? What if Julian was white with a blond, preppy haircut and over-priced jeans? Would you assume the same thing? Would we be here right now?

"I was looking for you," Julian said. "She thought I was headed for the door or something."

James picked up the jacket, revealing a large white disk attached to it by a short chain. "This is a huge security device," he said. "Do you really think anyone would try to leave the store with it?"

The round security guard answered. "Kids have done it before, sir. They don't care if they set off an alarm for a few minutes. If they think they can run faster than security, they take the

82

risk."

The store manager addressed Audrey. "Listen, miss," she said, her tone frank and patronizing. "Please keep a better eye on your nephew next time you're shopping with us. Maybe this won't happen again."

Until that moment, Audrey had remained uneasy but calm, confident of Julian's innocence, not at all surprised by the suspicions he'd raised or the store employees' reactions. She was accustomed to being treated cautiously by white salespeople and usually approached them slowly in turn, speaking softly and smiling, looking forward to the end of the interaction so she could escape their tense faces and rigid backs. Now, though, as the familiar heat of embarrassment crept up the back of her neck, Audrey grew desperate to end this incident. She gave the woman a curt nod and turned to leave, certain Julian would follow.

James, however, stood his ground. He stared at the manager. "What is your problem?" he demanded.

The security guard stepped toward him, but James continued to glare at the woman.

"Pardon me?" she asked.

"You heard me," James said, his voice rising. "You're treating Ms. Conarroe and her nephew as though they're not good enough to shop here. What right—"

Audrey's mind raced. She wondered if James was trying to impress her and Julian, or whether he really was upset—and surprised—by the manager's attitude. She glanced beyond their small circle to see two curious teenagers draw closer to them while a mother and her boy scurried out of the department.

James ranted on. Audrey sensed Julian's impatience, and grew more anxious to leave. She put her hand on James's arm, hoping to lead him away. Instead, he placed his hand on hers, as though to console her. "I'm a regular customer," he continued, "and I'm going to file a complaint with your district manager on Monday. I find your tone condescending, and your reaction to this whole situation insulting."

"Sir, I think you're overreacting," the manager answered, her face now flushed. "We were simply trying to safeguard our merchandise. You understand this is an expensive jacket."

"And I understand you assumed my—friend—could not afford to buy it, an assumption that was wrong. In fact, I was holding the money he'd saved from his summer jobs. Here,

83

Julian."

Audrey watched, her mouth open, as James took out his wallet, counted ten twenty-dollar bills, and handed them to her nephew. "Now you can get your jacket," James said, "if you still want it."

Julian stood with the bills in his hand, all the adults watching. A slow smile crossed his face as he pocketed the money. "Naw," he said, grinning now. "I like the Bulls better than the Knicks, anyway."

James patted him on the back as they turned to walk away. "No kidding?" he joked.

Audrey clamped her mouth shut and faced the store manager. "I can assure you this will never happen again," she said, her skin bristling with heat, "not because I see the need to keep a 'better eye' on my nephew, but because we'll never set foot in this store again."

She walked away with deliberate, steady steps, though her heartbeat raced. She caught up to James and Julian as they left the store and entered the mall. "Where are you guys going?" she demanded, her voice shaking.

James smiled. "To the arcade, remember?"

"You've got to be kidding."

He put an arm around her shoulders. "C'mon. We handled that pretty well. Put them in their place. Now Julian's got some cash to spend, so—"

Audrey stopped. "Julian, give the money back."

"What?" James pulled his arm away. "Audrey, really, I don't mind—"

She glared at her nephew. "You heard me, Julian. That was a great scene you two pulled, but now it's over. Give the money back."

Her nephew scowled as he dug his hand deep into his pocket. "This was just getting interesting," he said, pulling the bills out and handing them to James. He walked away and sat on a bench, staring down the busy hall with a sullen expression.

"Audrey," James said, still holding the money. "I don't mind letting him keep this, if it'll make him happy—"

"Make him happy? What thirteen-year-old wouldn't be thrilled to have $200 handed to him? Of course it would make him happy. What will you do next time you want to impress him, buy him a car?"

James frowned and put the bills back in his wallet.

Audrey sighed. "Please stop trying so hard. Really. There's no need to win him over."

He looked away, his lips pursed, while Audrey wondered what was going to happen next—and whether she had enough money for cab fare home.

"I wasn't trying to win him over," James said. "But I did think someone should stand up for him in there."

Audrey blinked, trying to absorb his words without reacting to them, infuriated by his suggestion she'd failed to defend Julian. I may not have declared my nephew's innocence to the entire store, she wanted to yell, but at least I didn't spout off like a fool.

"Maybe you're right," James added. "Maybe I should stop trying so hard." He approached Julian, patted the boy's arm, and signaled him to follow.

Audrey tagged along on the way to the arcade, envying their apparent camaraderie, overwhelmed by the sensation she was the only person in the shopping center who felt so low. It didn't matter what group she spied—high school girls in a pack, a young couple with a baby stroller, an older couple window-shopping—everyone else seemed content, cheerful, in good company. She waved James and Julian into the arcade and sat on a bench, content to people-watch for a while.

Two women approached from down the hall. Audrey knew at once they were sisters, and realized she couldn't take her eyes off them. They appeared to be Italian, like Pam, with olive skin and dark hair. They passed her, then paused before a lingerie store window as one whispered a joke that sent them both into peals of laughter. Audrey looked away to let their private joke remain private as the ring of their laughter echoed in her ears.

She had never considered herself and her sister best friends, but she had considered herself and Laura close. Close enough to enjoy a private joke, a good laugh, a long talk. Close enough to know each other's strengths and weaknesses, each other's best and worst moods, each other's pet peeves. Close enough to like each other as well as love each other, to crave each other's company, to miss each other while apart.

Audrey was halfway to the ladies' room before she realized she'd stood. She found the bathroom blessedly empty and banged into a stall where she sat on the toilet, feet tucked together on the floor, arms pressed into her abdomen. As her sobs escalated, she clamped her hand over her mouth to keep their echo from reverberating beyond the small space into which she'd locked herself. She surrendered fully to the force of her grief, then, letting it knock her breathless as she rocked and wailed.

Finally, she fell silent, still rocking, steadied only by the methodic placement of her fingers upon her tear-stained face.

Chapter Eleven

In December 1993, Laura confessed to her mother she felt "snowed in" whenever Julian was sick. She and Julian had just arrived in Florida to be with Yvonne for her first Christmas as a widow. While Audrey was due to arrive soon, Julian, feverish with the flu, slept in the guest bedroom near the townhouse's small kitchen.

"It slows everything down," Laura continued, "makes you change plans with no notice, and put off making plans for who knows how long. Suddenly all you can do is get through the day at hand."

Yvonne placed a cup of coffee in front of her daughter. Both women's eyes were pink at the edges, framed by light circles of gray. Laura wore sweats, very little makeup, and had swept her hair back into a ponytail. Her mother wore her hair and makeup as she did every day, neat and evenly done, yet the tired lines of her face belied any attempts to distract the eye.

"I felt the same way when Daddy died," Yvonne said. "Only I didn't just slow down, I stopped in my tracks. Life went on, my own life, without me. Days just sped along as if nothing had happened, while I waited for some signal I was ready to rejoin the living." She sighed and took her daughter's outstretched hand. "All you can do is rest a while," she added, "though sometimes it seems such a long while."

"Oh, Mom," Laura said. "I felt that way, too, after you called with the news. Like I'd had the breath knocked out of me. But I couldn't slow down, I just moved in a fog, trying to put up that front of normalcy for Julian, trying to think through the best way to help him understand."

A wry smile crossed her face. "He's almost thirteen, and I still treat him like a baby sometimes, especially when he's sick." Her hand remained clasped with her mother's while she spoke. "He woke up at the motel this morning saying he felt heavy, and I knew he had a fever without even touching him, he radiated that much heat. He gets such high fevers with even a minor cold. It always worries me. And it was so hard to make him get back in the car, even after we got the fever down. I'd convinced myself it was best to drive the rest of the way and get here, but I wasn't sure. He was such a good sport, never complaining, just moaning a little in the back seat. It broke my heart."

Yvonne nodded, still solemn. "He's an angel, Laura. I know you've had a time of it, raising him yourself. Daddy was so proud the Conarroe name would live on through Julian. He'd always worried about that, with no sons, or brothers, or male cousins on his father's side. Did I ever tell you that?"

"Yes," Laura assured her. "Many times."

"And you're a wonderful parent," Yvonne continued, determined not to be put off course. "You did the right thing. You always do." She paused and sat back a bit. "What would you have done in a motel room all day while he slept? Gone crazy with worry and more second-guessing, most likely." She nodded as though to defend her argument against naysayers. "You did the right thing."

Laura gave her mother's hand a squeeze. "It always helps to talk things over with you, Mom." She glanced around the kitchen. "It's quiet around her without Dad, isn't it?"

"Deathly quiet," Yvonne answered. "I never should've agreed to move into a retirement community, but that's what he wanted. I suppose he'd had his fill of young people from all those years teaching."

Laura brightened. "Move back home, then," she suggested. "Julian would love to have family close by. We both would."

Yvonne shook her head. "Those winters, Laura. I couldn't go back to that. And I'm not alone here. I've got friends, after so many years, though it's certainly not the same without your father. Nothing is." She paused. "I never realized how much I'd miss him, tell the truth. But when you lose someone who shared so much with you, even your memories . . ." She turned in her chair. "Did I just hear someone?" She frowned toward the kitchen door, which led to a few steps out the back of the townhouse, to resident parking. "Audrey didn't rent a car, did she?"

"She'd planned to."

"When will she learn to save money?" Yvonne scoffed. "I thought she'd take a shuttle. Or I could've picked her up at the airport; it's not that far."

Laura raised her hand. "Shush, Mom. She'll hear you. You know how upset she gets when you pick on her like that."

Yvonne's frown deepened. "I just wish she had better judgment, sometimes."

The door opened and Audrey appeared at the threshold to the kitchen, an overloaded garment bag draped over her shoulder, her business suit crinkled, her heels too high for traveling. "I'm here," she announced. "Time to put up the tree."

Laura rose to greet her with a hug, then relieved her sister of her garment bag. "How long are you staying?" she teased, lifting the hefty bag as though testing its weight. "A month?"

Audrey rubbed her sore shoulder. "I never know what to pack. It was pretty cold in Washington, but I figured it would be warm here, so I brought everything, just in case." She kicked off her shoes and settled into a kitchen chair. "Hi, Mom," she said. "Anything to eat? Forget the tree, by the way. I'm beat."

Yvonne got Audrey a glass of water. "There'd be no tree at all this year, if it weren't for Julian. I'm not sure I'm up to getting out all those boxes, looking at all that holiday paraphernalia, knowing last time I packed it all up, Daddy was still with us. If I'd any idea . . ." Her voice trailed off, prompting Laura to quickly approach.

"Is this too much for you, Mom? Our being here? Is this okay?"

Yvonne patted her daughter's arm. "Of course, dear. I'd be miserable without you. I'll just go lie down, while Julian's sleeping. Be back in a bit."

Laura let her mother go, watching her walk down the hall to her room. Audrey suspected her sister was tempted to follow Yvonne, to make sure she made it into bed, the light low, the covers pulled up. Laura was a nurse through and through, on or off duty.

She cleared her throat. "This is going to be harder than I thought," she said. "I've never seen her look so—"

"Fragile?" Laura returned to sit at the table. "The first holidays alone can be miserable," she said knowingly. She moved her untouched cup toward her sister. "You'll want to warm that up. Mom seems to think I like coffee all of a sudden."

Audrey pushed aside the water Yvonne had provided and

carried the cup of coffee to the microwave. "Maybe she mistook you for me. It's so hard to tell us apart."

Laura kneaded her forehead. "Are you going to be difficult the whole four days, or just this afternoon?"

Audrey grinned at her reflection in the humming microwave as the coffee warmed. She'd put on fresh makeup in an airport bathroom, highlighting her round eyes with a bright cinnamon shadow, dusting her angled cheekbones with expensive rouge she'd bought during a recent spree. She knew she looked good. It was one of those days she felt "on": she'd just been promoted at work, she'd been in a new aerobics class she loved for three weeks, now, and she'd flirted shamelessly with a grad student from George Washington University on the plane. The laughs they'd exchanged had given her a pleasant lift that lingered still. It was fading fast, though, in the somber home of her widowed mother, and Laura wasn't doing much to help.

Audrey sat back down with her sister. "You'd be disappointed if I let you off that easy," she said.

Laura shook her head. "Just . . . be nice to Mom. And give me a break, too, while you're at it. Julian's sick and I'm exhausted."

Like I need to be told that, Audrey thought. She'd never guessed Laura would grow to resemble their mother so much, but the lines of her sister's tired face were plain to see, and strikingly familiar, despite her brown skin. Audrey prayed she'd never inherit either of her parents' weary ways. How awful it would be to always look so tired of living. "I wondered where my favorite nephew was," she said. "Do you need anything? I've got a car—"

"No, I always bring medicine when we travel, just in case. He'll be okay by the time we open presents, I'm sure."

Audrey shrugged. "Always makes me feel better. What'd you get me, anyway?"

"You never could wait," Laura said. "I'd give you a hint, but it's not exactly purchased yet."

"What! Nice sister you are."

"Busy sister, I am. The clinic's short-staffed, so I've been working insane hours, then of course feeling guilty for neglecting Julian, so any spare time is spent with him. He's on a game kick, so I've played more Monopoly and Scrabble lately than anyone should ever have to play." She yawned a long, lazy yawn, then rested her chin in her palm. "A three-day drive to

Florida wasn't exactly what I needed."

"I still don't see why you drove. Mom offered to fly you down." Her sister's exasperated glance made it clear to Audrey that she'd failed to grasp some simple, but important, truth.

"I could never take her money," Laura said.

Audrey moaned. "You're too good, Laura. Really. And this is the most you ever complain. That can't be healthy." She bent her head to test her coffee, and escape her sister's amused, potentially condescending, smile for a moment. Finally Audrey mumbled the compliment she'd meant to pay, but now feared she was muddling. "I can't imagine parenting at all, much less alone," she said.

Laura crossed her arms and continued to assess her. Then she shrugged. "You'd be a great parent. An unusual one, maybe, but a good one. You're terrific with Julian."

Audrey raised her eyebrows. "How do you mean, unusual?"

"I mean you'd do things your own way. Not exactly Dr. Spock's way, and that would be fine." She gave her sister a weary smile of encouragement. "Seriously, you'd be a great parent."

Audrey laced her fingers around her cup, grateful to have a prop. "I'd still need a guy around, though, someone to pitch in, make it an even-Steven deal."

Laura shook her head. "No, you wouldn't. Really."

"Yes, I would, really. I know my limitations. I'd need help. Then I might be okay, as long as he wasn't an overbearing disciplinarian, like Dad was."

Laura stared at her sister, slack-jawed for a moment. "I can't believe you just said that."

Audrey shrugged, annoyed her confidences had suddenly turned against her. "It's true," she said, certain her face revealed her embarrassment. Eager to cover up, she realized the stupidity of her next words only after they'd spilled out. "Maybe you have a hard time admitting that because you were such a Daddy's girl."

"Maybe I have a hard time talking about this because Daddy's dead," Laura retorted.

Audrey swallowed hard. "You don't think I'm upset by that?" she asked, annoyed by her weak voice, which she now needed at its strongest. "You don't think I regret that he and I didn't get along, that I never had a chance to smooth things over with him?"

Laura tapped the table, and Audrey imagined her admonishing a patient who'd returned to cigarettes or blown a strict diet.

"You had plenty of chances," the decree finally came. "And you and Dad would've gotten along fine—"

Audrey shook her head.

"—if you hadn't always been so defensive."

"Of course I was defensive," Audrey snapped. "He loved to put me down. At least I didn't let him walk all over me."

Laura relaxed against the back of her chair. "Now what are you suggesting?"

"That you rarely stood up for yourself." Audrey studied her coffee cup as though its pale design fascinated her. When Laura did not immediately respond, she decided to pursue the topic, to see what her ever-composed, ever-confident big sister might reveal when pushed a little. "With Dad," she added, "or with Pritch."

Laura leaned forward now, one hand flat on the tabletop. "Harry and I," she said, her voice and gaze steady, "had very different points of view. Yes, I'd go out of my way to smooth things over sometimes, and yes, I did that with Daddy, too. I simply believe you show someone you care by making life easier for them, not more difficult."

Audrey tried to meet her sister's disapproving frown with one of her own.

Laura continued, her voice now an irritated whisper. "You've pushed a button, and I'm almost too tired to discuss this right now. Almost." She gave a curt sigh. "But I'm also sick of being pigeon-holed simply because I look on the bright side. I get this at work all the time. I'm often frustrated and upset by things, just not in public. Stereotypes are so common and convenient; I don't have the luxury of giving people more reasons to label me. I could cure cancer, and people would still look at me and see yet another single parent with brown skin."

Audrey peered at her sister. "What do you mean, you get this at work all the time?"

Laura shrugged. "At work, at college, at school when I was a kid. You know what I'm talking about. People read so much into your behavior. First semester freshman year, my roommate told me I 'acted white' because I wanted to be white, like her. Do you believe that? Harry often said I was 'unaware' of racial issues, so he made me feel I didn't act black enough. And did I ever tell you about the girl in third grade?" Audrey shook her head. Laura went on to tell of the only other black girl who'd been in her class. While her father was stationed overseas in the Air Force, Leticia Atkins had stayed with her mother and other relatives nearby and attended St. Therese's for one year.

"Remember those awful gym uniforms we had to wear?" Laura asked Audrey. "They were one-piece and had blue shorts and a blue striped top? I'd just want to change quick and get out of the locker room, but Leticia would corner me and want to comb out my hair. She'd run her fingers through it," Laura brushed an absent hand toward her ponytail, "and ask why it was so straight. Then one time, she stood there staring at my face, I mean really studying the shape of my eyes, my nose, my mouth, then declared she 'knew my secret.' 'What secret?' I asked.

"'You can't fool me by acting so white,' she said.

"'I'm not trying to fool anyone,' I said. 'Everyone knows my parents.'

"'But what are they?' she asked. 'What are *you?*'"

Laura shivered. "I hate that question. 'What *are* you? Are you adopted or something? Come from an island some-where?' It's like people need a tidy answer because they can't figure it out for themselves, and that drives them crazy. Don't you remember shopping with Mom and getting those looks?"

"I still get those looks," Audrey answered, "even when I'm alone. Or no looks at all. Like I'm invisible."

"Right." Laura's hands moved now as she spoke. "But back then, when we were kids, how were we supposed to know we didn't belong with a white mother? What were we supposed to think when cashiers scowled at us? I'd think something was wrong with me, like my face was dirty all the time."

While Laura rose to get herself a drink, Audrey recalled a memory of her own. She'd been about to walk into her sister's room one day after Laura had arrived home for a college break, when she'd glanced at a mirror on the far wall that revealed Yvonne with her eldest daughter, brushing Laura's hair. Audrey had watched, breath stopped, while her mother smoothed her hand behind the brush over the silken sheen. She knew her mother had always loved Laura's hair, and had seen Laura and Yvonne in long conversations before, but at that moment she'd been shocked and dismayed to see her mother and sister so relaxed together. Yvonne said something, sharing some confidence in low tones, and Laura listened with a serene smile. In the instant she knew she had to retreat before she was caught spying, Audrey wrestled with the jealous awareness she'd never shared a moment like that with her mother, and most certainly never would.

As Laura returned to the kitchen table, Audrey took a deep breath before exhaling her next words. "Your lighter skin did seem to make things easier for you."

Laura surprised her with her ready "Ha!" and wide grin. "I always assumed you knew better than that," she said, "but maybe it seemed that way, to some people. Still, it was no crystal stair."

Audrey's brow furrowed. "No what?"

A slow, knowing smile spread over Laura's face. "You never read the Langston Hughes collection in Daddy's study? I always loved that image of a crystal stair, from 'A Mother to Her Son.' When life's no crystal stair, only you can decide whether to keep climbing or to turn back. That's what I think. Sometimes, though, I get tired of working, day in and day out, just to make others feel at ease around me."

"You never make it look like work," Audrey said.

"Maybe that's why Harry thought I didn't care," Laura murmured. "I did, but I was more concerned with my own self-perception than with others' perceptions of me. Harry, though, he had no patience when he sensed someone disapproved of him. He'd rather clear out than try to change someone's mind. He said it never mattered what he did to make up to his father for all the wrongs he supposedly committed. It did him no good, so why waste the time? He was like that with his work, too, when an employer faulted him for no reason. He'd just as soon move on and start over rather than try to prove he'd been wronged."

Laura paused. "I still try to understand why he stopped on that stair, why he turned back. He must've believed he had no choice, must've lost all faith in everyone, including me." She sat with her shoulders round, head lowered to meet the tips of her fingers, which she pressed to her temple. "Maybe he wished I looked and behaved more like him, I don't know. At least he'd never suggest I wanted to be darker, like my roommate assumed I'd rather be white."

"She must've been a case," Audrey scoffed.

Laura shook her head with a wondering smile. "She was. I think she wished she could wave a magic wand and make me the perfect blond, blue-eyed, Barbie roommate. Then she wouldn't get that knot in her stomach every time she came back to the room, hoping I wasn't there, wondering what kind of voodoo," she widened her eyes and waved fingers through the air, "I was performing over her things in her absence."

Audrey laughed, but wondered at what Laura had suggested about her former fiancé. After thirteen years, Audrey remained baffled over Pritch's sudden disappearance, and was curious to hear Laura's theory. "Do you really think Pritch might've left because you weren't like him?" she finally asked.

Her sister shifted and stretched. "Honestly?" She spread her arms wide, then lowered her hands to her lap. "No. I'm fairly certain Harry left because of Daddy. Not because of anything Daddy said or did, though. Harry simply mistrusted him, from the start, because he was such a domineering father figure. That struck too close to home. Harry would've hated himself if he ever behaved like his father. "

Audrey nodded, but found it hard to believe Laura could remain so magnanimous toward Pritch after what he'd done. "You're right I never took advantage of opportunities to apologize to Dad," she said, staring again at her lukewarm coffee. "Actually, I'm still not sure he deserved an apology from me. But you do."

She glanced up to see Laura's perplexed frown.

"Apology for what?"

"I've always felt I let you down . . . you know . . . when Julian was a baby and you asked me to move in to help so you could go to night school?" Audrey glanced up again, sheepishly. "So I'm sorry—sorry I let you down. I just thought, back then, it was best to do what I wanted, you know?"

Laura waved a weary hand. "You didn't let me down. You did a good thing, for both of us. It forced me to depend on myself, which led me to see I *could* depend on myself. Even if I usually second-guess my decisions."

Audrey tried to relax as her sister paused. She'd hoped that voicing the apology might finally relieve some of the guilt she still felt over what she'd done. But now she knew neither her apology, nor her sister's calm words of comfort, could help.

"And don't beat yourself up about Daddy," Laura added. "He had high expectations of everyone."

And you don't? Audrey was tempted to retort. Just by your looks, your mannerisms, your daily, weekly, monthly good deeds, Laura, you set high expectations for everyone around you. But you would deny that, wouldn't you? You'd say any such effect was imagined, that you're simply making your way, happy to help any sorry souls you come across while you're at it.

"He never understood some people just do their own thing and get through each day," Laura continued, "wishing only for a little happiness and fun, verification they're loved, maybe, and needed. He believed you had to prove yourself, not just get along. He and Harry were a lot alike, you know.

"Harry had such pride," Laura went on, her eyes now dark with memory. "It bothered him he had no college degree. In fact, it's possible he never graduated from high school, he went to work so young after his father left. I never asked. But I know he loved the construction business. Just being part of the building process gave him a great deal of pleasure. He had this knack for how things stand, their structure, the heart of their balance. I told him when we first met that I wished I could work like that, with my hands. You know what he said?"

Audrey frowned. "What? What did he say."

"He said, 'I propose you do work with your hands, as a nurse, even as a nursing student, tending people every day. Nothing could be more gratifying than that.'" Laura beamed. "We were at Varsity Pizza on the Syracuse campus. He was working on an addition to the medical center. All the booths in Varsity were full and we were each alone, so we just sat at one of the long tables, eyeing each other, you know? And he'd ordered wings and was drinking a soda, waiting to be called up. They had this guy there who'd get on a microphone and say 'So-and-so, your wings are ready,' in this big booming voice. So the guy finally said, 'Pritch, your wings are ready,' and Harry went to get his order. By the time he returned, I'd got up my nerve to talk to him, so I said 'Pritch?' and he sat next to me and introduced himself as Harrison Pritchard, Jr., shaking my hand, very formal. I just smiled and said, 'I bet you were called Harry as a boy,' which made him grin, just grin. It was so sweet. I knew right then that deep down he was a little boy named Harry, and I wanted to take care of him."

"Kind of like picking up a stray."

Laura shrugged. "He was a stray, especially after his mother died that winter. A lonely boy pretending to be a strong, stubborn, loner. In the end, though, he didn't want to be babied or brought into the fold of our family. I thought that's what he needed, but he knew better than I what he needed, which was to be on his own."

"You can't blame yourself for trying to help him," Audrey said. "You've always been the nursing type."

Laura laughed. "You mean the compulsive helper-maniac type? I'm afraid that ties in easily with the compulsive drive to change someone. Harry and I were both set on changing each other. I wanted him to be more carefree and relaxed, he wanted me to be more aware and cautious. Maybe he finally decided I was hopelessly naive, and that's what drove him away. I suppose I'll never know."

"Never know what, Mom?" Julian entered the kitchen, then paused and hovered for a moment, as though uncertain it was safe to take another step.

Laura rose to guide him to a chair. "Why I'm so lucky to have such a wonderful kid," she answered. She kissed his forehead and frowned. "Time for more medicine," she murmured. "That fever's going to hang around a few days."

Julian stared at his mother in disbelief, then rubbed his eyes angrily. "I can't believe I'm going to be sick for Christmas," he whimpered.

"Poor sweetie," Laura cooed, embracing her son. "I'm so sorry."

Audrey got up to warm her coffee some more, suspecting Julian might be embarrassed by her presence as he cried to his mother. She busied herself by surveying Yvonne's kitchen, which remained as sparse as ever, everything clean, ordered, concealed, locked away in appropriate compartments.

Laura kept her attention on Julian. "Did the nap help?"

Her son sniffed. "My head feels like a ton of bricks and my legs are all noodly when I walk."

Laura smiled. "All noodly? Uh-oh, sounds like the dreaded noodle-legs disease."

Julian's cheeks rounded as his mouth curved into a feeble grin. "Mom, stop teasing," he moaned.

Laura retrieved a duffel bag from a corner of the kitchen. "Okay, but I'll still have to give you some anti-noodle medicine."

Julian crossed his arms on the tabletop and lowered his head to meet them. "Whatever."

Audrey moved to sit next to him. "Santa brings extra special gifts to sick kids, you know."

Her nephew raised his head slightly to acknowledge his

aunt. "Hi, Aunt Audrey."

Laura interceded. "We're way beyond the Santa stage, I'm afraid." She handed Julian two pills and a glass of water. "Take this, then it's back to bed until you feel like eating. The best thing to do is rest, right?"

"Because my body's telling me something," Julian added, swallowing his medicine and rising to leave. "So I need to listen." He shuffled toward the door. "I haven't believed in Santa Claus since I was, like, ten, Aunt Audrey," he added as he left the room.

Audrey winked at her sister. "I'll be sure to call and let him know."

She noticed Laura remained in the kitchen rather than follow Julian out to the hall as she'd followed their mother. "I know people with kids who are exhausted all the time, every day," Audrey said, watching her sister.

Laura slumped into a chair, but remained silent until she heard the guest bedroom door close. "It's the anxiety that kills me," she then confided. "I can deal with having limited 'me' time. I've always gotten more out of helping other people than babying myself. That's why I became a nurse. But the day-to-day worries, you know? Something as silly as a cold, which I know how to treat, for crying out loud, can drive me nuts when it affects Julian. I just want to spare him the misery."

"Wouldn't most parents?"

Laura stared past her sister. "Sometimes I think it's a good thing Harry left," she said, her voice a low monotone, "and I have no husband around to love me and need me at the end of the day, after I've cared for and cajoled and comforted so many others, including Julian." She smoothed her fingers underneath her eyes, as though to wipe away any shadows or other signs of weariness that might linger there. "Most days, I doubt I'd have the energy, or desire, to love him back."

Chapter Twelve

Audrey found James and Julian outside the arcade. She explained where she'd been, adding only that she didn't feel well. She suggested they cut the outing short and head home. The car ride was quiet, probably because they were all tired, she reasoned. After the brief friendly interchanges Julian and James had shared that morning, the two seemed to retreat to their own quiet corners. She wished they were all less moody, then decided what she wanted most was to take a nap.

They turned onto her street, and Audrey knew something was wrong. Pritch was parked in front of the house, his suitcases in the back of his pickup. He approached as they pulled into the gravel driveway and got out of the car. Then he greeted Julian, who squinted at him and looked away, and introduced himself to James. Audrey felt as though she'd brought a boyfriend home to meet her father.

"You're in town a while?" James asked.

Pritch frowned. "Had hoped to be. But there seems to be a problem with my living arrangement."

Julian stuffed his hands into his jacket pockets and eyed his father, his mouth set, his expression guarded.

"What kind of problem, Pritch?" Audrey asked, her voice flat. She shivered and led the others toward the house.

"It seems the problem lies in the tenant," Pritch said. "That being me. Or with the landlady's sudden fear of said tenant." He explained he'd found a low-rent apartment attached to a woman's house, but the woman's neighbor talked her out of renting to him. "The landlady was candid about it, said she'd prefer renting to a woman and all that, and she gave me my first month's rent back, though I'd used the apartment two days."

Audrey stepped inside, wondering where Pritch was

99

leading, what James was thinking, what Julian was hoping. She went to the kitchen to make some coffee, listening to James ask polite but hesitant questions regarding Pritch's plans.

"I'm not certain, tell the truth," Pritch said, excusing himself to follow Audrey into the kitchen. "That's why I'm here," he added, his voice low.

Audrey switched on the coffee maker.

"I don't like to broadcast my troubles to strangers," he continued. "But I haven't time to spare. I need to be out looking for work, not for an apartment no one wants to rent me."

"Are you leaving or not?" she demanded.

He shook his head. "It would kill me, to leave now. All I've thought about since Saturday is Julian, and all I want now is to know my son, to show him I love him and care for him. I knew my father, and despised my father, and right now I need to do everything I can to ensure my son doesn't despise me."

Pritch stood so close Audrey could see his pulse throb at his temple. She watched his dark eyes and hands move, and understood why her sister had loved this man.

"Where else have you stayed?"

"In a God-awful motel off Main Street. Don't make me beg, now. You know how it is. No one in this uptight town is going to rent squat to an unemployed black man."

"We've got plenty of room," she said, "if it's okay with your son."

Audrey returned to the front hall, where James still stood with Julian. She took in her nephew's steady glare. "Your father needs a place to stay," she said. "I think we should have him here for a while, until he finds a job."

Julian remained silent, prompting his aunt to doubt the wisdom of her suggestion. While she believed he and Pritch needed a chance to get to know each other, she didn't want to see her nephew hurt in any way.

"Audrey?" The sound of James's voice surprised her. "I'd better get going," he said, moving toward the door.

"I'll be right out." She addressed Julian. "He's family. Think about that."

The boy continued to glare at her. "You always ask my opinion," he growled, turning away to head upstairs, "but it never matters what I want, so why bother?"

Audrey kneaded her forehead for a moment, then followed James out to his car. She held her arms close around her against the cold, damp air.

James coughed. "Do you think this is a good idea?"

Audrey stopped short. "Unbelievable," she muttered.

"Yeah." James chuckled. "The gall of the guy—"

"The gall of all of you," she snapped. "Pritch for putting me on the spot like this, Julian for treating me like I'm an ogre because I made him return your money and now want to help his father, *his* father, and you for even suggesting you know what's best for me."

"Audrey, I—"

"I know, you're just watching out for me, worried about me living alone with a pain-in-the-ass teenager and inviting a strange man to stay here. I know, I'm doing everything wrong and you simply want to help. Well, I've had it with people telling me what's best, what I should and should not do. You want me to go away with you. Julian wants me to be like his mother. Pritch, I guarantee, wants me to stop seeing you and being such a bad influence on his son. How am I supposed to make you all happy? And why the hell should I even try?"

Audrey realized she was shaking, and that James's face was redder than ever. She took a deep breath and gripped her arms, painfully aware of the cold. "I'm sure you've had enough of all of this," she said.

He paused. "I can't . . ." He opened his car door. "I hate to see someone I care about get hurt, and I can't stand back and let that happen, when I think I can help. Know what I mean?"

You sound like my sister, Audrey thought. "I'm not a high school kid anymore," she said. "I'll be all right."

She watched his car leave, sorry to see him go, not at all certain she was doing the right thing. She turned to go back into her sister's house, back to her lost nephew and his homeless father, trying to piece together the bizarre puzzle her life had suddenly become.

Pritch waited in the front hall. For a moment, Audrey wished he'd disappear—decide staying in town was a bad idea, leave as abruptly as he'd arrived, just make things easier for her and disappear.

She sighed. "Julian still upstairs?"

Pritch nodded. "Give him time."

"Huh?" Her head jerked back and her eyes narrowed. "Don't tell me what to do as far as he's concerned, Pritch," she snapped. "You're welcome to stay for a while, but don't think you—"

Pritch held up his hands. "I'm not thinking anything, Miss Audrey. Truly." He flashed her a smile. "Trust me, eh?"

Audrey frowned, then gestured toward the living room. "Sleeping on the couch in there would kill your back, so we'll open Laura's room." She led him upstairs and took the unfamiliar turn into her sister's bedroom. "I'll get some sheets out." Audrey could hear her voice waver as she spoke, and knew her attempt to sound casual was failing. She wiggled the room's doorknob, the brass knob that didn't lock and rarely even latched correctly, and eased the door open.

The cold brightness of the room startled her. She had closed the vents a month ago, to keep from having to heat the room during the winter. The shade was still up, as Laura had always left it each morning. A shaft of weak sunlight peeked inside for a moment.

"You feel her presence, here," Pritch whispered. "Everything's still in order."

Audrey moved away from him, toward Laura's dresser. "Julian makes sure of that." She touched perfume bottles that stood ready for use, dust-free thanks to her nephew's steady attention. "I never come in here, but he does, when I'm not around."

Pritch took a deep breath. "I doubt this is a good idea, then," he said. "I'd best sleep downstairs."

Audrey shook her head. "No matter how hard he tries, he can't keep her locked in here forever." It's been eight months, she wanted to add. Isn't it time to move on?

"He's thirteen," Pritch said, his face long and drawn.

She shook her head again. "I know. He's thirteen. He's upset. He's in need of . . . something. Something I can't understand because I'm not a parent, something I can't give him because I'm not *his* parent. So where does that leave us? He's thirteen, I'm thirty-four, and we're both miserable."

Pritch wandered across the room. "I told you I don't have any answers, Miss Audrey."

She sat on the bed, on her sister's favorite quilt, tracing a star with her finger. "I don't want answers anymore," she said, her voice weary. "I want out."

"Out from what? Raising Julian?"

"No, no!" She slammed her fist into the mattress. "I'm telling you, Pritch, don't get any ideas about taking him away from me. He may think hanging onto his mother's run-down house and her room and her perfume bottles is going to keep her close, but what really keeps her close is *him*. He's all that's left of her, and she trusted him to me, me!"

Hot tears spilled onto her cheeks as her sobs returned from earlier that day. She gripped the quilt, frustrated by her outburst. Pritch stepped over and handed her a handkerchief, then sat silently beside her while she wiped her face and tried to stop crying. When he started to talk, she felt his words more than she heard them, and knew he was trying not to cry, too.

"You *are* a parent," he said. "In eight months, you've become a parent to Julian. You've been here for him when he's needed you most, and he'll always remember that. *I'll* always remember that."

She wondered what object on Laura's dresser held his stare as he spoke, what helped him keep his composure.

"Laura left Julian to you," he continued. "I understand that. I respect that. I am not here to take him from you. I am here to show him who I am. A boy needs to know his father. He may hate me, but he needs to know me and understand my strengths and weaknesses so he can know his own, and work with them for the rest of his life."

Audrey nodded, growing more confident about her decision to let Pritch stay.

He paused. "I do need to know I am free to speak up now and then," he added. "To try to help, while here."

Audrey remained silent as he met her gaze with a small smile.

"We're in this together," he continued, "learning to be parents, and I believe if we work together, Julian will benefit even more."

"What's your point, Pritch?"

He grinned. "Aah. I knew you'd be straightforward. Good. Now, hear me out before you fly off the handle, eh?" He stood and stepped away. "You and your sister were always . . . different, in many ways."

Audrey stood, too, and walked around the room, opening the vents.

Pritch continued. "But I think it might help if you'd be a little less emotional, perhaps, with Julian, and a little more reasonable when dealing with him."

"Reasonable?" She faced him. "You think I'm unreasonable?"

He held up his hands. "Uh-uh. Let me finish, eh? I'm sure you're reasonable most times but, well, take this—situation—with you and James—"

Audrey moaned. "I don't believe I'm hearing this."

"I just say it's sure to confuse the boy. What do you suppose he thinks when he sees you with James—that black men aren't worthy?"

"And I say," Audrey growled, "to you and to him, that my relationships have nothing to do with either of you. Nada. Zilch. Zero. Besides," she tilted her open palms upward, "it's not like I plan to marry James."

"Oh?"

Pritch's mocking grin made Audrey's heart race. Her fists clenched, she spun away from him, only to see Julian at the door.

"What are you doing in here?" the boy demanded. "Who said you could come in here?"

"Julian," Audrey began, walking toward him.

"You don't belong in here!" He glared at Pritch. "You don't belong in this house! Why don't you get out of here!" Julian ran out of the room and slammed the door, impeding his aunt's attempt to follow. Audrey grabbed the loose doorknob, then heard a car door close outside. She went to the window in time to see James step up to the porch. As the flash of his hair and jacket disappeared below her, she pressed her hand to the cold windowpane.

A second later she was back at the bedroom door, jiggling the knob again. When it refused to cooperate, she grabbed and tried to force it. The ring of the doorbell sounded from downstairs. "Open, damn you!" She grabbed the knob again, then shrank back as Pritch waved her aside. With a firm grip, he turned the worn knob, easily opening the door. Audrey slipped by him.

James stood on the front porch, a bunch of pale chrysanthemums in his hand, roots and all. "I was beginning to think you saw me coming," he said.

"Sorry, we were in the bedroom, and—" She shook her head, noting his raised eyebrows. "Never mind."

"Can I come in?" he asked. "I stole these from somebody's garden and they're probably hunting me down as we speak."

Audrey smiled as he stepped inside. "What am I going to do with you?"

"Keep me," he said, grinning.

"I keep trying to get rid of you. Back in high school when you wouldn't leave me alone, at Pam's party when you followed me home . . . Now you go and do this."

James placed the flowers in her hands and held them to his chest, pulling her close. "I'm sorry," he said. "I was driving away, then I stopped and thought, 'What the hell are you doing, Sullivan?' I want to spend as much time with you as possible, to really get to know you, Audrey. You're all I think about, all I want."

Audrey felt the beat of his heart, overwhelmed by the echoes of what he wanted, what Pritch wanted, what Julian wanted. At the sound of Pritch's footsteps on the stairs behind her, she stepped back.

Pritch stopped and glanced at them. "I thought I'd get my things from the truck." He paused. "Is everything all right here?" His frown settled on the flowers she held.

The contrast between Pritch and James intrigued Audrey for a moment. While Pritch with his dark, round face and square build blended into the shadows of the hall, James, tall and fair, brightened the open doorway. She beckoned James to come in further and stepped aside to let Pritch pass.

"Everything's fine," she said, giving him a quick, uncertain smile.

"Hm." Pritch walked by her and out the door.

James watched him go, his gaze steady but troubled. He pointed his chin in Pritch's direction. "This is still hard for me to accept," he said. "You have to know that."

Audrey laid the flowers on the stairs. "And you have to understand I'm doing what's right, not what I want."

He paused. "What do you want?"

To get the hell out of here, she thought. To escape, run away from all this, let someone baby *me* for a while. I want to sleep for three days, and wake up somewhere else, somewhere far, far away. "I want to go to that wedding with you," she said.

He smiled and pulled her to him. "The hotel's supposed to be beautiful."

Audrey wrapped her arms around his waist, wishing she could ignore the sound of Pritch's approaching footsteps, and the frown she knew he'd direct at them.

She realized James heard him, too.

"I can't tell you how happy you've made me," James whispered, letting her go.

Audrey nodded, mustering a weary smile, as Pritch reached the front door.

Chapter Thirteen

James picked Audrey up early the Saturday of his friend's wedding. Soon after they left, Julian sped down the stairs and out the front door—without breakfast, or a word to his father. The boy had announced his plan to stay at a friend's house when he learned his aunt would be away for the weekend.

Alone, Pritch stared at Laura's picture in the living room. He stared for a long while at the images the portrait presented—images of Laura's hair, her eyes, her mouth, her face. But he struggled to piece them together, to return in memory sixteen years to the first time they met, or the first time they made love.

Laura. He blinked, realizing he'd reached toward the picture. He knew what would happen if he touched it, if he let his hand pick it up, this lifeless image, this portrait that harbored nothing of Laura's true being. Though he'd blocked out much of his past, he could easily see the immediate future, the immediate impact of his decisions. He could imagine the crash of the frame and glass on the far wall, could see the crumpled photo amid the shards on the floor, could taste his own furious tears and hear his escalating curses. What frightened him, though, was what might come after, what might happen beyond what he could see.

He retreated to the basement to find his toolbox, his eyes dry but his face drawn despite the morning's early hour. The past week had been much more stressful than he'd anticipated. Audrey had been cordial but guarded, Julian abrupt and aloof. Pritch spent one night on the living-room couch, waking with a painful crick in his neck. While Audrey offered aspirin and suggested a heating pad, Julian had scowled, sullen over a bowl of cereal. That night, after a tiresome day chasing dead-end job leads, Pritch found his things moved to Laura's room. Though Julian never said he'd agreed to the arrangement, he never complained about it, either.

Sleeping in Laura's room proved more difficult than Pritch had suspected, however. He kept waking the first night, expecting to find her next to him. By the end of the week, he'd made it a habit to force himself to acknowledge, upon waking, that she was not there, that he would never see her again. He convinced himself he had no choice but to acknowledge this every day, to force himself to repeat it, even as he stared at her bedside table and the framed photo of her and Julian she had placed there.

During the week, Pritch had set aside a few hours to begin surveying the house, noting its biggest problems, fixing smaller things as he went along. He secretly hoped his job hunt and the house's work would take at least a month or so, long enough for Julian to give him a chance, perhaps.

In his survey of the house, Pritch first checked under the top of the toilet tank to see the date stamped on it with the manufacturer's name. This, he knew, would give him a good idea when the last new plumbing work was done, and he was satisfied to find the year 1979 printed there. If major plumbing work had been done in the past fifteen years, it was possible other improvements had been made as well.

He'd been surprised to find the house's foundation sound, with only a few small cracks requiring patching. No water stains were evident on the basement walls, discounting the likelihood of much leaking from the cracks, or much flooding through the years. The few things stored down there—an old dresser and a dozen or so packing boxes—were set on the floor, one more sign flooding had not been a concern, at least since Laura had moved in.

Now back in the basement, Pritch passed the monstrous fireplace. Its chimney joined the chimney of the living-room fireplace, forming a critical brick artery of support through the center of the wood-frame house. Huge cooking utensils lay on the dusty mantle. He tried to imagine what it had been like to cook meat, poultry, and pork from one's own farm in the core of one's own home.

Pritch opened his toolbox, pulled out string and a handful of tacks, and set to work. By tacking the string taut between opposite bottom corners of a girder, he checked for excess sag and noted girders that could use extra support. He then directed his attention to the ancient gas furnace, which held court in an ominous corner, grand in a gray cloak of dust. The house boasted a surprisingly modern heating system with custom ductwork, proof that at one time someone had invested substantial effort—and money—in it. Pritch suspected, though, that this was the original furnace, now long neglected. He located and cleaned the installation date and found he was right. Installed nearly thirty years ago, the furnace should have been replaced right after Laura moved in. Pritch frowned, trying to keep from thinking in terms of when Laura moved into the house. He and Laura had joked about where they might live after they married—he teasing they should settle in Rochester, though he knew she'd never move out of her hometown. When he suggested they find a trendy new condo with vaulted ceilings, she'd given him a look that made it clear she'd rather live in a barn. It didn't surprise him at all that, left to buy a place on her own, she'd chosen this house. He only wished he'd been around to take care of it with her back then, rather than without her now.

He carried his toolbox upstairs and grabbed his black leather coat before going outside to assess the exterior. On the front porch, he placed his toolbox at his feet and zipped his jacket closed. The sky was gray and the air still, the silence of the street broken only by an occasional dog's bark or a car trundling down the block. Pritch squinted, trying again to stop thinking of Laura living in this house, standing on this porch, marking each season's passing. Laura growing lovelier and happier as she lived another year in this home that suited her so well.

He pulled an awl and a pair of small binoculars from his toolbox, and left the porch. His inspection of the house's exterior took two hours. Pritch kept himself busy—and his mind off any thoughts of Laura.

With the awl, he probed rotting areas of siding, penetrating some deeply. While he noted a few bowed boards that could be nailed back and some small, shallow areas of rot that could be patched with fiberglass, he found most of the boards extensively damaged and in need of replacement. On the southern side of the house, brittle and cracked paint flaked off in sheets, revealing an even dingier shade of gray beneath it. He noted the need to have all the exterior paint tested for lead.

With his binoculars, he scanned the old, discolored tin roof, which appeared to be in decent condition. He knew any small leaks could be fixed easily by applying a coat of rusty metal primer and a couple coats of acrylic roof coating. Still, he wanted to get it inspected right away, in case major work was required. He decided that and the furnace should be top priorities. He continued to scan the roof and upper story for any problem signs, noting a gap at a joint near the chimney, and a crack in the chimney cap. He wondered when the fireplaces had been used last, knowing the cracked cap could admit water and cause a fire hazard if the masonry had deteriorated. An inspection of the gutters and drains around the house confirmed Pritch's growing suspicion the exterior would require the most attention. He finished his survey on the front porch and was about to go inside when a police car sped around the street corner, screeching to a halt in front of the house.

Pritch remained on the porch, confident any move he made would appear threatening. A memory flashed: Laura driving him home one night, pulled over for speeding, asking him to reach into the back seat for her purse. Pritch had sat dumbfounded, shocked she'd made such a suggestion. He knew well one misjudged move in the presence of a cop could hang a black man. Yet she thought nothing of asking such a thing of him while a state trooper flooded her Buick with light.

Two officers, one male, one female, both white, left the car at the curb and walked up the driveway toward the house. Pritch remained on the porch, his toolbox still in his hand, its weight wearing on his back. With a brief smile, he asked if something was amiss.

"A neighbor thinks you may be, sir," the male said. He was young, blond, working hard to sound friendly.

The woman, older, sallow, and curt, stepped closer to the porch. "Are you a contractor? A neighbor reported seeing a stranger poking around over here."

Pritch nodded. "That would be me." He gestured toward his toolbox, which he now lowered, slowly. Then he straightened, explaining he was a houseguest of the Conarroes and was inspecting the house during his stay. The officers peered at him from the foot of the porch steps. Pritch considered joining them on the sidewalk, but decided against it, still uncertain how they might react.

The woman took out a notebook. "Name?"

Pritch gave it.

"So are you a relative?"

Pritch nodded again, preparing for a lengthy explanation.

"That's him!" An elderly man limped down the driveway of the opposite house and crossed the street. Wrapped in a long, thick sweater, he moved quickly despite his limp, as though fueled by excitement. "That's the man I saw sneaking 'round here," he announced, one hand pointing.

The female officer beckoned Pritch to join her and her partner as they went to meet the old man.

"I'm Carlton Benton, live right there," the neighbor said, jabbing a finger toward his house. "Thank heaven someone in this neighborhood stays home days, no telling what trouble he might've caused. Right, officer?"

He addressed the younger cop, who looked to his partner. She answered for him. "Sir, please. We appreciate your concern, but Mr. Pritchard here—"

"Aha!" Carlton Benton screeched. "Just as I suspected! The folks that live here be named Conaroo or some such. French, I think, although . . ." He glanced at Pritch, then away sheepishly. "Never mind all that. What'd you book him for?"

The woman gave an exasperated sigh while her partner rubbed the back of his neck.

Pritch tried not to scowl at the man. "I'm certain I appeared suspicious, but Ms. Conarroe will be able to explain as soon as she returns from out of town—"

"Out of town?" The woman opened her notebook again. "You're a houseguest, but you're here alone?"

Pritch shook his head. "Not alone," he said. "I'm watching Ms. Conarroe's nephew, my son." He turned back to the neighbor. "The boy, Julian."

The woman scribbled in her pad, her mouth open to ask a question, when Carlton Benton screeched again. "Your son!" He waved an accusing finger. "Now I know you're up to no good, mister. That boy's never had no father 'round here."

Both cops stared at Pritch as he sighed and opened his palms to them. "Perhaps I could explain all this inside," he offered, signaling toward the house.

The woman put her notebook in her pocket. "Perhaps you could explain all this at the station." She instructed Pritch to get his toolbox and follow them to the squad car.

Resigned to the loss of his afternoon, realizing any arguments on his part would only lengthen the process, Pritch tried not to let the obvious upset him. He was simply grateful Julian was not home to witness this insult.

A car approached from down the street. Pritch frowned,

wondering how many curious neighbors were gawking at the sight of a strange black man being carted away by the police. As the car slowed and entered the gravel driveway, Pritch realized his son was staring at him from the back seat.

Julian jumped out of the car before it came to a full stop. Pritch noticed his swollen right eye and bruised, cut face at the same moment he heard his cry.

"Dad!"

The word shocked and enthralled Pritch, who stood as though stunned. For a moment, he forgot the police and their accusations, his lost job and uncertain future, and was aware only of his overwhelming desire to embrace his son.

Julian squinted as if blinded by sunlight, though the clouds remained low and ominous. He peered at the police car. "What—what's going on?"

Pritch forced himself to sound nonchalant, afraid Julian might retreat from him again if he sounded too anxious. "Nothing," he said. "A misunderstanding."

The other car passengers joined them—another boy about Julian's age and his mother. The female officer addressed Julian and motioned toward the house. "You live here?"

"Yes, ma'am," he said, his voice still hesitant.

"And this man's your father?"

Julian nodded. "He's visiting, for a while."

The officers glanced at each other. "We'll have to file a report," the woman said, signaling her partner to get in the car. "But I think we're all set here."

She thanked Mr. Benton, who retreated with a grunt, limping back to his home as quickly as he'd emerged from it. Then she addressed Julian again. "You're pretty banged up there. Run into some trouble?"

He shook his head, but appeared startled as his friend's mother spoke up.

"There was a fight at the school yard," she said.

"And you are?"

"Adele Spencer." She nodded toward her son. "Eddie and Julian were playing basketball at the high school when some other kids came along."

Julian interrupted. "It was no big deal."

"He needs some first aid," Adele continued. "I tried, but he kept asking to go home. His bike's at our house. I drove him over since I know his aunt's out of town."

Pritch thanked her, assuring her Julian would be fine with him. The female officer offered to drive by the high school to make sure the same boys weren't causing more trouble. She took out her notebook again. "Can you describe them?" she asked.

Julian poked the toe of his sneaker into some loose gravel. "My age," he finally said, "thirteen or fourteen, wearing jeans and stuff. I don't know."

She frowned. "Hair color? Race?"

As Julian hesitated, Pritch wondered whether his son was the only black child in his school.

"Brown and blond hair," the boy said, glancing at his father. "They're all white."

Both cars drove away, leaving Pritch and Julian alone for the first time. Pritch walked with his son up the driveway, explaining a neighbor had mistaken him for a prowler. "An honest mistake, surely." He waved toward his toolbox as they neared the house. "I was doing some work out here."

"This place is a mess, huh?" the boy asked. "Guess Aunt Audrey would be better off without it."

Pritch stopped. "How would you feel, without it?"

Julian looked away as a light drizzle started to rain down on them.

Rather than offer fatherly advice, Pritch tried to sound casual. "It's possible no one will buy the house, if that makes you feel any better," he said. "Regardless, it needs work, and I've promised to do what I can."

"Can I help?"

"Of course," Pritch said. "We'll check the attic next." He stepped over to his truck and pulled a battered hard hat out of the back. "For the nails in the low ceiling," he explained, pleased by Julian's curious smile as he positioned the hat on the boy's head. Pritch peered at the cut on his face. "Let's fix you up first, though, eh?"

In the bathroom, Pritch had Julian hold a bag of frozen peas to his swollen eye while he put first aid cream on the cut and covered it with an adhesive bandage. "I can teach you to sidestep a blow like that," he said, winking.

Julian removed the bag of peas and stared at his father. "You box?"

Pritch laughed and packed up the first aid supplies. "I

did. A lifetime ago. Before—" He glanced at his son. "Before I knew your mother. She never would have approved." He winked again, patting the boy on the shoulder. "And neither would your aunt, so mum's the word, eh? It'll be our little secret."

Pritch had not located the attic access yet, so he asked his son to show the way. Julian revealed a cramped staircase inside his bedroom closet.

They climbed the stairs and reached the attic, met there by a muffled chorus of taps from the steady rain that had begun to fall outside. Pritch showed Julian how to examine rafters for signs of rot, insects, and water damage by probing areas with the awl. When the boy hesitated to approach the far end of the attic, where his flashlight beam revealed layers of cobwebs, Pritch talked Julian through, bent low to avoid bumping his own head, the wide-board floor groaning beneath his feet.

He was pleased to find most of the attic beams in fine shape, despite their apparent age. "Another good sign," he said, patting a beam. "Not only is the foundation solid, but the roof has been cared for. Otherwise we'd have one rotted rafter after another up here." He found an old broom propped in a corner and used it to clear away more cobwebs, revealing a round window out the northern side of the house with a wide, shelf-like sill. Pritch chuckled. "Someone got a little creative here, eh?" He invited Julian to step closer, then rubbed dirt and grime off the glass, providing a clear view of the quickening rain.

"Wow." Julian stepped in front of his father to get a closer look. "You can see right over the house next door."

"Perhaps there was a view of the lake from here once," Pritch suggested. He followed the boy's gaze. "Imagine this house when it was first built, how glorious it must have been. A beautiful home, so well made, with such a tremendous lake so close by. Ontario's so big, surely it seemed an ocean in those days."

Julian stepped back. "This house is great," he said, "but I don't remember it ever looking beautiful. I wonder why Mom bought it."

Pritch bent over his toolbox. "I'm sure she had her reasons."

"Like you had reasons for leaving her?"

Pritch jolted erect, knocking his bare head against a beam. He steadied himself, dropped the ruler he'd retrieved into the toolbox, and signaled his son to follow him. "Time we talked,

114

eh?" he said, rubbing his bruised crown.

They returned to the boy's room, where Pritch sat on the bed, still rubbing his head, while Julian sulked in his desk chair. "Before I answer your question," Pritch began, "you need to know something about me." He leaned forward, resting his elbows on his knees, his fingers spread, their tips touching. "I never lie."

The boy snorted. "Everybody lies."

Pritch chuckled. "You mean you lie? To your aunt, sometimes?"

"Sometimes. I have to, to make her happy."

"Of course, you do *her* a favor when you lie to her."

"She gets so worked up over everything." Julian gestured toward his marked-up face. "She's going to freak when she sees this."

Pritch leaned back on one elbow. "I agree sometimes it may be easiest to stretch the truth. Like when you told the police you could hardly describe those boys, though you knew them from school. Am I right?"

Julian peered at his father, his jaw clenched. "You want to know the truth?" he asked, his voice tight. "The jerk who hit me likes the girl I like. He called me a nigger and said if I ever talk to her again he'll cream me." He sat forward, his face a tense mask of control. "So there, that's the truth. Happy?" He shook his head. "Everybody lies, sometimes."

Pritch pursued eye contact. "I do not. I decided a long time ago I could not afford to compromise my self-worth, my self-esteem," he tapped a finger to his chest, "by ever deceiving anyone, including myself."

They sat for a long moment, considering each other. Pritch breathed steadily, aware this crossroads was a critical one. "I have a story to tell," he continued. "You still like to hear stories, or are you too old for that sort of thing?"

Julian shrugged, but remained silent.

"I appreciate your tolerance for your old man's sentimentalities." Pritch allowed himself the luxury of a small smile. "So I'm your old man. Are you curious about my old man, your other grandfather, then? You ought to be. A person hardly knows himself if he knows little of those who came before him, eh?" He heaved a ragged sigh and placed both hands at his knees, as though bracing himself to finish what he'd begun. "Understand Harrison Pritchard, Sr., is not a favorite topic of mine. He was often cruel, in fact, and he abandoned my mother when I was fourteen. Cleared out the bank account, left her with nothing, disappeared. I dropped out of school and went to work doing odd jobs. Eventually, at sixteen, I landed my first construction job. I've learned a lot since then, including the need to remain true to one's self. To know when all else fails," he drummed lightly on his thighs for emphasis, *"you* can depend on *you."*

He stretched his legs, then crossed his ankles. "So onto your mother, and why I left her. Was I angry with her? She rarely even upset me, though there were certain topics on which we differed in opinion. Your grandfather, though, dear Dr. Conarroe—"

At this reference, Julian spoke up. "Grandpa died last year," he said, "from a heart attack."

Pritch paused. "I'm sorry to hear that, Julian. I know you loved him, and he you. I've had some time to consider what he meant to your mother, and I can only conclude she adored him as a daughter should adore her father."

"She did," Julian murmured. "They were really close."

Pritch leaned forward again, pursuing eye contact with his son. "But you have to understand something important here, something that may be difficult for you to even consider. Your grandfather did not get along with everyone."

Julian smiled. "I know. He and Aunt Audrey picked on each other all the time."

"Heh," Pritch chuckled. "Your aunt always was a bit outspoken, especially when she was young. Good, then you understand your grandfather could be difficult, sometimes."

Julian frowned. "You didn't like Grandpa, huh?"

Pritch sighed. "Let's say, in my youth, I had a hard time with father figures. I know it was unfair to take out my frustrations on your grandfather. But back then, when I first met your grandparents, when I was over my head in love with your mother," he noted his son's pleasure at this admission, "my frustration with Dr. Conarroe made perfect sense to me, and became an obstacle I found impossible to overcome. So I did the easy, cowardly thing fools in their youth often do. I ran from the problem rather than take it to task."

He paused, aware he'd fallen into preaching. "You've been very patient," he said. "And I have only one more thing to ask you to consider." He took Julian's continued silence as permission to go on. "I left your mother because I thought your grandfather considered me unworthy of his daughter, and I reasoned he might be right. I believed, in the end, my leaving would be a good thing for Laura. But," he took a slow, deep breath, "if I'd known about you—I beg you to trust, Julian, that if I'd known about you—I never would have left."

The doorbell rang, but they remained seated. Pritch hesitated until his son sat back and appeared to relax, his face now lined with an odd smile.

Pritch smiled, too, as he stood. "I've told you how I had a trouble, still have a trouble, trusting fathers. Now you need to decide whether you can trust *me*. Be aware, for whatever the worth, that I am truthful in all things I say. Always."

He stepped through the doorway, then back into the room. "As far as the bully goes," he added, tapping his chest again, "I've been there. You talk to your girl. I'll teach you to manage the bully."

Pritch went downstairs, his limbs fairly shaking from the varied emotions he'd contained in order to make it through his first talk with his son. At the front door, he found Carlton Benton, now dressed in a dripping rain hat and coat.

The old man held out a crumpled paper bag. "Been meaning to drop this over here, has to do with the house," he said, his words tumbling over themselves. "The last owner, an old friend of my late wife's, left everything to Ellen when she died. Had no other friends or family, just my Ellen. Anyhow, Ellen always said she planned to give these papers to the other girl, the boy's mother." He waved his hand impatiently. "You know the one."

Pritch nodded, accepting the package.

Carlton Benton cleared his throat. "Almost threw 'em out, but I couldn't." He poked a finger upward. "Knew Ellen was watching." He smiled weakly, then coughed. "Also wanted, you know, to apologize for the trouble," he waved his hand again, "this morning. Good to see someone fixin' up the old place."

Pritch smiled as Julian appeared next to him. "Ms. Conarroe is considering selling," he explained.

Carlton Benton paused and looked at the boy. "So you'll be moving, huh? I thought, now you're old enough, you might mow my lawn next summer. Make a few dollars? Boys still do that sort of thing?"

Julian brightened. "Sure."

A brief smile crossed the old man's face. "Fine. Well,"

he glanced from the boy to Pritch, "we'll see if you're still around, then."

Chapter Fourteen

Audrey refused to care that the drive to the wedding was hardly gorgeous that dark, drizzly Saturday. For at least twenty-four hours she was getting away, and she intended to enjoy her escape, no matter how brief and imperfect it proved to be. Reclined in the front seat of James's sedan, she drummed her fingers on her knee in time to the raindrops and the radio's low melodies, listening while her boyfriend, again the talkative one, confessed his varied woes.

His mother did nothing but complain, James said, explaining he'd moved back to his family's home when she took an apartment for seniors, but refused to sell. Since her move, she continually found fault with her apartment as well as with his upkeep of her house. Her complaints had begun to annoy him as much as his job bored him, and he was tired of both.

For a few silent moments, James and Audrey watched as the gray shades of the landscape—the empty fields, the paved Thruway, the overcast sky—passed them by. They switched lanes to go by a brown milk truck. Byrne Dairy—Since 1933, its side panel read. Back in the right lane, they followed a line of telephone poles that seemed to speed along with them. Beyond the poles, electrical towers marched for miles, sending off shoots to service towns of squat brick homes, whitewashed churches, strip malls, and sprawling office parks.

Audrey recalled traveling the same route with Laura and Julian one dry summer years ago. Petrified tree skeletons had stood in the middle of dehydrated marshes along the highway, testaments to the land's desperate need for rain. Julian, then three, had strummed a miniature guitar in the back of his mother's car, singing "Row, Row, Row Your Boat" and "Old MacDonald." A nonsense version of "Life's a Bowl of Cherries" had led Audrey and Laura to exchange surprised smiles as Julian's small voice serenaded them.

Audrey relaxed in the cocoon of the BMW's leather upholstery. "Let's keep driving and not come back," she said.

James took her hand, resting it on his leg.

"At least not for a few days," she added. "New York City's only six hours away. We could be there tonight, stay tomorrow, maybe come home Monday, maybe Tuesday. Who knows? Who'd care?"

"That's the problem," James answered. "Many people would care."

Audrey nodded, wondering if she'd ever learn to shoulder responsibility without growing so restless. She looked back out the window, this time focusing on beads of rain that traced a painful path as they clung—for life, it seemed—to the edge of the speeding car.

James stole admiring glances at Audrey all day, pleased with her outfit: a short-skirted emerald suit with long sleeves and French cuffs that added intrigue, as did her delicate earrings. He held her hand throughout the wedding ceremony, anxious to show his colleagues they were together. He scanned the room, making a mental list of people he hoped to see—or avoid—during the reception.

"What a gorgeous dress," Audrey whispered to him as the bride walked up the aisle. He nodded and watched Carol—a long-time colleague of his and an old friend of his ex-girlfriend, Bridgit. Then he looked around the room, this time in search of a very tall, very noticeable, blonde. He slipped his arm around Audrey's waist when he realized Bridgit was not there.

After the ceremony, they made their way through the receiving line that led into the ballroom. Audrey paused to compliment the bride while James waited to greet Carol's mother, who spoke with other guests. He noticed people looked twice at him and Audrey, especially women as they swished by in their satin and pearls.

The bride's mother finally addressed James, exclaiming how wonderful it was to see him. "And where is that lovely girl of yours?" she gushed. "Carol was so lucky to have her expert advice in choosing her gown. Will Bridgit be arriving soon?"

James cleared his throat and guided Audrey to his side. "I don't know, Mrs. Newman," he said. "But I'd like you to meet

Ms. Audrey Conarroe."

"Oh, my. How nice to meet you." The bride's mother briskly shook Audrey's hand before passing the couple on to her husband at the line's end. James wondered if she'd been embarrassed by her awkward reference to his ex-girlfriend, or shocked by the color of his new girlfriend's skin. Either way, he'd enjoyed her reaction.

Audrey raised an eyebrow at him as they entered the ballroom. "Did she expect you to bring someone else?" She lifted her chin, an amused gleam in her eyes.

"Well . . ." James shuffled his feet and adjusted his tie, exaggerating his motions. "As a matter of fact—"

She laughed and took his arm. "Don't sweat it, Romeo. Pam filled me in about your ex a long time ago."

He stopped. "You know about Bridgit?"

Audrey grinned and led him to the bar. "It's no big deal," she said. "C'mon. You need a drink."

A few moments later, James heard Bridgit's voice before she even entered the room. High, lyrical, and laughing, the sound of it sailed down the receiving line, into the ballroom, and straight to him, like a heat-seeking missile. While Audrey sipped Chardonnay and listened to him point out wedding guests he knew, James shifted so he could see the door, and watch Bridgit appear.

She brought up the rear of the line. Tall and lanky, she moved with the grace of a trained model, slowly and deliberately, but with ease. James thought of a modeling trick she revealed once, when she pointed out a woman in a short skirt stomping down a city sidewalk. "What a crotch walk!" she'd exclaimed, irreverent as ever, explaining women should brush their knees and ankles together when they walk, even if their thighs rub.

Bridgit hugged the bride while James recalled the curves of his ex-girlfriend's slender knees and thighs. Convinced the sight of her white ankles beneath the hem of her gown would floor him in a second, he resolved to concentrate on her face when she approached him. And approach him she would, he was certain.

James tried to focus on what he was telling Audrey as he glanced past her toward the door. Bridgit was flirting with the bride's father. As always, he wondered how she pulled off such conversations with so much charm when he knew she was terribly bored. Bourgeoisie, she once called their mutual friends and their families, comparing them to the jet-set crowd of her modeling days.

Some at the wedding, including members of the band assembled at the head of the dance floor, certainly wore conventional, inexpensive outfits. But many of the guests, as well as the bridal party, were decked out in elegant attire. James had chosen his best Armani suit for the occasion. A few men sported tuxedoes, and numerous sequined gowns sparkled through the crowd, despite the early hour.

James knew none of this would impress Bridgit. Now a buyer for a New York designer, she divided her time between apartments in Rochester and Manhattan, spending as little time upstate as possible. She'd made her growing distaste for her hometown clear to James when she broke up with him in the spring.

He realized Audrey had said something. "Hm?" he asked.

"Want to find our table?"

"Sure, sure." He noted the curious gleam in her eyes again.

"You're pretty pale, kiddo," she teased. "Even for an Irish boy."

He peered at her. "Funny. I was just, you know, thinking about things."

Audrey tapped her glass. "You're really nervous about this, aren't you?" she asked, the corners of her mouth turned up.

He smiled back. "And you really enjoy seeing me sweat, don't you?"

She shrugged. "I'm just here for the show."

He touched her elbow and directed her to their table. "All right, I'll come clean," he said, bent toward her in confidence. "I not only wanted to show you off here, I didn't want to come stag, just in case—"

"In case Bridgit showed up?"

"Exactly."

"And she just has?"

"Bingo."

"And I thought you wore that suit to impress me." She clucked her tongue. "My, this *is* going to be fun."

"Maybe for you," he said. "Maybe for you."

They reached their table, and James realized with relief that Bridgit was not seated with them. Instead, the table was full of people from his office. Audrey introduced herself to the woman next to her.

"I'm sorry," James said. "I should be doing that. This is Madge, Bill, Theresa, Sam, Derek, and Stella. These ladies all work for, I mean with, me—and they're all trouble. Don't believe a word they say."

Audrey embarked in a lively conversation with Madge, a droll redhead with an insatiable appetite for gossip, while James scanned the room as nonchalantly as possible.

"James," Audrey scolded him, turning from Madge with a grin. "Is it true you . . .?"

He raised a hand. "Uh, uh. Not a word, I'm telling you. Don't believe a word."

She squeezed his hand, holding it as she continued to speak with Madge.

Stella, seated next to James, leaned toward him with a quick smirk. "Didn't I see Bridgit come in?"

"Did you?"

Stella nodded across the room. "She's seated on the other side of the dance floor," she said. "Carol thought it best to keep you two apart, in case you weren't being civil with each other."

James raised his eyebrows. "Of course we're being civil."

"Well," she said, "now's your chance to prove it."

James knew from her smug nod that Bridgit was walking toward him. He pivoted in his seat, then tried to stand quickly but hit the table with his knee. He grabbed his water glass to keep it from toppling and noticed Audrey's amused stare. Certain she was perfectly aware what was happening, he suspected she found him highly entertaining, perhaps even laughable.

He looked up and focused on the color of Bridgit's dress: royal blue, the exact color of her eyes. He'd always had trouble arguing with her, over even the most trivial points, because of those eyes. She'd simply give him a sidelong glance, put her petite, slightly upturned, nose in the air, then shake her blond waves from her face and flash a disarming smile, abruptly silencing him.

Her gown shimmered as she walked across the bright, noisy room. Though he knew it wasn't the time of year for spaghetti straps—he'd learned a thing or two about fashion while dating her—James fully appreciated the effect of her dress as she

123

moved, her bare shoulders in harmony with her hips, her scoop neckline revealing just enough cleavage to pique interest. He caught sight of her slender ankles and gripped the back of Audrey's chair.

"Jimmy!" Bridgit exclaimed. She gave him a hug and a peck on the cheek while he patted her back, enveloped by the scent of her perfume.

Bridgit greeted the other couples at the table, then considered Audrey. James noted Audrey did not stand. Instead, she sat back in her chair, her legs crossed, one elbow resting on the table. It occurred to him that if she were to stand next to Bridgit, she'd probably be a full head shorter.

He cleared his throat. "Bridgit," he said, "I'd like you to meet Audrey Conarroe. Audrey, Bridgit Lochen."

James noted a twinkle of curiosity in Bridgit's eyes as she realized Audrey was his date. She quickly sat next to her in his chair, leaving him to stand. "Well, hello," she cooed, patting Audrey's arm, unruffled by the even stare Audrey gave her. "What a lovely . . ." Bridgit scanned her from head to toe, as though searching for something to compliment, "ensemble. I love to see Jimmy's old friends and meet his new . . . acquaintances. It's been much too long, hasn't it, ladies?"

The three other women at the table nodded, wearing what James knew were forced smiles. None had ever concealed her dislike for Bridgit, and each had privately revealed her relief to James following the breakup.

"She's so phony," Madge had said. "Too high on herself," Theresa had added. "Extraordinarily high-maintenance," Stella had concurred. With all his heart, he'd wanted to agree with them. But even after so many months, he considered their comments nothing but jealous stabs at a very beautiful, successful woman.

James remained behind Audrey's chair, partly to show where his allegiance lay, partly to keep from accidentally glancing down Bridgit's dress.

"So what do you think of Carol's gown?" Bridgit continued, not waiting for an answer. "Stunning, isn't it? I helped her pick it out. I can't believe I missed the ceremony, but she knew I might be late getting here from the airport." She winked. "You should've seen me change into this get-up in that cramped lobby ladies' room."

James tried not to imagine her changing into anything,

anywhere.

Bridgit went on. "I only hope Carol will be happy with the big lug. She's a lot braver than I am, that's for sure. It's so hard to know whether marriage is the best thing these days, you know? Then again, I've always been such a big chicken."

She shifted in her chair, running a fuchsia-polished nail along her neckline, and beamed at James. He held his breath.

"Jimmy, remember when I flew to New York on that little puddle jumper in that awful storm?" She tapped Audrey's arm again. "The plane dropped like a rock. I was a mess, screaming and hanging onto the guy next to me. As soon as I could get to a phone, I called Jimmy and bawled my eyes out, and the next morning he flew to the city to make sure I was okay. What a guy, huh, Audrey? That's our Jimmy, always someone you can count on for help."

"Or at least for a good laugh," Audrey said.

Bridgit continued. "Anyway, Carol's definitely braver than I am with this marriage stuff. Such a big step, you know? But she says it would be the best thing for me if I would settle down, rather than fly all over the world for this silly job. Then again, I told her, now I'd have to find a guy willing to live in France for a few years. Did I tell you, Jimmy? I'm being transferred to the Paris office. Believe that?"

"Really?" James exhaled slowly. Though he heard Bridgit review her pending plans, he couldn't process a word she said for a few moments. The stark contrast between the life his ex-girlfriend was leading and his own life startled him.

"I'll be leaving in a couple weeks," she added. "That's why I wanted to get here, to say good-bye—to everyone."

The band stopped playing in preparation for the introduction of the bridal party. James stepped back slightly as everyone else looked toward the door. What caught his eye, though, was not the scene across the room, but the immediate scene before him—his old lover beside the woman he hoped that night would become his new lover. A comparison was impossible to avoid—Bridgit's fair European looks were a stark contrast to Audrey's African appearance. What surprised James most was his desire to move on from the familiar, to recover once and for all from the dizzying effects Bridgit had always had on him, to move to a place of comfort with someone like Audrey. No, he thought, with no one but Audrey.

"Give me a hug now, Jimmy, huh?" Bridgit said as she

stood. "I've got an early flight in the morning, so I've got to eat and run tonight."

James tried to relax, determined to give her a friendly hug without being overwhelmed by the feel of her in his arms. "Take care of yourself," he said, his voice low.

Bridgit waved to the other guests at the table, barely acknowledging Audrey. "'Bye, all." With a final smile to James and a tap on his arm, she was gone.

James sat back down. "Is it warm in here?" he asked, tugging at his collar.

Audrey patted his flushed cheek. "Poor boy. You don't know what hit you."

He grinned. "Maybe a walk by the lake later will help me recuperate."

"It'll be a little chilly, don't you think?"

James raised his wineglass. "Not if we warm ourselves up first."

As Audrey reached for her glass, James found even her perfume more sincere than the showy, expensive scents Bridgit favored. He took a deep breath, letting Audrey's presence relax him as his ex-girlfriend's never could.

Audrey was relieved later when James suggested again they slip out for a walk. Restless after so many hours of meeting and conversing with strangers, she looked forward to the next stage of her escape. She'd found James amusing but endearing all evening, especially during his charade of calm while Bridgit turned him to mush with each sidelong smile, each wink, each tap.

Madge, the redhead, had wasted no time telling Audrey about Bridgit prior to her appearance at their table. "She's a class-A bitch, my dear," Madge had whispered, obviously enjoying the opportunity to enlighten her on the subject. "Once she realizes James is moving beyond her reach, she'll bend over backwards—literally, if you get my drift—to reel him back in. Not because she'd die without him, but just to prove she can do it."

Audrey knew James remained spellbound by his gorgeous ex-girlfriend and suspected he still harbored hopes of making up with her, perhaps even convincing her to marry him, some day. For now, though, she was determined to enjoy her time with him, however long that lasted. She simply wanted to enjoy herself, to have some long-overdue fun.

They crossed the hotel's wide lawn toward the lakeshore, holding hands, laughing as the heels of Audrey's pumps kept sinking into the wet ground. Dusk closed in around them. James walked ahead to search for a dry park bench while she continued to step gingerly along. Suddenly, her shoes sank deep into a patch of mud. "I'm stuck!" she cried.

James laughed as he returned to her. By the time he arrived she was doubled over, hysterical as she tried to jiggle a shoe loose.

"Ms. Conarroe." He remained in the grass beside her, both hands on his hips. "Do you realize you've found the only mud hole in a lawn the size of our whole town?"

Audrey reached for him and wrapped her arm around his. "Save me!" she cried, laughing harder now. "I don't care about the shoes, they hurt my feet anyway!"

"I don't know," he teased. "You got yourself into this mess."

Audrey pressed against him, her weight now full against his chest, her breathing heavy with her laughter. "Save me," she whispered. James lifted her out of her shoes and into his arms, then brought her back up the lawn to a patio, where they sat on a wrought iron bench. He held her on his lap as though she were a child. "My hero," Audrey proclaimed. "Your wing tips must have cleats."

"Right. Special order from Johnston Murphy. So you can wear them to a wedding and then play football in them." He shook his head. "No. Sometimes I'm just . . ." He pulled her close. "Sometimes I'm just incredibly lucky."

Audrey nodded toward her stockinged feet. "You know you'll have to carry me all the way inside now, Romeo."

"My pleasure." He kissed her, and Audrey leaned into the fullness of his kiss, enjoying the pressure of his mouth against hers, of her small frame arched against him. She pulled away and sighed dreamily, tilting her chin toward the sky.

The full moon broke free of the scattering clouds, the same clouds that had hidden the sun all day, blessing the wedding with good-luck showers. Bright and full, the moon perched on a wispy shelf, obvious in its unabashed, wide-eyed stare.

"Do you believe stars are loved ones watching over you?" James asked.

Audrey studied his face as he spoke, watching his eyes

absorb her, enjoying the slow realization she wanted him as much as he seemed to want her.

"I like to think my father's watching me," he continued, looking up to the few stars that had appeared, "watching me take care of Mom, and the house, and that he's proud of what I'm doing."

Audrey gazed at him as the weight of his words registered. She straightened and moved to sit next to him on the bench. "I wish I could say that, too," she said, determined for one night not to let her distress over her family overwhelm her, or keep her from what she wanted. "But—" She paused as her voice wavered.

"Give yourself time," he whispered.

"I just doubt Laura, or my father, would be happy with what I'm doing," she said, "what I'm wishing, if they were watching." She fought her growing frustration, her tears, her desperation. "I want to feel sure of something again," she added, incredibly tired of trying so hard to enjoy herself. "Anything."

James smoothed the edge of her face, tracing the line that ran from her cheekbone to her chin. Audrey pressed her hand over his, closing her eyes to stem her tears, to fully absorb his touch.

"Feel sure about me, Audrey," she heard him whisper. "Feel sure about me."

Chapter Fifteen

James noticed the older woman staring as soon as he and Audrey sat at brunch the next morning in the hotel's intimate dining room. Thin, pale, and brittle, she turned in her chair, ignoring her husband and meal for a full minute. At first, James thought she wanted to see what he and Audrey had piled on their plates from the generous buffet. He glanced toward the woman, who returned his quick smile and nod with a steady glare. James tried to ignore her and smiled instead at Audrey, who beamed back at him. He loved to see her so content, and wanted to keep her in such a mood. Despite only a few hours of sleep, she appeared refreshed and calm, not at all bothered by the woman's rude stare.

He poured syrup on his pancakes from a small silver pitcher as white-dressed servers bustled from table to table. Though he and Audrey talked while they ate, James couldn't stop wondering why the woman had seemed so disturbed. He looked her way, now seeing only the back of her head, her gray hair knotted in a chignon like his mother sometimes wore.

Certainly his mother would disapprove if she were to see him at a hotel brunch with someone like Audrey, he thought. Then he clenched his teeth, realizing he'd categorized Audrey as someone "unlike" himself, just as Margaret would, just as the older woman probably had. He knew he and Audrey made an unusual couple, but wondered at his sudden desire to somehow change that.

He sipped his coffee and recalled waking while Audrey still slept. He'd realized a liberating resolve to pursue this relationship with her, regardless of any concerns his mother might raise. All he wanted was to wake with Audrey every day, to always be there to help and protect her. She needed him in a way

Bridgit never had.

James reached for Audrey's hand across the table, then moved to sit in the chair next to her. When she looked at him in surprise, he leaned forward as though to whisper in her ear but kissed her on the earlobe, instead, pleased by her sudden laugh, her dropped fork clattering on her plate, the wondering stares directed their way from every corner of the room.

They strolled by the lake after brunch, cold October sunlight casting their shadows along the shore. Audrey replayed in memory the way their last walk had led them inside, to their first night together. James had proven to be an attentive, tender lover. And though Audrey hardly thought they'd begun a long-term relationship, she certainly intended to enjoy their time together. She awoke that morning to find him already awake, watching her. He announced they'd gained an hour as daylight saving time had "fallen back" overnight, and said he'd been waiting for her to help him celebrate their extra hour in bed. She embraced him instantly, happy to oblige.

Now, though, as they continued to walk along the lakeshore, concerns edged their way into Audrey's conscience. She began to worry Julian might arrive home from his friend's house to find himself alone with his father and retreat to his room to wait for her return.

James squeezed her hand, as though sensing her concern. She wondered that the sight of his handsome smile, the pressure of his kind hand, could cause her such joy and such heartache. How easy it would be to fall in love with him. How easy to let him take care of her, to share with him her many concerns, to ask for and wholly accept his help. He'd give it, she knew, over and over again, without hesitation. He was that type, the type that thrived on helping others, while Audrey remained skeptical of anyone so eager and honest, protective of her own sorry heart, to the bitter end.

She suggested they head back, wishing the morning sun would hold its place midway, willing time to fall back some more and leave them there for just a while longer, together and alone.

The drive home was quick, though relatively quiet, with soft music filling the voids between their sparse conversations. James seemed preoccupied, so Audrey sat back and enjoyed the final remnants of her brief escape in silence. She grew certain by noon both Julian and Pritch would be home, waiting.

At the house, James pulled her bag out of the trunk. When Audrey kissed him on the cheek, he grinned and promised to call later.

She kissed him again, this time on the mouth. "Don't worry," she purred. "I won't wait by the phone all day."

He opened his car door and winked. "I'm sure of that," he said, nodding toward the house.

Audrey followed his gaze to the front door, where Julian and Pritch now stood, her nephew with a baseball cap pulled low over his forehead. Though her stomach tightened into a quick knot, she waved to James before heading up the porch steps, determined to appear rested and relaxed after her time away.

Pritch returned her smile with a frown. "You had some calls this morning," he announced, his face grave. "I thought you'd be back earlier."

Audrey entered the house and dropped her bag in the front hall, her face hot. "I didn't know I had a curfew." She glanced at the written message he handed her. "Aunt Letty called? From Nashville?" She squinted at the piece of paper. Calls from her father's family had always been rare, coming only in cases of emergency.

Pritch cleared his throat. "It seems your mother has fallen ill there," he said. "Your aunt thought you'd want to know."

"What?" The thought of another family member in crisis was almost too much to bear. Audrey clenched the scrap of paper and raced to the kitchen telephone, which she quickly dialed. "I forgot Mom went there for a wedding." She stared at Pritch, who had followed her, as she waited for the call to go through. "Did Aunt Letty say what was wrong?"

"Apparently," he answered, "your mother had some sort of stroke."

"A stroke!" Audrey stared a moment longer, than stamped her foot. "Damn it! The damn answering machine." Pause. "Aunt Letty? This is Audrey. Thanks so much for calling. I'll leave here, New Bilford, soon. . . . I should be there tomorrow. I'll call on my way to get directions to your house—and to see how Mom's doing. Talk to you then."

Pritch had raised his hands by the time she hung up. "I don't think she meant for you to race down there now, Miss Audrey. I doubt there's anything you can do while your mother is in the hospital."

"Of course I'm going, Pritch. What the hell else am I supposed to do, sit around here and leave her there alone?"

"She's not alone."

"She needs me, anyway. And Julian, too. Julian!" She called to her nephew, who appeared beside his father. "Did you hear all that? Grandma had a stroke in Nashville. Let's pack so we can leave ASAP."

Julian frowned. "Why do I have to go? I've got two tests this week."

Audrey shook her head. "I can't ask one of your friend's moms to take you for God knows how long, Julian. And I can write you an excuse for school. I'm leaving in half an hour, and I expect you to be ready."

"I can stay here," he said, his voice a casual challenge.

Audrey stared at him. "Two days ago you refused to spend one night with your father. Now you're ready to spend at least a week with him?"

Julian looked away.

"We've come to an understanding," Pritch intervened.

Audrey raised an eyebrow at him.

"Julian agreed to give me a chance, and I promised to give him plenty of space."

Audrey turned an incredulous circle, both fists at her hips. "You two decided all this just this morning?"

"The boy spent the weekend here."

Audrey stared at her nephew again. "You lied to me?" She stepped closer, noticing his bruised eye. "What happened here?" she asked, lifting the brim of his cap.

Julian backed away.

"A school-yard scuffle," Pritch said. "Nothing—"

Audrey raised a hand. "He can tell me about it in the car. Right now, I have a dying mother in Nashville, so—"

"She's not dying!"

Audrey pivoted back toward her nephew. "I don't know that, Julian. I have no idea how she is. All I know is Grandma's in trouble and I want to see her and make sure she's all right. Can you understand that?" She glared at Pritch. "Can either of you understand that? I'm going, I don't want to leave Julian here, so Julian is going with me. Is that clear?"

Despite the looks of disbelief that met her pronouncement, Audrey stormed out of the kitchen. She retrieved her overnight bag and went to her room, where she gathered clothes from her dresser and closet, listening for the sound of Julian going to his room to do the same. Instead, she heard Pritch's slow, heavy steps ascend the creaking stairs. A moment later, he stood in her open doorway, hands clasped.

She continued to throw clothes onto her bed. "You know I can't leave him here with you," she said, willing her voice to remain steady.

"And you know it makes perfect sense to leave him here with me," he countered.

Audrey ripped open her lingerie drawer, adding bras and panties to her pile. "How can I be sure you two would be all right?"

He shifted his weight and cocked his head. "Why are you so certain we wouldn't?"

Audrey sensed an edge of urgency in his voice, in his stilted movements, and knew he considered this a unique opportunity to get to know Julian—without her interference. She snapped her head back, glaring at him.

"I'm beginning to regret inviting you to stay, Pritch." She saw him straighten his back, as though bracing for her attack. "Why do you want to cause trouble here? Don't you think he's confused enough already?"

He gazed at her, his eyes round and innocent, his hands open and extended. "Now, Miss Audrey, I'd think you'd appreciate the chance to get away for a while without Julian. Maybe your boyfriend could drive you in his nice sedan, make the trip a little easier on you."

"Lay off, Pritch. I'm not going for a joy ride. I'm worried about my mother down there, and I'm anxious to make sure she's all right. Now you can help me out and talk some sense into your son, or you can shut up and let me take care of things."

Pritch refolded his hands. "You're right, of course. You're right to be concerned."

"And I'm right to expect my nephew to come with me." She pulled an empty suitcase onto her bed, yanked it open, and began to fill it.

"You know he'd be fine here," Pritch said. "He'd be with his father, the most reliable person in his life right now."

"Reliable!" Audrey planted her hands in the clothes she'd pushed into the suitcase.

Pritch continued. "He'd be with family. That *should* be a comfort to you. As you should be comforted knowing your dear mother is with family. Your father's family, yes, but as far as they're concerned your mother became one of them when she married your father. Then again," he shrugged, steeling his gaze, "maybe that's what's troubling you. Perhaps you're right not to take your boyfriend along. Baby James would very likely be quite uncomfortable with your colored relations."

Audrey moved around the bed toward him. "Cut the crap, Pritch. You know full well the color of anyone's damn skin means nothing to me. All I'm concerned about right now is my sick mother, my stubborn nephew who refuses to come with me, and his cocky, pain-in-the-ass father who loves to preach about his perfect black skin and his many virtues. Well, I'm sorry, but all I know is you deserted my pregnant sister and fourteen years later still have no family, yet you insist you're the most reliable person in Julian's life right now. Can you imagine *why* I have a problem with that?"

Pritch had spread his feet and crossed his arms. Despite his average height, he now filled the doorway with his presence, and his boiling anger. His eyes narrowed and his words were clipped, but clear, when he spoke.

"Go ask your mother why I left Laura," he said, "and see what she tells you. Then you decide whom to believe, whom to trust. I left Laura because your father made it clear I wasn't good enough for his daughter. I left because I refused to join a family where I'd be a lesser member, unaccepted because I wasn't a lawyer or a doctor or an academic, because I worked with my hands and my heart, more concerned with the quality of my work than the size of my paycheck. You go to your mother and ask her what your father, a black man, thought of his daughter's choice for a husband."

Audrey pointed an accusing finger. "Don't even suggest my father disapproved of you because of your race, Pritch. That's beyond ludicrous."

"Believe what you wish. I only wish I'd had the strength to stand up to him, and the faith in Laura to ask if she'd stay with me despite his narrow view." He smiled a brief, bitter smile. "Respect is the key, Miss Audrey, and where that is lacking no love can exist. Your father had little respect for me, and I couldn't bear to live with that."

Audrey crossed her arms and glared at him. "My father was a good man."

Pritch shook his head, his gaze still steady. "Your father

134

was a confused man. He did himself, and his family, a disservice by marrying a white woman."

The swell of blood that made her head throb and her hand fly up to strike Pritch disturbed Audrey as much as his words had. She stopped herself, but only after she'd lurched toward him, bringing herself so close she could clearly see the lines of his condescending smirk and the redness of his now haughty, hooded eyes.

"Get out," she growled. "Get the hell out of my house."

He snorted, incredulous. "My son would have none of that now, I'm certain."

Audrey faced him for a full minute, inhaling deeply to slow her racing pulse, gritting her teeth to keep from giving him more ammunition in the heated, furious curses she ached to scream.

He met her gaze with a bored, matter-of-fact expression, as though daring her to speak.

Audrey blinked a few times, then chuckled. "You're really trying to trip me up, aren't you?" she asked, backing away. "Determined to test me. All for Julian's sake, of course." She picked earrings from a small jewelry box on her dresser. "Well I'm not biting, Pritch, so save your games for Julian. He's suddenly pretty eager to please you." She turned back toward him, at a safe distance now. "I plan to be back in one week, hopefully earlier, depending on my mother's condition. Just keep your bitterness toward my father to yourself, would you? Anything you say against him will tear Julian apart."

Pritch nodded. "You have my word that I have not, and shall not, say anything about your father that is untrue. Besides," he stepped into the hall and lifted his chin toward Julian's room, "your nephew is learning to accept the truth, regardless how painful. Eh, Julian?"

Audrey rushed to the door to see her nephew a few feet away, certainly within earshot, half his body in shadow, the other half illuminated by the hall's wall of windows. He faced her defiantly, his dimpled chin raised, meeting her stare with a steady, unnerving gaze that matched his father's.

She groaned, gesturing toward him, and glared back at Pritch, her raised hand shaking. "What are you thinking?" she demanded. "Why expose him to all this?"

Pritch's face softened, but his voice remained steady. "The truth is in everyone's best interest, Miss Audrey," he said.

"Lies simply delay pain, and ultimately add to it."

Audrey's voice was a near whisper when she spoke. "He's just a boy."

Pritch nodded. "Yes, but you see? Keeping the truth from him only makes his way more difficult."

She paused, wondering at her nephew's continued silence, fearing what he thought—about her, his family, himself—after all he'd heard. She looked back down the hall, saw he was no longer there, then heard his bedroom door gently close.

She sighed, exhausted but anxious to be on her way, though she'd been home less than an hour. "My mother. I've got to finish packing."

Pritch moved from the doorway. "I'm curious," he began, despite Audrey's frown, "about your opinion regarding your parents' marriage. It's important I know, really, so I don't confuse the boy if we touch on the subject while you're gone."

She zipped her suitcase. "All I know is that because my parents married, I exist, Laura existed, Julian exists. Can't you look past *your* narrow view to see that? To appreciate that my parents gave you two of the most important people in your life?"

Pritch walked around the bed to gaze out the room's window. "But your father robbed you—and Laura—of your heritage, hiding you away in this town," he said. "Maybe he thought he could protect you, but all he did was hurt you, hurt his people.

"If we keep intermarrying," he continued, "our race will cease to exist, will be whitewashed right into the rest of the anonymous crowd, until none of us knows who we are. And then all those survivors who came before us will die away as their names are forgotten, omitted from our children's history texts." He glanced at her as though he acknowledged her desire to end the conversation, but hoped she'd let him continue. "It would be such a shame," he said, "to forget all those who struggled, refusing to give in to a society hell bent on destroying them and their kind. They deserve to live on in our memories, or we will have defeated them as death never could."

His voice deepened. "At least I won't be a part of that," he said. "I won't stand by while my son comes of age believing that to marry white is to marry right, that he is unworthy because his skin is brown."

Audrey moaned. "I wondered where this was leading," she said. "I told you, my decision to date James is *my* decision. It has nothing to do with Julian. He is being raised to know his worth is not measured by his skin color."

"Huh," Pritch scoffed. "That statement proves how little you understand, Miss Audrey. Any black boy knows full well his worth is measured by the color of his skin, not the power of his brain or the size of his heart. It's the first thing people see, the first thing to register, the first thing to measure," he counted the crimes on his hand, "and no matter what he does or says or creates, when people describe him, they'll call him colored."

Audrey pursed her lips. "Why are you telling me all this?"

Pritch stepped closer to her. "Because, like it or not, you and I are bound in this life. Not only by our love for your sister, but by our charge to raise your sister's son."

Once again, Audrey found herself impressed by the intensity with which Pritch operated, the passion that drove his beliefs, his words, his actions. She took a deep breath.

"But as in any relationship," she said, "teamwork and *compromise* are required." Her eyes narrowed. "Agreed?"

She watched the lines of Pritch's face deepen and his mouth tighten as he appeared to struggle with the request made of him.

Finally, he gave a curt nod. "Agreed," he said, his voice now raspy. "Of course, agreed. We must be straightforward, as you said the other day."

Audrey pulled her suitcase off the bed, grateful when Pritch offered to bring it downstairs. A few minutes later, she followed with her overnight bag and went to the living room to get a road atlas off a bookshelf. Then she stood at the bottom of the stairs and called up to her nephew, torn between her desire to make sure he was all right and her belief he'd simply scowl at her again, annoyed by her concern.

"Good-bye, Julian."

She paused a moment, heard his muffled good-bye from behind his closed door, and tried not to feel hurt, or surprised, that he did not come down to see her off.

"Ugh," she muttered, heading to the kitchen, "I need to call work." After leaving a voice-mail message with the temp agency, she recorded a message on James's home answering machine saying she'd call from Nashville as soon as she could.

She hung up the phone and found Pritch in the kitchen doorway. He handed her a rolled packet of papers bound by a rubber band, explaining only that they were from her neighbor,

Carlton Benton, whose wife had received them from a former owner of Laura's house.

Audrey tucked the papers under her arm, promising to call in the morning. She paused before leaving the kitchen. "Tell me what happened to Julian, at the playground."

He explained about the fight, adding that he'd promised to teach Julian some boxing basics.

Audrey grimaced. "Terrific."

"He's a boy," Pritch said. "The only black boy in his school, I imagine. He needs lessons in self-defense."

"You said this was over a girl," Audrey reminded him, "not race."

Pritch shook his head. "It's always about race, Miss Audrey. You know that as well as I. You simply need to admit it, some day."

Audrey frowned, but paused again. "Listen," she said, gesturing toward the ceiling, toward Julian alone in his room. "I don't want to leave him here, but . . ." She willed her voice to remain steady. "I know I can trust you, because Laura did."

Pritch's face remained blank. "You can trust me," he said, "because I'm the boy's father."

Chapter Sixteen

An hour later, James listened to Audrey's message with concern and some confusion, wondering why she'd take two days to drive to Nashville when she could fly there in a matter of hours. He knew airfare would be high at such short notice, but wished he'd had a chance to at least offer to help pay for it.

He frowned at his mother, who had followed him into the kitchen. Though Margaret Sullivan stood only a few inches shorter than her son, she weighed much less. She ate constantly to keep her blood sugar at stable levels, but had lost quite a bit of weight during her recent bout with diabetes.

James reached into a cupboard for a box of low-salt crackers, which Margaret opened. She glanced at the sink full of dirty dishes.

"Really, Jimmy," she quipped, nibbling a cracker. "If you don't plan to marry soon, at least get a maid. I know you can afford one."

She rinsed a dishcloth and wiped the counters. "The house hasn't been this neglected in years," she said. "Your father never would have eaten in a dusty kitchen." She returned to the sink and dried her hands. "At any rate, we've got plenty of cleaning to do before my party next Sunday. This place is going to be full of people."

James cringed at the reference to his mother's abruptly planned sixtieth birthday party. He wondered which team the Bills were scheduled to play that afternoon, certain the party would force him to miss the game.

Margaret nodded toward the answering machine. "Whose mother had a stroke?" she asked, filling the sink with soapy water.

James stepped out of her way. "Do you remember a girl

I met in high school named Audrey Conarroe?"

His mother smoothed her sweater. "The colored girl?"

He nodded. "Right. The colored girl. She went with me to the wedding yesterday."

"What?" Margaret stared at him. "You didn't tell me you were taking anyone, Jimmy." She soaped a plate, her thin lips set together. "And you said you saw Bridgit there, and of course Carol and all her family. And all your friends from work? What in the world were you thinking?"

James leaned against the kitchen counter, not at all surprised by her reaction. He'd been inclined to defend his mother when Audrey suggested she was prejudiced, but now he recalled Margaret's words when she insisted he stop seeing Audrey in high school. She'd kept the conversation short, that day she caught James with Audrey in the mall, and closed it with no chance for her son to comment. "It's my job to guide you from poor decisions, Jimmy," she'd said. He'd known better than to question her true motives, much less argue against them.

"At least no clients were there." Margaret sighed, then glanced up at him. "Were there?"

He shook his head, wishing he could feel something other than contempt for his mother at that moment.

"Does it really matter?" He took a glass from a cupboard, filled it with cold water from the refrigerator, and placed it on the counter next to her.

She nodded, soaping another dish. "Yes, Jimmy, it does matter. When people see you with someone—like her—they think differently of you, of your judgment." She paused. "You're such a catch," she added, her voice lighter. "I wish you'd set your sights higher. I know your breakup with Bridgit was difficult—"

"This has nothing to do with Bridgit."

"Of course it does," she said. "You may not see it, but everyone else at that wedding certainly did." She shook her head and braced both soapy hands on the sink's edge.

James knew what she was going to say before she uttered the words.

"Oh, my nerves," she moaned. She glanced at her son. "I spoke with Bridgit's mother this morning, by the way."

James crossed his arms, anticipating his mother's next suggestion as a teasing smile played across her lightly lined face.

"Bridgit didn't go to New York today," she continued. "She's been called to Paris earlier than expected and will be gone by the end of the week."

James's face flushed hot and red. "Mom, would you stop scheming?" He moved away from her. "I won't beg her to marry me. She turned me down, and that's the end of it."

Margaret's smile widened. "Go see her before she leaves, Jimmy. What harm would it do? You could bring the ring with you, just in case. Bridgit's strong willed, but she's about to make a big change in her life. I'm sure she'd love to have you by her side in Paris. What girl wouldn't?" Margaret winked at him, an old trick to try to soften him up.

James stared at the floor, sure his mother would be crushed to learn Bridgit had scoffed at that ring, a cherished heirloom from his father's family. He thought of the small box tucked away in his bedroom and wondered how Audrey would react if he were to offer that ring to her.

A few hours later, James left his mother at her apartment, her cupboards refilled with groceries from a quick shopping trip. On the short drive home, he considered Margaret might have been right about one thing: it would do no harm for him to visit Bridgit, to say good-bye. Even if he and Audrey were to marry, there was no reason he and Bridgit couldn't remain friends.

He called her late that afternoon, startled after one ring to hear the sudden sound of her voice.

"Hello?" she answered, her tone abrupt.

"Bridgit," he sputtered. "This is Jimmy."

"Jimmy! How'd you know I was home?"

"My mom said your trip to New York was canceled for the week, and you're leaving for Paris early."

She laughed. "Word travels fast."

"Especially with our mothers on the grapevine." He took a deep breath. "I thought I could stop by, sometime, before you go."

"Sure," she said. "How's tonight?"

"Tonight?"

"Tomorrow night's booked, and the movers are coming Tuesday, so really tonight's it."

"All right," he said, pacing. "All right, tonight's fine. I'll be there, when? When's a good time?"

"Now's fine, really. The sooner the better."

James stopped pacing.

"You can help me move some boxes."

James drove through a rainy drizzle to Bridgit's apartment building on the outskirts of Rochester. He pulled into her street, scanning the shadows for a parking spot.

Though bare, thick branches in the crippled oaks and towering maples that lined the road blocked the dull lights of the old street lamps. James aligned his car with the curb under one tree as heavy drops pelted his hood from above. He got out and stepped around puddles on the sidewalk, wishing he hadn't worn his suede oxfords, though they went well with his new corduroy slacks. Certain Bridgit would notice, he'd also worn his cobalt blue herringbone shirt, the one she always said looked best on him.

Another tenant used his card key to open the locked entrance, allowing James to slip inside without buzzing Bridgit. He took the elevator to her floor and knocked, then remembered she never locked her door until she went to bed, a habit he'd always questioned.

He heard her yell from inside that the door was open. "Safety-conscious as ever," he muttered, letting himself in.

"In here," Bridgit called from the kitchen.

James found her kneeling on her counter, emptying a cupboard. "Will you ever learn to lock your door?" he teased.

She shrugged, her back still to him. "I know," she said, pulling a handful of half-burned votive candles from the cupboard. "I can't believe how much stuff I save," she added, tossing them into a trash can behind her.

She glanced toward him and whistled. "Look at you, all gussied up. Going to see Audrey later?" She winked and sat on the counter.

James flashed her a grin as he sat at her table. "Just wanted to leave a good last impression."

Bridgit moaned. "C'mon, Jimmy," she chided. "This isn't the last we'll see of each other. Promise."

She returned to her chore. "The movers say they'll do all the packing, but I don't want them to pack all this junk." She continued to empty the cupboard as she spoke. "I should tell them to get rid of it—burn it, sell it, give it away, whatever. But then I'd probably get to Paris and find all these boxes of crap delivered on my doorstep, with no room to put it all. Who needs it? I hear the apartments there are cramped little closets, anyway. Can I get you something? Not that there's much, but...." She signaled toward the refrigerator.

"No, thanks," he said, his voice higher than he'd expected.

Bridgit worked and talked, her lower back bared by her cut-off sweatshirt as she reached up to empty the cupboard, revealing her thin waist above the gathered line of her loose sweat pants. James tried to focus on something else in the kitchen, but his eyes kept returning to an alluring spot in the center of her lower back, a spot he was sure he'd tasted hundreds of times.

"I'm telling you, Jimmy," Bridgit continued, the sound of his name rattling him back into focus. He took a deep breath to steady himself as she sat again on the counter, facing him. "You surprised everyone by bringing Audrey to Carol's wedding."

She brushed back hair that had fallen loose from her thick ponytail, not at all sure what she intended to accomplish with this line of teasing, but enjoying the game, nonetheless.

"You should've heard Carol's mother when I got to her in the receiving line." Bridgit's face brightened with laughter, prompting James to return her smile. "What a riot! She was dying to tell me, warn me, I suppose, that you were there with someone else, especially since I was stag, but she didn't know how to tell me your date was black. She stumbled all over the place, trying not to say something 'inappropriate.'"

She imitated her friend's mother, her voice high and quivering. "'Have you met his new friend, Bridgit dear? She's perfectly lovely, to be sure, very *dark* and mysterious, really.'" She hooted with laughter. "She practically fell over herself to tell me. Carol just rolled her eyes. What a joke!"

James clenched his teeth. "Good to know we entertained everyone," he said.

Bridgit slipped off the counter and sat next to him. "I was laughing at Carol's mother, not you," she said. "Why so uptight tonight? We lived together for two years, and now you're sitting here like a scared mouse." She extended a manicured hand across the table. "You know, my mother was furious with me when we broke up. Said I blew my chance at a good catch. That's what she called you: a good catch."

She leaned back in her chair and stretched, tucking loose hair behind her ears, revealing her flat belly as her short top lifted with her arms.

James coughed. "Funny," he said, trying to sound anything but rattled, "my mother said the same thing."

Bridgit raised her eyebrows.

"That I blew it, losing you," he explained. "She practically begged me to come see you before you left."

He watched Bridgit's face, searching for signs that Margaret's assumptions about her vulnerability might have been accurate.

She surprised him by laughing. "My mother's petrified about my move to Paris," she said. "I'm sure she's been on the horn to Margaret every day since I told her I was going." She went to the refrigerator, where she stood for a moment with the door open, as though cooling off on a hot summer afternoon. Without taking anything out, she closed the door and faced him again. "She seems to think France is in another galaxy, and she's certain I'm terrified to move there alone."

"Are you?" James asked, his voice barely audible. "Nervous, I mean, about moving there?"

Bridgit snorted. "Tell you what, Jimmy," she said. "Why don't you come with me so everyone can stop worrying, okay?"

Her flip statement made James realize how much he'd hoped to find her vulnerable, eager to have him escort her to Paris, sorry she'd ever left him. He also realized his expression revealed all this to Bridgit, who beamed a mocking smile at him and then burst out laughing.

She raised a hand as he tried to speak. "No, no, Jimmy. Don't say anything. I was kidding." She slowed to compose herself. "Really."

James stood. "I know that," he sputtered, his face warm. He gestured toward the scattered boxes on the kitchen floor. "Didn't you say you had some stuff you needed me to move? I should get going."

Bridgit regretted that she'd upset him so quickly. She'd enjoyed seeing Jimmy at Carol's wedding, and was pleased that he'd called and stopped over. He was a nice guy, a sweet guy. There was no denying that. But Bridgit had remained unsure since their breakup that Jimmy really missed her, or that he'd ever forgive her for her awful timing. He'd just shocked her with that ring, and she'd panicked. She never wanted to break up with him, she just wasn't ready to get married. But how could she explain that, when he was in such a rush to settle down in his dinky hometown? How could she say no, but yes at the same time? He'd be better off with someone local, someone like Audrey, maybe, though she hardly seemed the straight-laced, stay-at-home type Bridgit thought Jimmy would want for a wife.

She shook her head, still mystified by his sudden proposal, still compelled to believe his father's death had propelled Jimmy in that direction. It was fun to have him here; she didn't want him to go. Would he stay if she asked him? Yes, she was sure he would. He was a nice guy, a sweet guy, but Bridgit knew, deep down, Jimmy was a sucker for blondes with long legs. Which made his surprise date at Carol's wedding all the more mystifying. What was he thinking? What did he really want?

She waved her hand. "A few boxes I can take care of, in the bedroom. Don't worry about it."

James glanced at his watch, paying no attention to the time. "All right, then," he said. "I really should go. Take care." He gave her a quick hug.

"I'm sorry, Jimmy," she said. "I have a lousy sense of humor." She placed her hand on his arm. "You and Audrey look terrific together, by the way. Comfortable, like you're old friends."

James peered at her, wondering if the maternal grapevine could have possibly imparted this information to her so quickly. "We are old friends," he said, "from high school."

Bridgit's face brightened again. "A girl from your past," she mused. "I see." The teasing glimmer returned to her eyes. "Any long-term plans?"

James shook his head, certain his face had flushed scarlet.

"C'mon," she chided. "You can tell me."

"No plans," he said. "Not yet, anyway. She's got plenty going on. I don't want to complicate things."

Bridgit's grin widened. "You're such a martyr. Go for what you want and see what happens, why don't you?"

James peered at her again, trying not to marvel at her flawless face.

"I just worry about you," she continued. "I feel bad, you know, about our breakup, and want to make sure you're happy."

James stopped himself from laughing at her confession, wanting to believe she truly cared for him. "It's hard to say where things are going with Audrey," he began. "She's got a lot going on, especially with her nephew. She's his guardian, and I'm not sure—"

"Not sure you want an instant family?"

James paused, his mouth still open from his unfinished sentence. "I, uh, I don't know," he admitted. "I don't know what my problem is." He headed to the hall to get his coat.

Bridgit followed. "Maybe they could move in with you for a while," she suggested, "so you could try it out, see if it might work."

James gave her a questioning look as he put on his jacket. "It's not just her nephew, okay?" he said, suddenly impatient to end the inquiry he'd invited, to keep his private thoughts—and doubts—private. He placed both hands at her shoulders. "Listen," he added, "I appreciate your concern, but . . . Maybe it's too early, for all this. Anyway, I need to go." He gave her a peck on the cheek, then pulled away. "Lock up after me, would you?" he added, forcing his voice to sound light.

Bridgit opened the door for him. "Just don't let your mother keep you from getting what you want, Jimmy."

He stopped, halfway into the hall, and stared at her. "What makes you think—?"

Bridgit tilted her chin upward with a confident smile. "I know her, that's all," she said. "And I know how much she wants a redheaded grandchild."

She locked the door behind him, then sank into a chair. She couldn't bear returning to the mess in the kitchen, and wanted to think a few more minutes about Jimmy, now that he'd gone. His reaction to her glib suggestion he go with her to Paris had been priceless. She knew it would be fun to have him there. Hell, she mused with a wry smile, it was fun to have Jimmy anywhere, any time. Could he be serious about Audrey? She seemed nice enough, and yes, she was pretty, with those exotic dark eyes and those cheekbones up to her ears. Bridgit decided Audrey could've been a model, if she'd been taller. Her plain, short hairstyle remained a puzzle, though. Couldn't she straighten it, and grow it out?

Bridgit shrugged, loosening her hair out of her ponytail, raking it free with one hand before pulling it back out of her face. She tried to imagine what the children would look like, if James and Audrey were ever to have any. She laughed at the thought of a pale, redheaded little Jimmy and a dark little Audrey with cropped hair. Sure they'd be cute, she mused, but wouldn't they all be black, like Audrey? Would Jimmy really want black children? She stood to stretch, spying her reflection in her picture window, certain of only one thing: a white woman with long blond hair didn't ask such things, didn't even suggest them. Not unless she wanted to be labeled a raging racist, that is. She'd just have to wait and see what Jimmy did next.

James darted through a steady downpour, now cursing that he'd worn his good shoes, as Bridgit's words rang in his ears. He pulled out his keys just as two figures wearing black clothes and ski masks appeared from behind a nearby tree. One grabbed his arm and slammed him against the tree; the other jabbed what felt like a gun into his back. Then the first mugger retrieved his dropped keys and unlocked his car while the other patted his pockets until finding, and removing, his wallet.

Gasping at the taste of blood in his mouth, James tried to focus, startled by the sound of his car starting. Ordered not to move by a low, feminine voice, he grappled with the possibility the person threatening him was a woman. He pressed his eyes closed as she extracted the gun from his back, the sound of her footsteps and the slam of his car door echoing in his aching head as they drove away.

He turned in time to see his car disappear around a corner. James stood a minute, the rain driving at him, until he realized he could do nothing but return to Bridgit's apartment.

She swore when she saw him. "For God's sake, Jimmy. What'd you do, run into a truck?"

"A tree, actually." He went to her bathroom, where he studied his face in the mirror, relieved to find he was bleeding only from a few minor scratches. His head throbbed as he dried himself with a towel.

Bridgit pressed close to him, reaching up to the medicine cabinet for some first aid cream. "You ran into a tree?"

He shook his head, explaining what had happened, leaving out his suspicion he'd been held up by a woman.

"Shouldn't you call the police?"

He closed his eyes as she dabbed cream on his scratches. "After I call a cab. I just want to get home and go to bed."

Bridgit placed a consoling hand on his arm. "I feel like shit," she said.

"You do." His attempt at laughter made his head throb more.

She laughed with him. "That I gave you such a hard

time, before." She opened a box of Band-Aids. "Sometimes I wish I could keep my stinking mouth shut, you know?"

James let her take care of the cuts, watching her face as she tended him, discerning the scent of her hair above the smell of the plastic bandages. He enjoyed being so close to her, if only for a few moments.

She pulled away to inspect her work. "I'm no nurse, but that should do," she said, replacing the supplies. "Need some aspirin?"

He nodded. "Whatever you've got."

"C'mon in the kitchen."

He took the pills at the kitchen table. "I better call that cab," he said. "I'll have to borrow a few dollars, though."

She gave him the phone and left the room. He dialed information and she returned with her purse, a bunch of bills in her outstretched hand.

He smiled carefully as he made the call. "I said a few dollars, Bridgit. For the cab ride, that's all."

She caressed his arm. "I feel terrible about this, Jimmy. But at the same time, I wonder if it's fate, you know?" She caressed his hand now. "I hated seeing you leave, earlier, and really liked taking care of you, just now. I guess I . . . I miss it. I miss *you.*"

He squinted at her, uncertain exactly what she had just admitted, or suggested, trying to memorize the number the operator was providing while Bridgit's eyes danced in front of him. His stomach sounded as he realized he hadn't eaten dinner and tried to remember if he'd had lunch. While dialing the number he thought might get him a cab company, he wondered at the flashes of light he was seeing, then at the sudden darkness—and Bridgit's odd screech—as his head dropped to the tabletop.

Chapter Seventeen

Earlier that afternoon, Audrey had swung her sister's old Buick onto the gray highway. Since the car shook at high speeds, she was forced to keep a steady sixty-mile-an-hour pace.

She raced along, struggling with myriad emotions: anxiety regarding her mother, smug pleasure regarding her sudden progress with James, worry edged with fear regarding her nephew and his father.

Confident Pritch and Julian would get along without her, despite her arguments against the arrangement, Audrey worried they might get along so well they'd resent her return. She imagined them living together, a father-and-son team joking over breakfast, saying good-bye as Julian left for the bus stop and Pritch drove off to work, getting home late for dinner and talks about sports, homework, weekend plans. Certain she wouldn't fit into such a picture, she puzzled over her emerging fears—and hopes—that Julian might choose Pritch over her.

She cringed at the thought of Pritch discussing her family with Julian, worried he may have already influenced the boy to think ill of his grandfather. Audrey shook her head, amazed she'd defended her father so fiercely after so many years of fighting with him. Still, she couldn't imagine that he'd ever intentionally hurt Laura by sending her fiancé packing. "He was a good man," she said aloud. "A good man who had a hard time relating to certain people while others found him fascinating. That should sound familiar, Pritch."

Audrey sped through the city limits out of Buffalo, passed last-chance signs for Niagara Falls, and headed down I-90 toward Pennsylvania, parallel to the eastern shore of Lake Erie. The monstrous lake remained hidden by dense trees, but Audrey knew it was there. She'd written a report on the area in high school, and remembered snippets of information from her research. Her father had mentioned that this strip of I-90 follows a section of the Underground Railroad, the road to freedom for countless slaves.

Thoughts of the Underground Railroad made Audrey think of her dream fugitive. Hadn't thousands of fugitives trudged through rivers and streams, as that woman did, to hide their scent from bounty hunters' dogs? Hadn't they run all through the North, to keep from capture and return to furious, vengeful owners, until they finally reached freedom in Canada? Audrey tried to recall more details from her father's brief explanation of the Railroad, but remembered most clearly how he abruptly stopped talking, brushing away her eager questions.

The odometer clocked the miles as the hours continued to pass. Audrey tried to imagine traveling the same route on foot, undercover and possibly with children, ill-equipped and starving, driven by blinding fear.

She shivered as she drove farther south, wondering how she'd find Nashville. She had no childhood memories of the city, only of her father's family in their big farmhouses far from town. Audrey had her suspicions, however, that Nashville was a backward town, a town so ingrained in the ideals of the Old South that she—and others like her—would never stand a chance of really fitting in there.

She entered Pennsylvania. "One state down, three to go," she muttered, already tired of driving. The sky had grown more overcast, and the dim sun now threatened to dip behind trees early, as though anxious for the day to end. Audrey jabbed at the climate controls, hoping the heater hadn't died yet.

The Buick's radio had been broken for years, so she listened instead to a concert of rattling sounds from the car's various loose knobs and levers. She had teased her sister about the Buick many times, but Laura insisted she couldn't sell the car that had gotten her through nursing school, just as she couldn't live anywhere but in her hometown. The sentimental ties were too strong for her to break. Audrey also suspected Laura couldn't afford a new car. The only time her sister had splurged, she believed, was when she bought the house, and even then she'd found a bargain in an old place no one else wanted.

She reviewed the path she'd follow, through Columbus and Cincinnati, past Louisville and finally into Tennessee. Her father was once offered a teaching job in Cincinnati. Audrey remembered how excited she and Laura had been about the prospect of moving so far away—as though Ohio were an exotic land. Her parents hadn't been so receptive to the idea, though. She recalled a conversation she'd heard between her father and a colleague of his, another black man and a Southerner, who came to the house occasionally for dinner. Only with this particular friend did Audrey ever hear her father discuss his life down South, his Tennessee accent suddenly thick and rolling, like a secret part of himself he kept hidden until a fellow Southerner coaxed it free.

That night, he'd explained his decision not to move his family to Cincinnati. "It's a divided town," he'd said. "One foot in the North, the other in the South. A confused place—neither black nor white, and uneasy in between."

Audrey had eavesdropped from the living room, pretending to read, her eyes wide, her hopes fading. She wondered if her father ever found his mixed daughters as confusing.

"I moved north to escape all that," he continued, scraping the legs of a chair along the kitchen floor. "My girls don't belong in the South, memorizing Civil War battlefields in school, drilled to bow to every authority figure they come across, with yes-ma'ams and no-sirs, calling their teachers Miss this and Miss that, like slaves who know their proper place."

Audrey heard him spit the last words out with disdain as she slipped upstairs to her room, still harboring hopes her father might change his mind.

She smiled as she drove along. Western New York had always been a place she wanted to escape, especially as she grew older and more aware of its idiosyncrasies: the depressing cloud cover that hovered for months while warm lake air competed with the ground's wintry temperatures; the storms that dumped mounds of snow in their yard in the middle of spring, bruising early daffodils, burying brave crocuses.

It occurred to Audrey an early snow could fall in Rochester before her return trip. She wondered how she'd feel if a blizzard or other problem kept her from driving back. Her stomach tightened, the thought of being kept from Julian for any reason troubling her. Her thoughts shifted to her ill mother—and the possibility of losing her, too—as she headed toward Ohio.

Near Louisville, Kentucky, Audrey stopped for the night

at a motel. She got out of the car exhausted, consoled by the warm night air that differed so much from the damp, chilly weather she'd left that afternoon.

She slept fitfully, dreaming of snowstorms and runaways. The next morning, still tired and stiff from the long drive, she decided to make two phone calls—one to Pritch and Julian and the other to her aunt for directions once she arrived in town.

She called her aunt first, anxious to find her home. Audrey had made previous calls at various stops, all picked up by an answering machine, with a male voice identifying the reached residence as "Miss Letty Mason's." She reached the machine yet again, so Audrey left a message stating she'd arrive in Nashville in a few hours and would call at that time for directions. Then she dialed her own number, wondering if she was still in the Eastern time zone.

Pritch answered with a clipped hello. Audrey asked if Julian was still home.

"He's off to school," he replied. "Isn't he usually, by eight?"

Audrey paced impatiently. "I wasn't sure of the time there. Never mind. I'll call back later."

"Where are you?"

"Kentucky. I should be in Nashville this morning."

Pritch chuckled. "You're a speed demon, Miss Audrey. I'd no idea." He paused. "James called yesterday."

"Oh?"

"He's concerned about you, of course, after the way you sped off. Said he'd like your aunt's phone number."

"Did you give it to him?"

"I didn't think it was appropriate, really. I assured him you'll call when you're able."

Audrey frowned. "How's Julian?"

"Stop fretting over Julian, now. He's fine. We're fine. We've already got plans to take in a film after his exams Thursday."

Her frown deepened. "Great. Just—don't keep him out too late."

"You can count on me, Miss Audrey," he said. "Count on me."

"Humph." Audrey hung up and grabbed her bags, anxious to get going. Dazzled by the Kentucky sun as she crossed the parking lot, she was startled to see trees with so many leaves, still. "It probably never snows here in October, either," she mused.

The lush, rolling hills of the landscape soothed Audrey as she drove. She swung south of Louisville, past horse farms and acres of open pasture, imagining what it would be like to live here, so far from a teeming city or suburban sprawl. Audrey had always been convinced her hometown was the worst place for her, not because she'd suffered traumatic events or been the subject of ridicule there. She simply failed to feel certain about herself there, and had found her footing and direction only after moving away. Now, though, she knew moving away would mean moving Julian, too.

She wondered how difficult it would be to move far from James. She tried to take comfort in the fact that he'd called Pritch and was concerned about her; that he felt compelled to check up on her. She had to admit, though, in the privacy of her sister's rattling car, that she found such attention a bit suffocating.

"Enjoy this," she said to herself, following a curve.

Wooded hills stretched into the distance. Audrey drove past a billboard plastered with the sunny face of Colonel Sanders, a sign directing travelers to the birthplace of Abraham Lincoln, and another noting that she'd crossed into the Central time zone.

The echo of a song she'd heard on the drive home from the wedding with James rang in her head, and she realized the irony of humming Paul Simon's "Graceland" as she drove toward the Tennessee border. James had played the tape in his car, and now she wished she had it—and a working tape deck. He'd been eager to please her, then and throughout the weekend. She decided with a smile that he'd certainly succeeded Saturday night in bed—and again Sunday morning.

Her smile faded as she remembered Pritch had considered it "inappropriate" to help James reach her. "Jerk," she muttered, accelerating to pass two cars. The Buick shuddered, forcing her to slow down as soon as she pulled back into the right lane. The car behind her then sped by her, its horn blaring.

Audrey frowned, suspecting Southern drivers rarely tolerate errors from drivers with Northern plates. She refused, however, to take her eyes from the road when other drivers passed her, especially in the South. Racial divisions were too easily measured, she reasoned, and short tempers too easily triggered for her to do anything to call attention to herself here. She thought back to the department store scene, when she'd cringed as James bellowed about how poorly she and Julian were being treated. She'd realized then how naive he was about the reality of race relations, even in a Northern town.

The police siren startled Audrey from her reverie as she neared the state border. Assuming the cruiser would pass her, she slowed and edged toward the side of the road to give it room. When it flashed its lights and closed in behind her instead, she groaned and pulled over to stop on the dusty shoulder. A green highway sign a few hundred yards ahead read "Nashville, 30 Miles."

She cursed under her breath while the officer sat in the cruiser, checking her plates, she assumed. She pulled her license from her wallet and glanced at the registration sticker on the windshield, relieved to find it up-to-date.

Finally, the trooper left his car, his tall frame unfolding as he stood, his tan face lined and stern as he approached. Audrey had hoped for a young black female, though she doubted such officers were common in this part of the country.

She lowered the window, trying to decide which "face" to put on—the smiling, amicable face she wore at work to keep her coworkers at ease, or the concerned-citizen face she wore when things went wrong and she didn't want to accuse anyone with her frown, which she knew could be formidable. She chose the concerned-citizen face just as the policeman's waistline, adorned with his holster and weapon, filled her side-view mirror.

He stared at her through reflective sunglasses. "Ma'am?" he drawled, as though expecting her to question him.

Audrey handed him her license before being asked for it. "Is something wrong, officer?"

He peered from her to her picture license, then tapped his pen on his closed notebook, which he held at her eye level. Audrey glanced at the notebook cover, the sight of the Ku Klux Klan sticker on it making her want to laugh and vomit at the same time. She swallowed, her hatred for the cop and all he represented burning a hole in her gut.

"Do you know how fast y'all were going there, ma'am?" he asked, flipping his notebook open.

His words took a moment to register as the situation grew more and more surreal to her. She shook her head. "No—sir," she mumbled. Her tongue had grown heavy and numb, keeping her from explaining the car couldn't go above sixty without practically falling apart.

"Sixty-five in a fifty-five zone, ma'am," he announced, clucking his tongue.

She bit hers. "I didn't realize," she replied, as icily as she could.

He wrote her a ticket and handed it to her with her license, flipping his notebook closed again and tilting it toward her. "Best be more careful when traveling so far from home, ma'am," he added with a wry smile.

She nodded, refusing to thank him, exhaling as he retreated. She waited for his car to pull out and away before allowing herself to move, then glanced at the ticket—$100 fine. She threw it to the floor, then twisted the keys in the ignition and gunned the accelerator. When the Buick sputtered and quit, she tried to start it again, this time tenderly stepping on the pedal, praying the car would jolt back to life.

Five minutes passed with more failed attempts before Audrey decided she must have flooded the engine. She rubbed her eyes, then her forehead, cursing the state trooper, her sister's damn car, her sick mother, everyone in the state of Kentucky, and finally, herself.

Resigned to the fact that she needed help, she gathered her purse and jacket, locking the car as she stepped out. She stretched, relieved she wasn't far from the next exit. She could see a mom-and-pop gas station and headed for it, praying they owned a tow truck.

It was nearly noon by the time she got to the service station. She walked in, bombarded by smells of oil and gasoline, and forced a feeble smile at the older man behind the desk.

He grinned back. "Need help?"

Audrey let her smile broaden. "How'd you guess?"

The man, introduced as Joel Senior, turned out to be a knight in greasy work clothes as he had little to do and a well-oiled tow truck behind his shop. He drove Audrey to pick up the Buick and towed it back to his son, Joel Junior, who solemnly examined it. Joel Junior's diagnosis, however, was far from encouraging. "She needs a major overhaul, ma'am," he stated, his twangy voice soft around the edges, his concern for the ailing vehicle evident.

Audrey cringed. She'd already wasted another hour, and knew she couldn't afford whatever a "major overhaul" would involve.

Joel Junior discussed the Buick's various mechanical problems while Audrey listened and nodded, trying to act as though she understood what the hell he was talking about.

"How much," she sputtered, "how much would all this cost?"

The Joels glanced at each other, as though calculating figures in their heads and trying to see if they concurred. Audrey held her breath.

Finally, Joel Senior spoke. "Probably too much to make it worth fixin', ma'am, tell the truth," he said, his voice earnest. "I can get a buddy to pick it up for scrap, help you make a little money on it instead, if you like."

Audrey groaned and sat in a dingy chair near a rack of outdated, dog-eared magazines. She rubbed her temple, then glanced up at the two men. They waited patiently, as though understanding how difficult it is to send a beloved vehicle to the big scrap yard in the sky.

With a sigh, she stood again and asked to use the phone.

Audrey spent the next hour emptying the Buick, leafing through old copies of *People* magazine, and waiting. She'd finally reached a cousin at her aunt's home when she called, and from him learned her great-aunt had spent much of the past two days at the hospital, and her mother was improving steadily from her minor stroke. She also learned her mother had suffered no paralysis and would be released from the hospital in a matter of days if her improvement continued on track.

Assured her aunt would be at the station to pick her up soon, Audrey had collapsed into the chair near the door. Guilt over the loss of her sister's car threatened to overwhelm her, as did the empty sense she was losing touch with everything Laura had cherished—the old house, the old car, even Julian—at an alarming rate.

Audrey fought the sinking sense of loss that knotted her stomach, knowing it would quickly shift into uncontrollable weeping if she didn't keep it in check. She tried to focus on Julian. For eight months, she had concentrated all her energy on providing for her sister's son, on preserving the life he'd always known, the life his mother had given him. And in eight months, that life had continued to unravel beyond her control. Charged with the responsibility to protect and nurture her nephew at such a critical time, Audrey felt certain of only one thing—that she was failing him, and her sister, on all fronts.

A silver Oldsmobile pulled into the parking lot. Audrey had been told her Aunt Letty would arrive in a silver sedan driven by another young cousin. She went outside, smoothing her worn sweatshirt and faded jeans, wishing she looked more presentable, especially when she saw her great-aunt get out of her car.

Though in her eighties, Aunt Letty appeared steady and self-assured in her towering frame as she walked across the parking lot. She reached toward Audrey with open arms, her floral perfume caressing her grandniece almost as perceptibly as her embrace. "My, my," she breathed into Audrey's ear, smoothing her back as they hugged. "You've been through so much, sugar. My, my, my."

Audrey let the woman rock her in the middle of the dusty parking lot, in the heat of the warm October afternoon, her eyes and throat pressed closed against the tears and sobs that threatened to rack her body as soon as she let go. She drank in her aunt's soothing words, feeling, hearing, even seeing behind her closed eyelids the essence of her Southern-bred father in their sweet, rolling echoes.

Chapter Eighteen

Audrey watched wearily from the back seat of her aunt's car as they crossed the state border into Tennessee. Her cousin, introduced as her aunt's grandson Nathan, drove. Letty spoke of Audrey's mother.

"We'll stop to see Yvonne first," she announced.

Audrey had hoped to have a few minutes at her aunt's house to recuperate from the drive, to put on some makeup and change clothes. She leaned into the plush velour of the car's seat and tried to relax. She imagined her mother in a hospital bed and could only see her poised and commanding, her brown hair perfectly styled, her bracelets rattling as she spoke. Yvonne was not the type to wear a drafty hospital gown and eat bland food without complaint. Audrey expected to find her restless and anxious, eager to escape.

Letty chuckled. "Yvonne's had the nurses hopping like horny toads," she said, shifting in her seat to smile at her grand-niece.

Audrey smiled back weakly, her stomach churning with anxiety over the prospect of seeing her mother within the half-hour. She began to suspect she'd been foolish to race to Tennessee before learning if she truly was needed. She gritted her teeth, suddenly certain Yvonne would be more annoyed than relieved to see her.

The skyline of Nashville surprised Audrey as they approached down I-65, through the backside of the city with its warehouses and barges lining the wide Cumberland River. The cityscape was much more modern than Audrey had expected, with its fair share of shiny skyscrapers. Aunt Letty pointed out the newest building, a blue-black reflective monster with two antenna-like attachments in either top corner.

"They call that the Batman building," she quipped. "We'll take you the scenic route to the hospital, past some of the governmental sights. Farther down is where they're erecting the new stadium, where every football fan in town hopes some Texas team will come to roost. This city has changed so, with folks from the East Coast and California eatin' it up with their Crazy Horse Saloons and Hip Hop Cafes."

Nate, silent through most of the trip, shook his head at this comment. "You mean the Wild Horse Saloon and the Hard Rock Cafe, Grandma."

"Whatever," Letty snorted. "I just bet Audrey here won't even recognize the old neighborhood."

All Audrey could remember of "the old neighborhood" was her late grandmother's house, where Aunt Letty now resided as the family matriarch. The youngest of her generation, Letty was the last survivor of her siblings and cousins, and Audrey suspected she now had the final word on all family matters, big and small.

They crossed a bridge over the Cumberland. Audrey spotted a few small riverboats tethered to a dock as Letty described some of the sights she'd hoped to bring Yvonne to see during her week stay.

"Your father never had any patience for sightseeing," Letty explained, "so Yvonne's never really seen anything Nashville has to offer." She turned again with a wide grin. "Not that I'd take her to the wax museum, of course."

The hospital soon loomed ahead, a huge gray facility with a prominent cross on its side. Audrey considered eating some of the packed food her aunt had brought for her, but decided against it, at least until the visit was over.

Inside the hospital, Audrey noted the nurses' sweet accents and kind greetings as Letty led her and Nathan to Yvonne's room. Yvonne sat in bed, looking anything but regal. For a moment, Audrey didn't recognize her. With her hair clean but flattened to her head, her face bare of makeup, and her small frame sunken into the bed, Yvonne appeared frail, vulnerable, and far from well.

Audrey felt compelled to hug her, but hesitated. She sat beside the bed instead, silent while Letty explained how she'd gone to Kentucky to pick her up after the Buick had expired. Audrey watched her mother's face, wondering what Yvonne thought while her aunt—satin black and boisterous—described

159

how her daughter had come to be delivered to her in this strange city.

"What a story," Yvonne said, her voice startling Audrey with its clarity, despite her frail appearance. "I told you in February that car wasn't going to last another year."

Audrey cringed at the reference to February, when she'd last seen her mother during the weeks after Laura's death. Letty and Nathan excused themselves, telling Audrey she could find them in the waiting room down the hall when she was done. Yvonne straightened, pushing herself up with both hands. Audrey attempted to adjust the pillows behind her, but managed only to tug at one halfheartedly.

"So this is what it takes to get you to come see me," Yvonne said, eyeing her daughter.

Audrey gave a feeble shrug. "Florida's a long way from Rochester, Mom."

Yvonne smiled. "So is Nashville, dear. What in the world did Letty tell you, that I was on my deathbed down here? God forbid I die in Tennessee, of course."

"I got a message you were in the hospital. I had no idea how sick you were, that's why I left so fast."

"Before making a few phone calls?" Yvonne sighed heavily. "You always were the impulsive one."

Audrey avoided eye contact. "Who'd you have to bribe to get a private room?" she teased. She knew her mother would never tolerate sharing a room with another patient, especially if it meant having to listen to daytime television, which she'd always despised.

Yvonne waved a weary hand. "They just put me in here. Where is Julian staying, while you're gone? You didn't leave him alone, did you?"

Audrey blinked, realizing she was not prepared to tell her about Pritch's return. "No," she said, "he's not alone. He's with—an adult."

Yvonne straightened further. "Who? Who's he with?"

Audrey stood, not because she meant to, but because her nerves had sprung her legs into motion. "Pritch has been back in town, for a little while now—"

"Harrison Pritchard! Audrey Elizabeth, don't even tell me you're trusting your nephew to stay with Harrison Pritchard. For goodness' sake—"

Audrey raised her hands toward the ceiling as she paced

the room. "Fine. Fine, Mom, I won't tell you."

Yvonne pressed her forehead and smoothed back her hair, her hand shaking slightly. "Where in the world did he come from?" she asked, her voice so low she appeared to talk more to herself than to her daughter. "Certainly he doesn't expect custody, after all these years?"

Audrey sat back down. "Mom, please, calm down. All I need is for you to have another stroke."

"All *you* need—"

Audrey frowned at Yvonne, who peered back at her with an expression Audrey hadn't seen in years. She knew it all too well, though—a dark, doubting look that made it clear her mother was being patient as a saint while being tried as no martyr ever had.

Audrey explained how Pritch had arrived on their doorstep, and how far Julian had come already in accepting his father. She stated her belief they needed time to get to know each other if they were going to establish any kind of lasting relationship.

Yvonne scoffed, clearly unconvinced. "So now you're a family psychologist."

Audrey resumed her pacing, exasperated. "He's a good person," she said, wondering at her statement after being so angry with Pritch that morning. "He's also very eager—about Julian."

"Who wouldn't be?" Yvonne asked, her voice rising. "Julian's a wonderful boy. Anyone in his right mind would be thrilled to raise him."

Shocked by the force of her mother's glare, Audrey chose not to acknowledge the accusation hidden in her heated words.

"I just don't understand," Yvonne continued, "how you could leave him there alone."

Audrey dropped her hands to her side, resigning herself to being misjudged, once again. "He's not alone, Mom," she said. "He's with someone who cares about him."

Like it or not, she wanted to add, he's with family.

Audrey found her great-aunt had been correct: She hardly recognized the neighborhood her father's family lived in south of Nashville. Suburban developments had cropped up in every open field in the town of Brentwood. The clan's main house, a rambling farmhouse along what used to be a quiet dirt road, remained much the same. But the sound of the traffic that came into its open windows and the crowded view of houses and a nearby mall gave the old homestead an entirely different atmosphere from the rural, secluded one she vaguely remembered.

What was familiar was the hustle and bustle of the house, inhabited not only by Letty but by her youngest nephew, his wife, and their two teenage sons. Other relatives who lived in smaller homes on the family's land arrived and departed in steady succession throughout the early evening.

Everyone had something to eat at Letty's—while seated at a table, propped against a counter, or moving from conversation to conversation in the full kitchen. The smoky-sweet smell of barbecue filled the house, greeting visitors as they approached the back door, tempting them as they entered the kitchen, guiding them, finally, to the wide dining room table, where a weekend feast had been spread. Audrey recalled such dinners from her childhood visits, and remembered the first time a cousin had told her and Laura they'd be having barbecue that night.

"I love barbecue chicken," Audrey had replied, surprised by the cousin's laughter.

"Not barbecue chicken," he'd explained. *"Barbecue."*

Audrey and Laura had shrugged, discovering later they were having strips of pork in tangy sauce for dinner, as well as homemade slaw, salads, beans, and cornbread, with pies and cobblers for dessert.

Now drowsy from her long trip, Audrey opted to skip dessert tonight, and was relieved when the crowd began to thin. Everyone had been friendly and polite, inquiring about Yvonne and Julian, reminding her how sorry they'd been to hear about Laura. Many had attended her father's funeral in Florida, and those who'd grown up with him insisted Dr. Benjamin Conarroe had been the finest man to ever live.

Grateful but eventually exhausted by such conversations, Audrey slipped away from the kitchen and wandered into the parlor, where she rubbed her palm along the smooth, dark banister that led upstairs to various bedrooms. Everything in the home was dark, and cool, and comforting, from the hardwood floors and the rugs that muffled them, to the cushioned settee in the parlor and the thick banister. Audrey tried to imagine her father as a boy, racing through these rooms, banging in the back door and upstairs to retrieve some treasure. But she could see, most clearly, Laura lounging on the settee, Laura with her brown face pressed against a screen window to smell the summer rain, Laura skipping out that same back door to join their cousins as they chased fireflies in the dusk. Audrey could see, because she'd been the one watching, always watching, while Laura led the way.

Soon after dinner, Audrey retreated to the guest room in the back of the main floor. She unpacked, setting small things on the mahogany dresser.

In the morning, she rolled over as her aunt clamored in the kitchen. She peered at the alarm clock on the nightstand, realizing with a moan it was barely after six. A few moments later, unable to fall back asleep, she thought of the papers Pritch had given her and reached for them, pulling off a snug rubber band that broke as she tugged at it. Browned, curled papers spilled across the bed. She leafed through them, noting a few dates in formal script at the corners of some pages, and realized they'd come from a personal diary written in the mid-1800s. She wondered if the diary belonged to the original owner of her sister's house.

Audrey arranged the pages according to the dates, glimpsing notes as she did. Then she read from the beginning, improvising in sections that had been worn or torn through the years.

The first entry was dated 1849. The diary primarily covered household maintenance and repairs, with occasional notes detailing the weather, the progress of seasonal harvests, the health of various farm animals. Eventually, though, in entries dated in the 1850s, Audrey read more personal notes about sons who'd been born, and about the family's efforts to tame some of the wilder areas of their land, referred to as "the high pasture" and "the back woods."

Some entries were short, and long gaps of time passed between quite a few. One entry in early 1853 discussed a child "born still," a daughter whose casket was built with the wood of an oak tree off the property, and who was mourned in a wake held in the "great room." Audrey guessed this referred to what they now called the living room in her sister's house, the wide room that led off to the right from the front hall.

She read on for an hour, skimming many pages that discussed particulars of the land or farm. In longer entries dated from 1854 on, however, she began to see references to "chattels," "dry goods," and "U.G.R.R." Puzzled, she took a break from reading to join her aunt for breakfast.

Letty glanced up from her morning paper as Audrey entered the kitchen.

"Come, child." She gestured toward a chair next to her. "Everyone else is out the door already. You slept so late, you must be starved."

Letty filled a coffee cup from a pot on the counter. She placed it in front of Audrey with a sugar bowl and a small creamer. "Eggs this morning?" she asked, still moving through her kitchen.

Audrey spooned sugar into her coffee. "Cereal or toast is fine, Aunt Letty. Whatever's easiest."

"Easiest, schmeasiest," Letty scoffed. "I still hold by the old notion a stomach needs something hot in it to start the day. I'll have eggs ready in no time. Here," she slid the front page toward her niece. "Peruse *The Tennessean* while I whip somethin' up for you, now."

Audrey glanced at the paper, noticing the morning's forecast. "It's still so warm, for October," she said. "Does summer ever end here?"

Letty chuckled as she gathered eggs from the refrigerator. "Lordy, no," she quipped. "Tennessee summers last forever, long as New York winters, I reckon." Back at the stove, she lifted and tipped her black iron skillet, coating it with melted butter. "Going to see your mother this morning, or later?"

Audrey frowned. "I hadn't even thought that far yet, tell the truth."

Letty laughed. "Do tell, dear. Do tell!"

Audrey grinned at her aunt's mirth and watched as Letty cracked two eggs at a time on the skillet's edge. They hit the hot pan and sizzled, a sound Audrey found both energizing and relaxing. Her stomach grumbled at the promise of indulging in a hearty breakfast.

A few moments later, she dove into a meal of scrambled eggs, toast and jam, orange juice, and homemade applesauce. The more she ate, the more food Letty placed in front of her. Her aunt moved from one part of the kitchen to another, telling tales about relatives Audrey didn't even know she had, making Audrey feel as though her presence there were as common as the sunlight streaming through the window.

Letty finally sat. "Speaking of New York," she said,

"your cousin Barbara Ann is studying up there, in Manhattan, getting some business degree or another."

"Her MBA?" Audrey suggested.

"That's it," Letty nodded, "her MBA. She's smart as a whip, that one. Just like Rose was."

Audrey glanced up, intrigued by a reference to her own grandmother, Letty's older sister.

"Did Grandma Rose go to college?"

Letty let loose a whoop of laughter. "College?" she nearly screeched. "No, honey, there was no such thing as college for colored girls 'round here back then. Huh. We're lucky we got schooling at all."

Audrey felt her cheeks flush. "I forgot," she mumbled, "how different things were then."

"Like night and day, sugar," Letty declared. "Like night and day. Did you know I was born premature? And there was no such thing as an incubator back then, no sir. Mama put me in the oven to keep me warm. God's truth, she did."

Audrey raised an eyebrow at her aunt.

"Your grandmother, though, she didn't need schooling anyways," Letty continued. "Smart as a whip she was, and a beauty to boot. What she wanted most of all was to become another Josephine Baker. You know, that famous dancer who went to Paris and caused all the ruckus? Oh, she was big, larger than life, and a poor girl from the South, no less. Yessir, Rosie knew she could be another Josephine, if she could get a break. Then Daddy found all the clippings she'd saved about Josephine and threw them into the fire. Oh, how Rosie howled. She had a temper all right, but Daddy was fit to be tied a daughter of his was reading about a dancer like that. Rosie still had her sights set, though, to run away to Paris some day. Of course, then she turned eighteen and fell in love with your grandfather, and that was the end of that. You're named after her, by the way."

Audrey stared at her aunt.

"Yes, yes. Her full name was Audrey Rose, but we all called her Rosie. You never knew that? Lordy, your daddy never told you that? Shame, shame, Benji."

Audrey was shocked to laughter to hear her father called such a boyish name. He'd always been Benjamin, Ben, Dr. or Professor Conarroe, but never had she heard anyone refer to him as Benji, not even her mother.

Letty shook her head as she cleared Audrey's dishes

from the table. "He always was the stubborn one." She glanced out the kitchen window. "Oh, fine. Here's George."

Audrey heard footsteps outside and expected another cousin to enter from the back porch. When the door opened, though, she was surprised to see a white girl walk into her aunt's kitchen. The girl flashed an easy, broad grin, inviting Audrey to assess her cropped dark hair and wide blue eyes, as well as her muddy jeans and sneakers.

Letty introduced her as George, a local college student who helped with the few horses the family kept in a back stable.

"George here's a history buff," Letty boasted, "and a specialist on local history. I asked her to stop by to meet you, so she can show you around while you're in town, if you plan to stay a bit."

"That depends on how Mom does over the next day or two," Audrey said. "I also have to figure out how to get back home."

George spoke up. "Midterms were last week, so I can slack off a little the next couple days." She flashed another smile. "Let Miss Letty know when you'd like to go sightseeing, and she'll give me a holler."

Audrey peered at the girl, intrigued by the way her Long Island accent mixed with her easy, Southern words. "Actually," she finally said, "I could use your help another way, if you're into history. I've got some papers from an original owner, I think, of my sister's old house in New York. I'm trying to figure out what they're all about."

"When were they written?" George sat at the table.

"Mid-1800s."

"And they're confusing?"

"Wait." Audrey stood. "I'll get them. I just started a section where they use the abbreviation U.G.R.R., and—"

George's face lit up. "Underground Railroad. That's what U.G.R.R. stands for. Maybe your sister's house—"

Audrey stared at the girl, shocked at the suggestion, and how much sense her disturbing dreams suddenly made. Before hearing the words, she knew without a doubt Laura's house had been a stop on the Underground Railroad, and her dream fugitive had sought refuge there.

Chapter Nineteen

Audrey returned with the papers, enjoying the breathless sense of her excitement. She grinned at Letty and George, who sat at the kitchen table, then spread the papers across the specked tabletop.

She pulled out an early reference to the "U.G.R.R." and read aloud: "Warren learned we were to receive the U.G.R.R. chattels and dry goods tomorrow evening. The quilt is hung. Still, we shall hardly sleep for fear of missing the signal."

George, stretching to read with her, nodded eagerly. "That's what they called the runaway slaves," she said. "Chattels were men, dry goods women. They used other terms, too. I wonder what their signal was, a few knocks and a password, I bet. The quilt was probably left on the clothesline outside, or over a fence. Ever seen a log cabin square?"

Letty spoke up. "It's a simple block pattern, with a small square in the middle."

George wagged a finger. "Right, and the color of the center square was usually red, a symbol of the fireplace, the hearth, at the heart of the cabin. But some Railroad agents hung log cabin quilts with dark or yellow centers in each square, signaling their stop was safe, that no bounty hunters were on the premises. If the quilt wasn't seen during the day, the fugitives knew it wasn't safe to approach the house that night. They might hide in the woods, or their Railroad conductor might guide them to another, safer, place."

Audrey shivered while she and George leafed through more pages. "I can't believe this was going on in my sister's house," she said. "It's kind of eerie."

"Here's a good one." George pulled out another page. "From the next month, in June." She also read aloud: "Not a week passes without new visitors from this mysterious road. We are prepared at all times, but hardly find the extra preparations burdensome. Our friends' relief is palpable as soon as they escape the night air."

Audrey's great-aunt sat with arms crossed over her chest, her dark eyes now somber. "Plenty folks helped on the Railroad," Letty said, "freed blacks, Quakers, Masons, all sorts—but don't forget there never would've been a Railroad if those slaves hadn't dug deep for the courage to escape in the first place, knowing they'd be set upon something fierce if they were caught."

She paused, and when she spoke again her voice was slow, as though the words hurt. "I still know colored folks who have a hard time looking a white person in the eye," she said, "and not long ago at all white folks on the streets of Nashville expected coloreds to make way for 'em, even if it meant a cripple had to step clear off the sidewalk into the gutter." She nodded for a silent moment. "Thank the Lord times change, though I'll never understand why any of this hell," she gestured toward the scattered papers, "ever had to pass in the first place."

The papers revealed no diary entries during that winter, with the next entry written in the spring. "It's mostly about the crops and the animals and what survived the winter," Audrey said, scanning it. She stopped at a reference to one of the children in the house, Joshua. "Listen to this," she said.

"Joshua bid me sworn to secrecy before telling what he'd witnessed. Woken from slumber by sounds from the cellar, he pushed my rocking chair from above the trap door and—with much trouble, I am certain—lifted the door to investigate. When he peered down the stone steps into the darkness, he was shocked to find three pairs of eyes staring back at him. The boom of the slamming door woke us all frightfully, but the source was soon discovered and Joshua returned to bed with his brother. He swore never to investigate any sounds arising from the cellar, and I do not expect to find him near the trap door ever again."

George grinned. "Where's the trap door?"

Audrey shook her head. "It must be covered by something. I bet Julian, my nephew, knows where it is, though. He knows every cranny of that house." She glanced at the kitchen clock. "I could read these all day," she said, "but I'd better get in the shower and go see Mom." She gathered the papers. "I'm so excited about this I forgot I don't have a car. Is there one I can borrow, Aunt Letty?"

Letty waved her hand. "What's mine's yours, darlin'," she said, rising from the table. She gestured toward George. "But if you'd rather not drive around a strange town, your tour guide here could chauffeur you."

George surprised Audrey again with the ease with which she addressed her, as though they'd been friends for years.

"Happy to," she said. "Let Billy muck the stables this morning."

On the way to the hospital, George explained that Billy, her fiancé, had been working for Audrey's aunt since he was a teenager. "He's practically part of your family," she said. "Spends all his spare time out there with those horses. Letty adores him." She paused. "He's black, you know."

Audrey raised an eyebrow at her, curious she felt compelled to add that fact. She was about to say George seemed young to be engaged, but thought better of it.

"He's older," George continued. "He goes to Vanderbilt, too, to the medical school. I'll drive you around the campus later, if you like."

Audrey nodded. "Have you set a date yet?"

The girl beamed, but shook her head. "We just got engaged," she explained, "and my family's still . . . getting used to the idea."

"Hm. They're not thrilled, huh?"

George laughed. *"Far* from thrilled. He's older, he's black. I tell my mother she should be happy I'm marrying a doctor, but I just get this *look."*

Audrey nodded. "I know the one," she said, glancing out the car window.

George talked on about Billy and their plans while Audrey studied homes they passed. She marveled at some of the larger brick houses, admiring the manicured lawns and flower beds.

They reached the main avenue into town.

"My grandfather has the biggest hang-up over all this," George continued. She slipped into a guttural Yiddish accent. "Vhat do you mean, she's not marrying a Jewish boy? No Jewish boys in that whole university? Not one?"

Audrey burst out laughing.

"He's caused me trouble from the very start," George

added. "I'm named after his father. Not Georgina or Georgette, just George."

Audrey glanced at her, incredulous.

"Really," the girl continued. "The ultrasound tech said I was a boy, and when I turned out to be a girl, Grandpa Sol walked right out of the hospital without seeing me." She waved her finger in the air. "But I still had to be named after his father."

"I thought my family was strange."

"Oh, your family's the best," George proclaimed. "At least Letty's clan. They treat Billy like a son, and me like a daughter. Never gave it a second thought. Most people can't do that, see past differences, I mean."

Audrey sighed. "Tell me about it."

George glanced at her. "Prejudice sucks, huh?" She entered the hospital parking lot. "Misconceptions, misunderstandings, anxieties, fears, hatred. All over a person's skin color, accent, mannerisms, anything that's different. It's bizarre. Beyond bizarre."

Audrey assessed the gray cross on the building's side. "It's beyond everything." She turned to the girl. "Does it bother you that your family's so upset?"

"Sure." George parked the car. "My grandfather's threatened not to give us a dime if we get married, and we're talking a hefty sum, but I figure I'm doing what's right marrying the person I love. Say I don't do this and find out twenty years down the line everything would've worked out, my family would've come around? I mean, my family's my family, they're stuck with me. I'll camp out on their doorstep if I have to, to see them, but I'll lose Billy forever if I let them push me around. All that'll leave is two more lonely people in the world. How does that help anything?"

Audrey tilted her head. "So you're doing this to make a social statement."

"Ha," George snorted. "Is that what I sound like? I'd try to stop world hunger first. It'd be a lot easier." She reached in the back seat for a green knapsack and pulled a bottle of water and a box of animal crackers out of it. "I mean, they want me to choose, Billy or them. That stinks." She opened the box and offered some cookies to Audrey. "So I say no, I won't choose, I want both, and one way or another, that's what I'm going to get. They'll get over it."

"I hope so," Audrey said, declining the offered snack.

"Don't Jewish families hate to see their kids marry outside the faith, though?"

George nodded, munching. "Sure, but we'd raise our kids Jewish. We've talked about that. Billy's even offered to convert, but I don't want him to, for my sake. It doesn't seem fair."

"Wouldn't that make your family happy?"

"I don't know. That's one question I'm afraid to ask, to tell you the truth. I don't want to learn how prejudiced my own family might be." She gulped some water. "I mean, I understand the religion concern. It's like with blacks, right? People worry there are fewer practicing Jews and fewer true African-Americans because of people intermarrying. I understand that. History hasn't been kind to either group, know what I mean?"

She chewed another cracker. "I should write a paper on slavery versus the Holocaust, tying in the Underground Railroad and the way blacks and whites and Jews and non-Jews helped each other, when it really counted."

Audrey frowned. "Many would argue whites caused all the trouble in the first place."

George nodded, her face animated as it had been in Letty's kitchen. "That's why I need to write about this, to prove a point, to unearth some facts about the way the different races worked together. There's good in all people, you know." She glanced at Audrey. "That's one thing Billy and I talk about a lot. The positive aspects of all this, the amazing family we'll start, the example we'll set."

"You sound like a woman with a mission again," Audrey teased.

George laughed. "You know what I mean, right? Letty told me about your parents. You grew up with the best of both worlds. That's what Billy and I want to give our children, appreciation of the issues facing different groups, different people. It'd be great if everyone was mixed, then we'd all have to really listen, not only to the sound of someone's voice, but to the words they're saying, in order to understand them."

Her crackers and water in her lap, George peered at Audrey with the solemn earnestness of a child, a hopeful child beginning to acknowledge the possibility that ideals may lie beyond her reach.

"That should count for something," she said. "Shouldn't it?"

In the hospital, Yvonne was tired and quiet. After twenty minutes of awkward, choppy conversation, Audrey wished her mother would return to her normal, feisty self and start complaining about something. As Audrey rose to leave, her mother suddenly spoke up. "I'm going to fly back to New York with you." Yvonne lifted her chin, as though defying her daughter to deny her request.

Audrey straightened. "You are? I mean, are you sure? Sure you feel strong enough?"

With a flick of her wrist, Yvonne explained she was eager to see Julian. Audrey said she'd planned to rent a car to drive back, but Yvonne insisted on paying for both of them to fly. "The wedding is Friday night." Yvonne directed her daughter to get her credit card from her purse and call an airline. "So get the first flight out Saturday morning."

"Are you sure you're up to all this?" Audrey asked. "I know you'll be discharged Thursday, but—"

Yvonne raised a hand. "I came here for a wedding, I'm going to a wedding," she said. "Then I want to see my grandson."

The kitchen phone's ring that evening startled Audrey, though its sound was muffled as it reached her in the back bedroom. She laid the diary page she'd been reading aside and went to the door to see if the phone might be for her. She'd left her aunt's number for James on his answering machine, but he'd yet to call.

Letty signaled to her from across the kitchen, where the phone hung. Audrey stepped quickly to accept the receiver from her. "Hello?"

"Audrey." James breathed her name with relief.

She leaned against a counter, threading the coil of the telephone cord through her fingers. "Hey, stranger. Nice to hear your voice."

A long sigh whistled in her ear.

"I can't even tell you how good it is to hear yours," he said. "It feels like weeks have passed since Sunday. A lot has happened since then, too. I may have a buyer for your house. Wait, though. How's your mother?"

Audrey filled him in on Yvonne's recovery with minimal details. "What buyer?"

"A fixer-upper, a real handyman. Recently hired by Xerox, but he wants to live away from town. I drove him by yesterday and he's nuts about the place."

"Pritch showed it to you?"

James snorted. "I didn't even bother, we simply drove by. We'll need to arrange a showing right away."

"But that's impossible."

"Impossible?"

"To put it on the market already. It needs a ton of work."

"This guy can't wait long. His wife's expecting and she's anxious to move into a house."

Audrey reached for a vinyl kitchen chair and dragged it across the floor toward her. "James, wait. I've got this diary. It was written by early owners of the house."

"A diary?"

"It's amazing. Seems the house was a stop on the Underground Railroad."

"Terrific. Something else to add value to the old place. This guy's the type who'll eat that up."

Audrey sat. "I still don't want to rush anything. I'll be back Saturday afternoon. We can figure it out then."

"So you're leaving Friday?"

"Saturday morning. Flying, not driving. My mother's coming with me, and she wants to fly."

"What about your car?"

Audrey pressed a palm to her forehead. "I forgot, you don't know all this stuff. So much has happened. The Buick bit the dust on the way down." She told about her ticket and visit to the repair shop, but decided not to mention the sticker on the trooper's notepad.

"Funny," he suddenly said, "that we're both car-less, I mean."

"What?"

"My car, it was stolen the other day."

"You're kidding. From where?"

"Near downtown. No big deal, insurance will cover it and all that. I came out of a client's office and, I don't know, it was gone." He paused. "Listen, you'll be back in time for my mother's birthday party Sunday, at the house."

Audrey hesitated. "I doubt she'll want me there," she said, intending to be flippant but realizing too late her voice sounded weak and nervous.

"*I'll* want you there," James said. "Actually, I wish only you were coming. I swear Mom's inviting half the town."

"Your house is certainly big enough."

"Too big," he said, an odd edge to his voice. "I've been thinking, if this sale goes through on your house, you and Julian could move in with me for a while, if you want. Like you said, I've got plenty of room."

Audrey paused, her hand, still entwined in the telephone cord, suspended in midair. "Move in with you?"

James cleared his throat. "Yeah, why not?"

She could picture him pacing through his house with his cordless phone, staring into a mirror as he raked his free hand through his hair, braced for her reaction.

She lowered her hand to her lap. "James. Really. Think about it."

"I have."

"Everyone would object to this. What would your mother say?"

"All I care about is what you say."

She glanced out the window as the warm night closed around her aunt's house, trying to imagine how she appeared, seated in the old, scarred kitchen. The yellow light of it held her in place as she struggled to point herself in the right direction, guided by a kind voice from so many miles away, a voice that held so much promise as it beckoned her home.

"Julian," she answered, her own voice distant and dreamy. "Julian makes this complicated."

He hesitated, and she wondered again if he stood in front of a mirror, his hand now still as her own.

"You need a commitment, right?" he suddenly asked, his tone upbeat.

She remained silent, waiting.

Though low, his chuckle rang in her ear, and his answer came so quickly and joyfully she heard its echo for hours after they said good-bye.

"Maybe that can be arranged, Ms. Conarroe," he said. "Maybe that can be arranged."

174

Chapter Twenty

"What would Laura think?" Yvonne demanded.

Audrey studied her mother, who sat on Letty's front porch swing. Discharged from the hospital that morning, Yvonne insisted by noon she couldn't bear the heat in the house on the unusually warm October day, and bid her daughter join her on the porch. Audrey had followed, suspecting her mother wanted to talk in private. Rather than join Yvonne on the swing, though, she stood at the porch railing.

"I have no idea," Audrey replied. She wasn't surprised her mother had stewed for three days over the fact Julian had been left alone with his father.

The swing creaked loudly. Audrey could remember sitting out here—her grandmother in the kitchen, her sister off exploring with their cousins—listening to cicadas strum in high branches on a sweltering summer day. She turned to face the yard, concentrating on an overgrown, spiky shrub in a corner, trying to imagine its name, or what kind of flower it might blossom with each spring.

A warm breeze sent a rusted wind chime near a front window clanging.

"Does it really matter?" she asked.

The swing stopped, and Audrey tensed.

"Yes," Yvonne hissed, "it certainly does matter, Audrey Elizabeth. Your sister expected you to care for her son just as she—"

"No." Audrey spun toward her mother. "She didn't expect that. She knew I'd do things differently, but she still trusted me with him."

Yvonne peered at her daughter for a long moment, then looked away. The air hummed with the noise of nearby traffic while the two women remained on the porch, silent together, but aloof.

Finally, Yvonne spoke again. "I often disagree with the way you do things," she began. Her face had relaxed, though now she sat on the edge of the swing's seat. "I think you've known that for a while."

Audrey refused to nod, or comment.

"But this time," Yvonne continued, "maybe I can help." She took a deep breath. "In fact," she added, "for Julian's sake, I think I should."

"Help?" Audrey wondered why her mother was suddenly smiling, grinning really, like a young girl delaying the delivery of a secret.

"Your father invested part of his retirement savings in an expensive life insurance policy a long while back," Yvonne said. "Apparently he thought I'd want to be a rich widow. Anyway, after his funeral was paid for, I put the rest away, to have something to leave you and Laura."

Audrey tried to imagine where her mother was leading.

"Now I know Laura started a little nest egg for Julian for college," Yvonne continued, gently rocking, "but that probably won't be enough, so some of this will have to go to that fund. But the rest . . . well, I certainly don't need it, and after I heard about your car breaking down I lay in that hospital bed thinking. Why not liquidate all that and give it to you now, rather than make you wait for me to pass on? So I get socked with some taxes. There will still be plenty left over."

Audrey lowered herself into a plastic patio chair near the swing.

Yvonne went on. "You need a new car, and that house should have been renovated years ago, but Laura never had the money to do that kind of work." She stared toward the yard. "I'm beginning to wish I'd done this right after Daddy died, to help Laura, when I could."

"Laura never needed help," Audrey said, her mouth dry and her voice shaky.

"And you never learned to ask for it."

Audrey cleared her throat. "I'm going to sell the house."

"What?"

Audrey sighed, her stomach cramped with anxiety. "I can't find a decent job in that town." She rose and moved back to the porch railing. "The place is dying. Even with money from you, how long can I take care of Julian without a good job?" She glanced at her mother, who now glared at the porch floor. "We already have an interested buyer."

"You what?"

"I've been seeing someone who works in real estate. He's got a buyer who—"

"Have you slept with him?"

She frowned at her mother.

"This person you're 'seeing.' If you've slept with him, you're not just 'seeing' him, are you?"

Audrey sighed, exasperated. She'd never discussed sex with her mother, and she didn't intend to begin now.

Yvonne shook her head. "Julian can't be expected to move away. Not now, not after all he's been through."

"Then when?" Audrey stepped toward her mother. "When in God's name is the right time to get him to a better place, a better life? When he's fifteen, sixteen, twenty-one?"

As her mother stood to face her, Audrey stepped back, nearly losing her balance. Yvonne's small blue eyes met hers, disturbing as ever when they flashed with such anger and disapproval.

"When he's had time to come to terms with the loss of his mother, that's when," Yvonne said. "When you've learned to help him face his grief, rather than turn your back on your own."

She waved a hand in the air, as though dismissing her daughter. "Sell the house and go wherever you wish, then," she said. "Leave the Northeast altogether or move in with this salesman you're 'seeing.' Go wherever you want. But Julian should come live with me if you're having such a hard time with all this. What he needs now is stability, and if you're going to take away the only home he's ever known so soon after he's lost his mother, then he needs to be with someone else, someone he can trust."

Yvonne spat out her last words. "And that someone certainly is *not* his father."

The wedding ceremony the following evening lasted less than thirty minutes. At the reception, Audrey sat with her father's family in a small hall decorated with pink and white streamers. A three-piece brass band serenaded them from a platform stage at the head of the room. Two tables away, another one of Letty's grandsons—too young to be a groom, Audrey thought— beamed

177

in a silver tuxedo beside his new wife. Letty sat beside them in a place of honor while the rest of the family filled three tables, with five more reserved for the bride's family and the newlyweds' friends.

Couples moved on and off the dance floor, many of the younger relatives clowning around with each other as the band picked up the evening's tempo. Audrey thought of Yvonne, who had attended the brief church ceremony and then returned to Letty's house to rest and prepare for their flight. Audrey found it hard to believe they'd be leaving in the morning.

She'd spent some time during the week sightseeing with George and shopping for an outfit for the wedding, but Audrey had enjoyed the hours she'd spent with her Great-Aunt Letty most. Letty repeated her same routine each morning, filling Audrey in on family business while filling her coffee cup, telling stories of family lore while scrambling eggs and grilling bacon.

When Letty wasn't cooking, she was reading, always reading. Biographies, her favorite books, lay in odd places throughout the house, with most lining the shelves of the small library.

One wall of the library displayed framed photographs dating from early in the century, just as Audrey remembered from her childhood visits. She picked out her father among the smiling cousins in two photos, and noticed the new pictures that had been added. Audrey decided to send Letty a photo of herself, Laura, and Julian, from their last Christmas together.

Only this past week did Audrey learn her favorite portrait on the library wall portrayed her grandmother with Letty. While Rose, seven years Letty's senior, sat demurely in a high-backed chair, Letty stood beside her, her folded hands set lightly on her sister's shoulder. Despite their plaited hair, stiff bows, and high-collared, long-sleeved dresses, the girls appeared relaxed—even joyous—as they shared the spotlight, their uplifted chins presenting sure smiles to the camera. When Audrey mentioned how much she loved that portrait, Letty stopped to gaze at it with her, and said she still remembered that day.

"I was so proud," she said, her voice a low tremor. "So proud simply to be near Rosie, much less have a picture made with her. I cherished everything she gave me, every look, every word, every single moment, all my life." She patted Audrey's arm, a retrieved book in her other hand. "Such a shame I never told her that."

"Cousin Audrey." Jolen, another cousin, drew her back to the reality of the reception, his smile wide, his white teeth gleaming. "My friend, the professor, is here." He waved to a slim black man who had entered the hall. Audrey assessed the professor's shined shoes and double-breasted suit, not at all surprised to find an academic dressed so fastidiously. Her father had always been quite attentive to his appearance.

Jolen greeted his friend while Audrey reviewed what her cousin had told her about Professor Orlin Williams, the newest—and youngest—faculty member at Fisk University and a specialist in African-American history. Jolen had insisted his friend would be very interested to learn about her house and its history as a stop on the Underground Railroad.

As soon as he was seated next to her and served an overflowing plate of food, Professor Williams asked about the papers she'd been given regarding the house. He nodded eagerly while she described the diary entries. "Certainly a find you have there," he said, slicing into his chicken-fried steak. "A very exciting find."

He described some of the Underground Railroad safe houses he'd read about in his studies, and mentioned he'd like to visit one some day. "I can't imagine the thrill of discovering a filled-in tunnel in a cellar, a secret room behind a bookcase, or other evidence a building had been used to shelter fugitives."

"You're welcome to visit," Audrey offered. "I can't imagine there are many in Tennessee."

Professor Williams corrected her. "There were some in the state, to help escaped slaves from the Deep South. In fact," he raised his steak knife like a scepter, "two abolitionist newspapers were published in Tennessee in the 1800s, one as early as 1819. That's quite a surprise to most people." He sipped his wine. "It's also a surprise to people that many agents on the Railroad were black. They weren't all white Quakers set out to save the poor slaves. You mentioned the coded quilt practice. That actually originated on the plantations, with slaves teaching each other the codes of the different quilt patterns and hanging the quilts out to dry when it was time to follow certain directions."

"Is it possible white abolitionists eventually used quilts the same way?" Audrey asked. "The writing in this diary sounds, I don't know, white."

The professor glanced at her. "Be leery of assumptions,

my dear. So many myths have been passed down. And there's still so much to learn about that era. Many escaped slaves' stories were told to and written by white abolitionists, who very likely gave the stories a certain point of view that made them appear the heroes. The wretched fugitives were the true heroes of the day, I insist."

Audrey found herself compensating for the fact she'd already eaten by drinking plenty of wine while Professor Williams enjoyed his meal. She set her glass down, determined not to wake up in the morning with a hangover, just in time for a long flight with her disapproving mother.

"You know," the professor continued, "if your house was a stop on the Railroad, it should be put on a historic register, to safeguard it. So many of these places are being torn down."

Audrey cleared her throat. "Actually, it's going up for sale."

He frowned, prompting Audrey to add she planned to make considerable improvements before selling it.

"I'd contact the historical society, first," he suggested. "They'll have guidelines stating the home can be restored, but not renovated. No tearing down walls or anything," he added. "You're in the Rochester area?"

Audrey nodded.

"They'll be very interested, I'm sure, with Frederick Douglass's history there and all."

She laughed. "I can't get over the fact I learned nothing—nothing—about Frederick Douglass or the Underground Railroad, through fourteen years of school there. Maybe a blurb in a book, but nothing I remember. And there we were in the middle of it all."

Professor Williams cut into what remained of his steak. "The white man's version of history," he said, his voice flat. "We'll be fighting that battle for years to come."

The music and laughter in the room suddenly grew louder. A jubilant young man, his shirt collar open and his face flushed, gyrated in the middle of the dance floor, encouraged by the claps and cheers of other guests.

"To Master Juba, the greatest of all dancers," Professor Williams declared, raising his wineglass in a toast.

Audrey raised her glass with a laugh. "Who?" she asked, as the noise subsided.

"Master Juba, the biggest draw in New York's Five

Points honky-tonk district in the 1840s," he explained with a wry smile. "Couldn't drink in the white man's fountain, but he sure as hell could dance on his stage."

Audrey smiled back. "Sounds like you enjoy your work."

"Immensely," he replied. "Especially at a school that takes our history seriously."

Intrigued that he included her in his collective "our," Audrey found herself oddly grateful her mother was absent.

The professor continued. "I'll never work under a white administrator again," he announced, startling Audrey as he leaned closer, his voice a husky whisper. "And if I'm lucky," he added, "I'll only work with sisters as lovely—and enlightened—as you."

Asleep next to her mother that night, Audrey dreamed of the fugitive again. Silent, the woman sat in a ring in a dank cabin, watching with others as Master Juba, the greatest of all dancers, danced on the dirt floor despite the chains that bound his feet. With a determined grin, his eyes bright and proud, he bid the others to celebrate with him, to sustain him with their cheers and laughter.

The dream continued with Letty's voice insisting blacks had been the brave ones on the Railroad while the fugitive escaped again, this time with bound bare feet. She struggled to wade through shallow water as crippling muscle cramps traveled from her sore legs through her back, radiating into arms already weighted, her entire body now a knot of pain and fear.

Only with a struggle could Audrey finally rush to confront the fugitive, to help, to guide her to the safe house with the coded quilt and the stone cellar under the trap door. And only then could the dreamer see the fugitive's face and recognize it as her own.

She arrived at the house and banged on the door, begging to be let in, hoping to be welcomed by her brown-skinned sister, fearing instead she'd fall into the arms of her red-haired lover, or her sister's ebony lover, or the exuberant professor, his black wing tips shined to a gleaming glare, or even her fair mother, her white skin glowing, her steel-blue eyes reflective as the racist police officer's sunglasses.

The door opened and she recognized her nephew's face, blank as her own.

Audrey jolted awake, the silence of her aunt's house enveloping her, the presence of her mother in the bed with her buoying her and weighing her down in the same moment.

She caught her breath, realizing how anxious she was to get home.

Chapter Twenty-One

The plane carried Audrey and Yvonne above the clouds, the houses and highways of Nashville disappearing behind a hazy shroud. Audrey cringed at the thought of Laura's Buick, left behind in a Kentucky scrap yard. Surely the money from her mother would make life easier now, she reasoned, helping with the house and the purchase of a much more dependable car. Still, she remained discouraged over losing such a tangible tie to her sister.

What was it about Laura's *things,* Audrey wondered. She peered out the window in vain search of answers among the clouds, her arms tight around her waist. Had Laura cast some spell over them, owned them so completely they possessed elements of her, making them impossible to discard? Perhaps, she reasoned, Laura not only owned things, she placed such emotional value on them that they belonged to her even in her absence, and in her absence, were no longer whole. People, too, Audrey mused, considering in turn her own displacement—as well as Julian's, Pritch's, even Yvonne's—since Laura's death. Every person Laura had embraced, comforted, claimed so completely now faced an uncertain future devoid of her love. Each stood incomplete in her absence.

Audrey pressed her arms into her abdomen to help maintain her composure, grateful for the window and the space she'd placed between herself and her mother when she'd found the third seat in their row empty. She and Yvonne had exchanged few words since their argument on Letty's porch, and they spent the morning of their departure avoiding each other as much as possible. The extra seat on the plane offered yet another opportunity to remain distant.

She opened a magazine and pretended to read, calmer

now, but worried about their arrival and how she would find Julian, Pritch, the house, even James. After less than a week away, Audrey suspected everything had changed, all the players having taken advantage of her absence, all the players—including her mother—having some kind of agenda to pursue once she returned home.

An early-season snow squall greeted them in Rochester. As the plane touched down on the slick runway, Audrey grew anxious to see Julian, to make sure he'd been all right during her time away, to know he'd acquired no new scars.

A bitter gale wailed and frigid air shocked passengers awake when they entered the drafty ramp to their gate. In the airport, Audrey spotted Pritch right away, the only dark face among the small crowd of eager friends and relatives waiting to hustle the late travelers home.

Pritch slowly rose as they approached him. "Miss Audrey," he said, with a shadow of a smile. He greeted her mother. "Mrs. Conarroe."

"Mr. Pritchard," Yvonne responded, her voice icy as the weather.

Pritch gestured toward the carry-on bag she held, but she moved past him before he could offer to take it. Audrey handed him one of her bags and walked beside him, following her mother down the hall. "How are the roads?" she asked.

"Treacherous," Pritch replied. "I only hope things clear soon. My friend in Philadelphia reports his company has an open position. I interview there next week."

Audrey quickened her pace to keep up with him.

"I may ask Julian to go with me," he added. "He says he's never been."

Audrey nearly dropped her bag. Ahead, her mother stepped onto the descending escalator to the baggage area. Audrey and Pritch followed. "I don't know—"

"He'd be away a mere weekend," Pritch scoffed. "We'd leave Thursday after school, so he'd miss only one day."

"But why? I'm sure you'll be busy Friday—"

"Two meetings, in the morning."

"Doesn't he have a dance at school?"

"He says he doesn't plan to attend. Really . . ." They left the escalator and followed Yvonne to their carousel. "I do not intend to kidnap the boy."

Audrey shook her head. "His grandmother will be against this."

Pritch stopped a few feet from Yvonne's back as the carousel rumbled to life. *"Your mother* has nothing to do with this."

They turned onto Adams Street, the wipers of Pritch's truck pumping against the driving snow. Audrey squinted out the window at the strange car parked in front of the house, then remembered James had said he might stop by that evening. She fought the urge to push past Pritch to get out as soon as he turned off the truck's engine.

They walked carefully up the sidewalk, Audrey noticing the way had been cleared, salt put down on icy patches, the outdoor light left on. They reached the porch as the front door opened, thankful as extra light from inside the house illuminated their way.

Audrey finally relaxed at the sight of James there, waiting. He appeared pleased to see her, too, his gaze and grin welcoming her home. When she stepped closer, however, when his broad, easy smile dimmed and his eyes darted toward her mother, toward Pritch, then toward the floor, she sensed an odd imbalance. She brushed aside her doubt before she could name it, willing it to dissolve.

Noise filled the front hall as Yvonne and James were introduced, coats shed, luggage pushed aside. Pritch walked back toward the kitchen, where Julian could be heard talking on the phone, while the rest of the group moved to the living room.

Audrey switched on two lamps and invited James to sit with her on the couch. Then she noticed the faded scratches and bruises on his face. "What . . .?" she began, reaching toward them.

He patted her hand. "Nothing. I was helping my mother, in her apartment, and a shelf fell. I got a little banged up, that's all." He gave Yvonne a sheepish shrug. "I'm not much of a handyman."

Yvonne laughed. "Neither was Audrey's father, dear."

A loud whoop came from the kitchen. Julian sped into the room, his face flushed, his eyes bright with victory.

"I did it!" He stood in the middle of the living room, his arms as wide as his smile. "I asked Tina Alani to the dance, and she said yes! She said yes! Hi, Grandma!" He rushed over to hug

185

his grandmother. "This is incredible!" He let out another whoop and spun around. "Yes!"

Pritch entered the room as Yvonne asked who Tina Alani was.

"The most gorgeous girl at school, Grandma. Really. I can't even believe she talks to me, and now she's going to the dance with me. Uh!" The boy paced, both hands clasped at his chest. "I'm in love, serious. Dad, sorry I can't go to Philadelphia with you. This is amazing, though, isn't it? I gotta call Eddie!" Julian sped back toward the kitchen, his father watching him go.

"Philadelphia?" Yvonne peered at Pritch.

"He's got an interview there next week," Audrey explained. "But I was pretty sure Julian wouldn't be able to go."

"Why would he?" Yvonne snapped. "Dance or no dance, I certainly don't see the sense in that idea."

Pritch frowned. "Julian inflated the air mattress for me, so Mrs. Conarroe," he signaled toward Yvonne, "can sleep in the master bedroom." He nodded, then left the room.

Yvonne smoothed her hair from her face. "Well," she announced, "we'd better get some dinner." She addressed James. "Care to join us?"

"I'd better go," he said, standing, "before a snowplow buries my rental car out there. I only hope everyone can dig out in time for our party tomorrow afternoon. Did Audrey tell you about it, Mrs. Conarroe?"

Yvonne followed him and Audrey to the door. "Why, no, she—"

"You should come. My mother would love to meet you."

Audrey cringed. "I don't know if Mom feels up to a party, really—"

"Of course I do, dear. Don't interrupt." She gazed at James. "I'm sure I'd love to meet your mother. See you tomorrow, then." She waved, bracelets jingling, and headed toward the kitchen.

Audrey handed James his coat. "Thanks again for coming," she said. "I hope Julian didn't give you a hard time when you got here."

He shrugged. "Not at all. Maybe you should bring him to the party, too. Mom would enjoy meeting your whole family."

"She would?"

He kissed her quickly. "Sure."

"We can't all go in Pritch's truck—"

James slipped his coat on. "I'll pick you up early, how's that?"

Audrey squeezed his hand and leaned close. "I wanted to ask you about that buyer—"

"Don't worry about all that. I'll fill you in tomorrow."

"But—" Audrey tried to stall him, to keep him close a moment longer, now that they were alone. She placed her hand on his arm, surprised by the pressure of her grip, the sudden lump in her throat, the tears that threatened.

"The roads," she finally said. "You'll be okay?"

"Promise," he said, kissing her once again. He left, his promise hardly reassuring as she continued to puzzle over his bruised temple and cheek.

Audrey found her mother at the kitchen stove, heating soup and assembling grilled-cheese sandwiches. Pritch read a newspaper while Julian talked excitedly into the phone. The smells from the food made Audrey's stomach growl.

"You must be exhausted, Mom," she said. "Go lie down. I'll let you know when this is done."

"Nonsense, I'm fine. That James is a darling, by the way. Why didn't you tell me about him?"

Pritch snorted and turned a page of the paper. Audrey decided not to remind her mother of their discussion on Letty's porch.

"Don't you ever buy vegetables?" Yvonne continued. "I couldn't find one. Buy plenty next time you shop, so I can make real soup. This canned stuff is nothing but salt and water, really."

"It's a miracle you found anything to cook," Audrey said. She opened the refrigerator. "Then again," she added, surveying the stocked shelves, "we seem to have plenty." She addressed Pritch. "How much do I owe you?"

He continued reading. "Consider it part of my rent."

Audrey shut the refrigerator as Julian hung up the phone.

"Rent?" Yvonne frowned at her daughter. "I thought he was just helping in your absence."

"He's helping with the house, Mom. Whether or not we sell this place—"

Her mother raised her eyebrows. "So now you're reconsidering?"

Audrey frowned while Pritch glared at Yvonne. "I'll remain," he said, "as long as I'm needed."

Yvonne banged a spoon on the edge of the soup pot. "Then," she replied, "so will I."

Audrey cleared her throat. "Mom has some money saved that I can use on the house, so we can get right to work. Maybe that'll help speed things along."

Pritch returned to his newspaper. "How convenient."

Audrey noted Julian's lined brow and the anxious way he looked from his grandmother to his father. "Hey," she blurted out, trying to distract her nephew. "The diary. I forgot about the diary. Hang on."

She left to retrieve the packet of papers, then returned and spread them on the kitchen table. Pritch and Yvonne remained silent, their faces grim. Audrey addressed her nephew as he leaned over the papers with her, describing what she'd learned about the house and its history as a station on the Underground Railroad. She pulled out the page about the young boy and asked if Julian knew where the trap door was located.

"Sure," he answered, "in the dining room. Mom showed it to me. It's pretty heavy, though. She couldn't lift it."

Pritch followed them to the dining room. "The wood's likely warped a bit, after all these years," he said, "or perhaps swollen from trapped moisture." After they moved a few chairs and the small dining table, Pritch rolled an old wool rug off the area Julian indicated.

The boy quizzed his aunt. "What's under there?"

"A cellar, I think." Audrey said, excited by the prospect of discovering something described in the diary. "It must be separate from the basement."

The trap door measured about four by three feet and had a tarnished ring bolted to it. While Pritch slowly pried it loose, Audrey moved a floor lamp as close as its cord would allow. When the trap door was finally raised, she directed light toward the revealed opening, gaping at the series of stone steps that matched the walls of the cramped, secret cellar. She imagined the boy, Joshua, peering down them, only to find wide eyes staring back at him from the base of that makeshift staircase.

"Wow," Julian said, voicing his aunt's awe.

"That's where they hid runaways," Audrey explained. "And the woman, the one who wrote the diary, said if anyone came when they had fugitives here, she'd move a rug and her rocking chair over the trap door and sit there knitting." She shivered. "What a draft. Let's close it up."

Pritch stood, his hand braced to hold the door open, and stared down the dark steps long after Audrey had switched off the lamp.

"Dad?" Julian said, studying his father.

Audrey returned to the edge of the opening. "Disturbing, isn't it?" She followed Pritch's gaze into the dark cellar. "I've dreamed about it," she said, "about one slave in particular, a woman running, then finding refuge here. I dreamed about her before getting the diary, and now it all makes sense. I'm sure she was safe here, for a while, thanks to the people who once owned this house."

Pritch slammed the door shut. "You make it sound rather romantic, Miss Audrey," he hissed. "Then again, your life is quite romantic and rosy these days, isn't it?"

Audrey glared at him. "We're all in this together, Pritch. Black and white, or in between." She gestured from her nephew to herself. "Regardless of race, people who respect each other help each other out, in times of need."

"What . . . what are you guys talking about?" Julian sputtered.

"Yes." Yvonne spoke up from the narrow passageway separating the kitchen and dining room. "I'd like to know the same thing."

Pritch fixed his gaze on Audrey. "Perhaps someday you'll realize many whites who helped back then actually remained racist," he said, "and that, in different ways, the same age-old problems still exist."

"Don't you think I deal with that every day?" Audrey demanded. "We were never exempt, Pritch. No matter how 'protected' you thought we were. Not even Laura with her lighter skin."

"Audrey Elizabeth—" Yvonne scolded her daughter and reached for Julian.

"No," the boy said, refusing to let his grandmother lead him out of the room. "I want to hear this."

Audrey peered at Pritch, daring him to challenge her. "You may think I'm naive," she said, "but I won't let my own doubts dictate the people I date, or respect, or love." Like George said, she wanted to add, I've got the best of both worlds, with one foot in each and compassion for both sides.

"Respecting people," Pritch proclaimed, "and pleasing them out of fear are two different things, Miss Audrey."

"What about loving someone," Audrey said, "no strings attached? Doesn't that count for anything?" She turned away and retreated to the kitchen, where her mother and nephew soon joined her. A moment later, she heard Pritch head upstairs.

Yvonne set the table while Julian sat in a chair, watching his aunt. "I want to understand all that," he said, signaling toward the dining room.

Audrey tried to smile. "It's hard to understand, Julian," she said. "It's all so complicated."

"Not really," Yvonne interjected, ignoring their stares. "At least now people talk about these things, more than they ever used to. Take back when your father and I dated . . ."

An hour quickly passed as they ate dinner and talked. Audrey marveled at her mother's sudden inclination to reveal so much about herself, suspecting her stroke—and other recent events in their family—might have affected her more than she realized.

Yvonne spoke at length about her German parents, Pennsylvania farmers whose strict ways led her to leave home at eighteen, in search of a city far enough away to be exciting, close enough to be comforting. She'd landed in Rochester, working in a corner store, waiting for Prince Charming to walk into her life.

She admitted she didn't recognize him at first in the kind colored man, a young professor at the University of Rochester, who came in for the morning paper every now and then, and eventually every day. Benjamin Conarroe impressed her as a soft-spoken Southerner, a shy, sweet, lonely person, and Yvonne looked forward to their talks. She enjoyed the challenge of drawing him out, learning about the troubles he faced in such a conservative workplace, listening to his plans for the future.

After months of sharing coffee breaks and soon cocktails after work, Yvonne said, they went to a friend's party and got wonderfully drunk. When they woke up the next morning in each other's arms, Benjamin proposed on the spot.

Yvonne winked at Julian. "Your grandfather was noble to a fault, dear," she said. "The poor thing had no choice."

She explained while Ben's family insisted they marry back in Nashville, her family was nowhere near as receptive. Yvonne wrote home with the news, sending a photo of her and her fiancé. The letter was immediately returned, the photo cut in half. She never tried to contact them again.

Audrey spoke up. "If Dad's family was so receptive,

why didn't we visit more often?"

Her mother shrugged. "Those visits were never easy," she admitted. "Daddy was so self-conscious there. He assumed, I think, that most colored people, including his own, thought less of him after we married."

"Pritch thinks Daddy didn't think much of *him,* you know," Audrey said. "He says that's why he couldn't marry Laura."

"What?" Her mother's eyes narrowed. "Ridiculous," she said, pausing as she inclined her head toward her grandson. "Do we have to discuss this in front of—?"

"C'mon, Grandma," Julian protested. "You just told me all about you and Grandpa. I'm old enough."

She took an exasperated breath and glared at her daughter. "Harrison left because Laura was pregnant."

Audrey shook her head. "He didn't know that, Mom. He left before Laura even knew."

"Of course he's going to say that now. I—"

"He's not lying. He says Dad didn't approve of him because he worked with his hands, not at a desk all day."

"If only I could convince you how ridiculous that sounds," her mother said. "Your father was pleased when Laura started to date Harrison. Pleased she chose someone like him, a black man. But Harrison turned out to be quite different, so your father was still guarded with him, unsure of his intentions."

She glanced again at Julian, then back to Audrey. "The problem lay in the lack of respect Harrison appeared to have for us. Daddy thought he held us in low esteem, because we were mixed. We hoped after the wedding things might change, but then Harrison disappeared—"

"He had his reasons."

Audrey shifted to face Pritch, who stood in the kitchen doorway.

He handed her a piece of paper. "You had a phone message yesterday, from the Moon Resort. Your application is under consideration for another position, it seems."

"Another position? Where?"

"Here, of course," Pritch answered. "The gentleman on the phone said you're the top candidate. They'd like to interview you again next week."

Audrey read the familiar contact name, wondering what the new position entailed, wishing it were a weeknight so she wouldn't have to wait so long to call. She smoothed the note on the table, then looked at Pritch. "Join us?"

He remained standing. "I've already explained this to Julian, but you two deserve insight into my past behavior as well, it seems."

Yvonne set a bowl of hot soup at the empty place setting. "Have a seat, Harrison, and something to eat. I can hear your stomach growling from over here."

Pritch paused, then sat at the table. "All right," he said. "Now, where to start . . ."

"Tell them what you told me, Dad," Julian suggested. "About how mean your dad was, and how you thought Grandpa was mean, and didn't want you to marry Mom."

Pritch replaced the spoon he'd just picked up. "How I misunderstood your grandfather, Julian. I never said he mistreated me." He gestured toward Yvonne. "From what I heard earlier, he misunderstood me, too."

Audrey thought of the discussion she'd had with Laura, that Christmas before she died. "She was right," she said aloud.

All eyes turned to her. "Laura," she explained. "She told me you hated your father, and probably left because you had a hard time with Dad and decided you'd be better off on your own."

"She said that?" Pritch asked.

"Just last year."

He shook his head, both hands now in his lap. "She understood more than she let on," he murmured, his gaze distant, his face somber.

Yvonne rose from the table. "And loved you more than you knew, young man."

Chapter Twenty-two

Audrey's excitement about the call from the Moon Resort, the discovery of the trap door, and her family's airing out made it impossible for her to sleep. She stayed up later than usual, reading the diary, and was surprised when Julian stopped by her room with a small collection of papers—and some of Laura's clothes.

"I thought you were in bed," she said. She spied in her nephew's bright eyes evidence he remained excited, too.

"Grandma was putting things in Mom's closet, so I went through some boxes in there, looking for these." He handed her the papers. "I thought you'd be interested."

Audrey had him sit on her bed beside her. "What are those?" she asked, perfectly aware the sweaters he carried had also come from that closet.

Julian shrugged. "I saw them, and, I don't know . . . Mom loved these sweaters. I bet she'd want you to have them." He offered her a soft cardigan. "Grandma thought you'd look nice in this one."

Audrey sighed, fingering the cardigan's sleeve. "It's just not me, Julian," she said, sorry to see his face redden, wishing she could find the right words to explain what she feared—to herself as well as to him.

She slipped the sweater on, expecting to be overwhelmed by the grief inherent in wearing it. Surely it was wrong to wear Laura's things, feel at home in her house, love her son as though he were her own. Surely these acts testified to an acceptance of the fact that Laura indeed was gone, never to return. Surely, Audrey ached to cry, she should continue to grieve rather than make plans to enjoy living, when her sister had been so much better at doing that—and so much more deserving.

She slipped the sweater on, comforted by its weight and the way it wrapped her in such a tangible reminder of her sister. "She's with us all the time, you know," Audrey whispered to her nephew, stroking the sleeve now. "With you, me, Grandma, even your dad. All the time, now that she's gone. Funny how that works, isn't it?"

She took the other sweaters and patted his hand—such a big hand compared to the one she'd held on outings with him and his mother just a few years ago—then signaled toward the papers he'd given her.

"They're mostly copies Mom made at the library," Julian explained, "and at the historical society. I went with her a couple times. She copied old newspapers and stuff. Someone once told her the house might've been a stop on the Underground Railroad, so she wanted to check it out."

Audrey set the sweaters aside and leafed through the pages, surprised to find sheets filled with her sister's handwriting.

"She took lots of notes," Julian added, "but didn't find much. She said there wasn't a lot to go on."

Laura had put everything in chronological order. Audrey found a short article she'd circled from an 1847 edition of the Rochester *Democrat:* "Teaching Couple to Leave Day School for Orleans County Farm." The article described Warren and Nell Morris, two popular teachers who'd announced their intent to leave their positions. They planned to farm land they'd purchased from a Robert Anderson, and would leave their school the following year, when they'd built their house. The article went on to note the couple's associations with the local Anti-Slavery Society, a small organization established in 1838 with a Quaker teacher as its president.

"Wait," Audrey said. "Warren." She reached for the diary. "The woman who wrote this, her husband's name was Warren. I'm sure of it." She shuffled the papers, searching. "There it is!" She pointed to a diary page. "Julian, these are the people. Do you believe this?"

Her nephew, who'd been leafing through his mother's papers, pulled out a copy of another article. "They're in this one, too."

Audrey scanned the piece, which noted the Morris couple again, and described their home. "Situated within a few miles of the Great Lake called Ontario, the Morris homestead features a grand home with two large fireplaces and acres of fertile farm-land."

"Our house," Audrey murmured.

The article repeated the couple's ties to the Anti-Slavery Society. It also noted that Warren Morris's father, William, had settled in Rochester, "the Flour City," in 1820, "after a daring escape from bondage on a Virginia plantation."

"From bondage? These people weren't Quakers, after all." Audrey stared at her nephew. "They were black."

Long after Julian had gone to bed, Audrey continued to read through the pile of papers. Finally, she reminded herself of the party for Margaret Sullivan the next day, and tried to get some sleep.

She'd never had such vivid dreams.

They spilled over each other throughout the night. In one dream, Audrey sensed she was in her sister's house, but found it even more dark and cold than usual. She followed a light and the promise of heat to a wood-burning stove in the kitchen. Nothing within the kitchen appeared familiar, yet Audrey felt at home. She thought she saw Laura in a coarse, heavy dress, bent to feed wood into the stove, then realized as the woman straightened that it was Nell Morris.

Warren Morris banged through the back door, a man of average height with dirty overalls, an ill-fitted coat, and a large hat that covered his face. Audrey noted his dark, worn hands as he removed his hat.

"They're on their way, now," he told his wife. "How do the others fare?"

"They've been fed," Nell answered, "but are exhausted. They'll require additional days before they can travel."

Warren paced, agitated. "We cannot keep them long. What if more should come?"

"Why such concern?" she asked in alarm. "What did you see?"

He waved away her questions. "No need for worry. No signs anyone's caught on. We are safe and our friends are safe here. Keep the lantern in the attic window. We'll make due if more arrive."

Nell pulled papers from a pocket inside her skirt and sat at the far end of the kitchen table, where writing utensils stood, ready for her to use.

Her husband frowned, his dark face, though young, suddenly lined. "Such risks, now—"

"Such stories," she interrupted. "They tell such stories, I have to write them, so they'll not be forgotten. Tragic, unimaginable cruelties: rapes, whippings, lynchings, families torn asunder, as well as everyday trials: cramped cabins with dirt floors frozen or muddied by seeping rain, sickly babes wrapped in rags, food snatched and gobbled. They've never eaten warm sugar in March, worn woolens, sat to a meal with those they love, if they reside with those they love. Is this a way to live, Warren? Does a beast even deserve such treatment?"

He shook his head, awed as always by his wife's range of emotion, her frank despair over common injustices. Still, he continued his appeal. "If your writings were found—"

She tucked them back away. "A farm wife's scribblings are of no interest. But to please you and ensure safety, they'll remain hidden from all eyes but my own."

Later, the woman wrote: "So reckless, placing my own family at risk. This I know. Warren trusts these pages will never again surface, and I shall honor that trust. Such a drive to write, some days, to fill coarse pages, to move my hand and free my mind, to order things and list them, to let them loose to fall as they may. My own lost child, my dear daughter, would understand. To her all this would have been told, to her all this would have been entrusted. Without her, I am compelled to communicate with the hereafter, with readers now only imagined.

"Yes, we break God-forsaken laws to serve a higher cause. And yes, I shall continue to document our efforts, to confess, to champion that cause. These acts of lawlessness and compassion take time, this writing itself is an investment. Sure proof of our passions, our insistent pursuit of what is right, with so much else tugging at a person every day, such exhaustive routines, and yes, the threat of discovery. The fact I spend stolen moments, the fact I write now in a silent house full of sleeping family and friends, sacrificing needed rest, surely all this equates to a conviction, I say. And simply because I say, and share, and swear by my conviction of what is right, I write—for my own self, perhaps, in truth—to fill a secret, insistent need, a base desire, my own hopeful dream."

Audrey tossed and turned, her breaths quickening as her dream shifted outside the house to another night, to the edge of woods, to someone watching.

The farm beckoned. Its promise of shelter and food, God-given, life-sustaining food, proved almost too tempting to resist. Some sort of illness had set in, and fever fogged the senses. Still, the hidden remained hidden. He'd been told of the couple who ran the farm, teachers with hearts of gold and skin as black as his own. He'd been assured they'd take him in and arrange for his transfer to a launch at the lake, where he'd be ferried the final way to Canada, to true freedom. Still he hesitated, and searched the scene for signs of deception. He listened for the horrific echoes of baying hounds or horses' hoofs, straining for any clues that he'd been foolish to trust strangers, that he'd stumbled an ill-fated way, that his return to captivity was imminent.

Then the lantern in the attic window was lit, a simple, silent beacon he'd been assured would indicate when he could safely approach. He understood the wife hung a coded quilt in warm months, but in this season of cold, long nights, the lit lantern beckoned runaways. His knees weakened and threatened to fail him. When his resolve returned, he crept from the shadows.

The house loomed. He smelled the smoke from its chimney, heard the farm animals in the nearby barn. Every step across the frosted ground crackled, amplified in the night air. He could not reach the back door quickly enough.

He rapped the signal and stepped to one side, prepared to bolt should anything seem amiss. The teacher, whose skin indeed was blacker than his own, opened the door and signaled him to enter, no words spoken.

The man moved without knowing his body operated. He dressed in the clothes the wife gave him, devoured bread, stewed rabbit, other victuals he hardly took time to name or taste as he ate. Finally, his stomach filled and his head heavy with fever, he was wrapped in blankets and instructed to rest near the fireplace, assured he'd be removed to a secret cellar if needed. He relaxed, trusting his fate to the kind teacher, the son of yet another escaped slave. The fire leaped and hissed, lulling him to complete, consuming sleep.

Other eyes refused sleep, however, and continued their watch from the woods. Another runaway viewed the wide farmhouse, spied the lit lantern, smelled the smoke, heard the animals. But his steps made no sound, as he'd been trained by an Indian friend to tread on the balls of his feet, like a fox, to trick his pursuers using the rabbit's cunning, to survive on the season's sparse offerings as do the deer. This man defied exhaustion, denied himself the luxury of such a weakness. A blacksmith, he carried the expanse of his strength and breadth of his body with no concerns of discovery. He blended with shadows, became them.

A blacksmith and a murderer, he feared neither bounty hunters nor lawmen. The final blow of his hammer, the final blow he'd taken to his old life and self, had destroyed a cruel master who'd personified the slave trade, who'd represented all the evil, inhumane acts the blacksmith ever witnessed. Vowed never to return, the blacksmith would shred any hound that tracked him, any man that dared threaten him with capture.

He'd watched the other runaway enter the house and knew it was a safe place, though he'd spoken to no one of it. He sought help only to receive direction, to learn the fastest way to freedom's border. He'd refuse anything else and depart immediately upon learning the way.

The blacksmith moved across the yard, a shadow of a presence. The farm animals fell silent. He knocked at the door, unaware of any signal, and was greeted shortly by Warren Morris armed with a rifle.

The blacksmith stood firm, despite his shock at realizing the stranger's race.

"State your name and business, or be on your way," Warren Morris ordered.

"I require only direction."

"You lie. You're a slave catcher here to plague an innocent man and his family in the mean of the night."

"Might I note we're of the same color, sir."

Warren Morris glared at the blacksmith from behind the rifle, which remained raised. "Color counts for nothing to those who would profit from betrayal." He cocked his chin to the left. "Canada lies due west, if direction is indeed all you seek."

The blacksmith backed off, palms open, then slipped away to the woods. As the night swallowed him, images of the brave stranger remained with him. He'd carry these as far as Buffalo, where the blacksmith would in short order join others devoted to guiding lost souls across the freedom border. He'd never return to the land of his misery, but he'd remain where his strength and cunning could help others—and where freedom lay within easy reach, should it become necessary to finally claim it.

Audrey woke the next morning, anxious to read her sister's papers. Though unaware Laura had ever kept a journal, Audrey suspected these pages included much more than findings regarding the house. Beneath a list of organized, detailed notes, she found a sheet of flowing handwriting. "I love to imagine this house as it was, back then," she read. "I dream about it, about the people who possibly lived here, the other lives these walls have witnessed. I like to think the house was waiting for me, after being empty for a while, waiting for me to walk in the front door and claim it."

Her own name was mentioned a few paragraphs later:

"Audrey called, outspoken as ever. Something about work. She puts in such long hours. I understand what's driven her to be so independent, namely Daddy's dogged determination to set her straight. Still, I miss her. I miss the way we get along, now that we're older. Sisters know so much about each other. We're witnesses to each other's lives, even if we watch in silence for so many years. Then when we're older, we reflect that secret knowledge to each other. I find that very comforting."

Audrey read this paragraph many times, amazed by her sister's words, saddened by their mutual inability to express, out loud, how much they'd loved each other. Laura's use of the word "witness" reminded Audrey of a page of the diary she'd read the previous night. She pulled it out, wishing she could share the beauty of these words with Laura, certain her sister would have been moved to tears by their sincerity:

"I've lit the lantern in the attic window," the entry read, "the signal to fugitives hidden in the woods. As autumn progresses, the flow should slow, unlike in summer, when most considering escape take heart in the warmer temperatures and their increased chances for survival. In winter, only the desperate take flight.

"'This is a safe place,' the light tells them. 'Take comfort here.' And when they arrive, I want to hold them safe rather than send them off to another unknown. I ache to say to all our friends, 'Stay. Join our family and have us nourish you, call this house your home, let these solid walls bear witness to you and your loves and the dreams that have brought you here. Stay,' I want to beg. I cannot, yet I wish to whisper in every ear: 'Stay.'"

Chapter Twenty-three

On the drive with James to his mother's house, Audrey marveled at how bright everything appeared, now that the storm front had passed. Record cold temperatures had moved in overnight, and the sky was perfectly clear. Not only did the day look promising, she decided, but suddenly the future did, too.

Audrey told James everything that had happened the night before, continuing to talk at the house while she helped him arrange tables for the caterer. She glanced at her boyfriend from time to time, and was pleased to find him smiling.

Finished in the living room, they stood back to survey their work. Then James announced he had good news of his own: The potential buyer of Audrey's house had requested an immediate, informal showing.

"You could sell by owner," he suggested.

Audrey took a deep breath. "That's another thing," she said, grinning now. "I think I want to keep the house."

James frowned.

"Don't you see?" she asked. "If I get this job, there's no need to sell. Julian's going to be so excited when I tell him. Everything's falling into place."

James held up a hand. "Maybe, in case everything doesn't pan out, you should show the house to this one guy. He may make an offer you can't refuse." He adjusted a chair. "Actually, he may make the only offer you'll ever get."

She took his hand, lacing her fingers with his. "Things are changing," she said, "for the better. I can feel it, for the first time, you know?"

Audrey hesitated, despite her eagerness to tell James why she felt this way. She'd learned so much about the history of the old farmhouse and why Laura had been drawn to it, from her sister's own writings as well as from the diary's browned pages. And she suspected she'd have a hard time letting go. She wanted to share all this with James, but did not, preferring to hold such secrets safe in her heart rather than risk having them waved aside.

She watched him adjust a few more chairs and decided instead to change the subject. "I'm not sure Julian will come today," she said, smoothing a white tablecloth. "He wasn't thrilled with the idea."

James shrugged. "I guess most kids would feel that way about a sixty-year-old woman's party."

They removed punch glasses and stemware from the dining-room china cabinet and brought them to the kitchen to wash. Audrey filled the sink. Her hands deep in the soapy water, she commented his house appeared tidier than ever. James admitted his mother had insisted he hire a cleaning service.

"I doubt she's changed much since we were in high school," Audrey said, rinsing a wineglass.

James stepped up behind her, took the glass, and placed it on a dishtowel on the counter. He slipped his arms around her waist. Audrey leaned back into him as she dried her hands, his breath on her neck and the smell of his cologne close and comforting. She turned her face, then, to rub her cheek against the lapel of his suit jacket.

He smoothed her arms. "This sweater's so soft."

Audrey smiled as he raised his hand to the jewel neckline of the peach sweater, one of Laura's favorites.

"So soft." He sighed.

"Feel this." She smoothed his hands down to her black velvet skirt.

"Mmmm," he murmured, caressing her hips.

As they slowly swayed, Audrey turned to him and tilted her face up to his, reaching to his hair. Any sense of time or a schedule or even a reason for their preparations dissolved as she relished the pressure of his embrace and the urgency of his kisses. But as her fingers traveled from his hair to his bruised temple, James drew away, as though startled.

"Does it still hurt?" she asked.

He shook his head. "No. Yes, a little." He stepped back and touched his face. "Nothing to worry about," he added, studying his watch now. "My mother should be here soon. Maybe we'd better—"

Audrey peered at him. "Are you okay?"

"Just a little anxious," he said.

"Anxious?" She tried to identify his true state, but his eyes and expression revealed only a confused mix of emotions.

He ran a hand through his hair, then rubbed the back of his neck. "There's something I want to talk about, before anyone else gets here." He looked again at his watch.

Audrey stared at him, afraid to blink or breathe, her mind careening through the possibilities of what he might say. Her week away had left room for anything to develop, or fall apart.

He sighed, his shoulders relaxing as he moved back to her. "I missed you."

She smiled. "I'm here."

James traced a finger along her temple. "I mean I really missed you. Every day you were gone seemed like a week. It was all so familiar. I hated it."

He ran his hand along her cheek, his voice lower when he spoke again. "In high school, when we broke up," he said, "it was hard, not to see you anymore. Just like that, you were out of my life, and I let it happen. I don't want to make that mistake again. Ever."

She watched him, wondering, as he slipped his hand into his jacket pocket. Suddenly terrified he might propose, Audrey recalled his promise of some sort of "commitment" and was relieved to hear the front door burst open downstairs.

"Jimmy!"

She eyed James, assuming his mother had arrived, then frowned, realizing from the noise in the foyer that Margaret was not alone. She followed James to the top of the small staircase that led to the foyer. At the foot of the stairs, Margaret Sullivan grinned before moving aside to let two other women join her.

"Look who's here," she announced.

A trio of perfect smiles and sets of bright eyes beamed up toward Audrey and James, who gaped at the sudden sight of Bridgit. Flanked by Margaret and the other woman—a petite, impeccably-dressed version of herself—Bridgit radiated self-confidence and sensuality from her head full of blond waves to the tips of her trim leather boots.

James stammered a greeting and invited everyone upstairs. Audrey squeezed his hand, despite her initial inclination to move away from him.

Bridgit led the way, slipping off her fur-collared coat and

tossing it into a nearby chair, revealing an elegant gabardine suit. She gushed a greeting and explained her move to Paris had been postponed yet again. "All my junk's been shipped already," she said, "but the agency insisted I put off my departure, God knows why. Anyway, I'm staying with Mother, and since she was invited to the party, Margaret was nice enough to include me. Wasn't that sweet?" Bridgit took Margaret's arm and drew her close, saying how thrilled she was to help her celebrate her birthday. James cleared his throat and gestured from his mother to Audrey, his voice faltering as he introduced them.

Margaret extended a hand, which Audrey shook cautiously, expecting someone to say this was all a bizarre joke and she was now free to leave. She tried to convince herself the woman was not intentionally looking down her nose at her.

Relief arrived as the doorbell rang. A three-member catering team bustled up the stairs, their arms full of dishes and trays loaded with food. As they made multiple trips outside to bring in more provisions, Audrey wondered if Margaret had indeed invited half the town.

It was nearly two o'clock when the food was laid out and the bar set up. Audrey had successfully avoided further contact with Bridgit and Margaret, grateful for the diversion created by the caterers and the arrival of early guests. She was surprised when James ushered Yvonne upstairs with Julian—and Pritch. He introduced them to Margaret, who entered into a lively conversation with Yvonne while James returned to the beckoning doorbell.

Julian wore his best dress pants, a shirt and sweater, and a bored frown. Audrey noted he now stood almost as tall as his father. She leaned toward him. "You don't look happy to be here," she said.

His expression remained blank. "I'm not."

Pritch glanced at him. "But he remains aware etiquette sometimes calls us to overcome such reservations. Eh, Julian?"

Audrey wondered if Pritch had come to help his son endure this party, or to prove he was willing to overcome his own reservations by attending. Either way, she was pleased by their presence.

Margaret's voice changed its direction. "Yvonne," she announced, gesturing toward Julian, "this must be your handsome grandson."

Yvonne beamed. "My pride and joy."

A heavy sigh escaped Margaret. "Funny, isn't it? We grow older anticipating being surrounded by grandchildren." She swung her arms wide, nearly spilling her tonic water. "But my two girls are out of state, and Jimmy here has some sort of aversion to marriage, it seems."

James appeared at Audrey's side. "Mother," he growled, drawing out the "r" in mock warning. "Can I get anyone a drink?" His offer politely declined, he directed folks to help themselves at the bar.

Audrey scanned the room for Bridgit, wondering if she'd heard Margaret tease James about his aversion to marriage. She spotted her a few feet away, talking with her mother and two other women. Bridgit met her gaze, and Audrey's pulse quickened. The whole house seemed full of people all of a sudden, with noise from dozens of escalating conversations reaching an unbearable level. Audrey marveled that the large house could feel so cramped. As her skin began to itch under the weight of her sister's sweater, she blinked, realizing she'd been staring.

Bridgit smiled and glanced toward Julian and Pritch. Audrey braced herself, as though anticipating an affront on her family, then took a deep breath and tried to relax. Bridgit and her mother broke away from their conversation and drifted toward Margaret.

Margaret beamed at Bridgit, pausing in mid-sentence to introduce Yvonne. When Yvonne began to introduce her daughter, Bridgit announced she and Audrey had already met.

"That's true," Margaret explained. "When we first came in."

Bridgit nodded. "And at Carol's wedding."

"Oh yes, Carol's wedding," Margaret echoed, frowning now.

Yvonne addressed her daughter. "You went to another wedding?"

"Last weekend," Audrey answered. "Before I left for Nashville."

Bridgit wagged a finger. "I told Jimmy I bet he'll be the next of the old gang to get hitched." She cupped a slender hand at her mouth. "He needs someone to look after him," she said, winking at Audrey, "to keep him from getting mugged and robbed again, huh?"

"Mugged!"

Margaret's exclamation sounded through the house as

conversations hung suspended for a silent instant. Though most guests quickly returned to greeting each other, many continued to glance toward the curious group at the party's center.

James had reappeared at Audrey's side. "Mom." He directed Margaret to a chair, his concern evident in his lined brow. "Here, sit. What's the matter?"

An awkward pause lingered while Bridgit's mother rushed to get Margaret a glass of water. Yvonne, Julian, and Pritch stepped aside. Audrey didn't move.

"You were mugged, Jimmy?" Margaret stammered. "But you told me—"

James shook his head. "I didn't want to worry you, Mom. It was nothing. They wanted the car."

Audrey looked more closely now at the scratches on his face. "They mugged you outside a client's office? In the middle of the day?"

"I'm so sorry, Jimmy." Bridgit's voice, uncharacteristically weak, interrupted. "I thought they knew."

Audrey glared at her. "It seems only you knew," she said. She sensed Margaret's cold stare, knew James had straightened beside her, heard her family's conversation falter a few steps away, and saw only Bridgit's narrowed eyes and cocked chin.

"I was there," Bridgit answered.

James filled Audrey's view. For a moment, she believed he'd appeared magically, as though to waken her from a bad dream. Before she could focus, before his anguished face could remind her she was indeed living this moment, Audrey realized she had fallen for Jimmy Sullivan again, just in time to be betrayed by him again. Her head rang with the empty echo of his confession that he'd missed her unbearably while they were apart.

"Were the police called?" Margaret demanded.

James nodded wearily, still watching Audrey. "I couldn't give very good descriptions, though. It was pouring, I barely saw a thing."

"You must have seen *something,*" his mother screeched. "At least whether they were black or not."

The shock of the woman's words stunned Audrey. She glanced toward Yvonne, noting her mother's furious scowl and quickly turned back. Audrey blinked as Margaret's words fully registered, then stepped away to follow Yvonne across the room.

James touched her shoulder just as Pritch appeared

beside her. "Time to go, Miss Audrey?" he asked.

She faced her nephew's father, taking brief comfort in his obvious concern.

James moved closer to her, his voice urgent. "Wait. Audrey," he said. "There's something, remember? Something I need to ask you."

He reached back into his pocket, but Audrey placed her hand on his arm, stopping him.

He stared at her. "But I want—"

Audrey gazed at him, her voice small and tight when she finally spoke. "Are you sure?" she asked, her brow furrowed. "Sure what you want, and why you want it?"

You're better off in your own little world, Jimmy, she ached to add. Safe and secure with familiar faces, familiar ways. Don't ruin that just to prove a point. And don't pretend you love me, when you really don't know.

She let go.

Downstairs in the foyer, she retrieved her coat from the closet and led her family out the door.

Julian caught up to her on the front sidewalk. "Aunt Audrey." His breath escaped in a series of rapid puffs that hung between them in the icy air. "Wait."

She frowned at her nephew, realizing even as she did that his face seemed older, more somber than ever.

"Not now, Julian," she growled. She pulled her coat close around her, wondering how they were all going to squeeze into Pritch's truck for the bitter ride home.

"Yes, now," Julian said, his voice deeper than she'd ever heard it.

He gestured toward the house. "If you just broke up with James, because of me, I need to tell you something." He stared at his aunt, wide-eyed. "I could go with Dad, if he gets that job in Philadelphia. It would be okay."

Audrey exhaled, willing away the tingle in her nose, the itch of her eyes.

"Don't you see?" Julian leaned toward her, his voice strained, his fists plunged deep into his coat pockets. "You won't have me to worry about anymore, so you can do whatever you want."

The boy continued to stare at her, his eyes revealing how much courage it had taken to speak those words. And while Audrey suspected he remained unsure about his future, she realized he deserved a say in what happened to him next, a chance to make a decision that would affect his life in a world that had spun so far beyond his control.

Certain her mother would love to take her grandson back to Florida with her, Audrey was grateful for Yvonne's silence. She heard Pritch cough and hoped he understood the situation as she now did, for his son's sake.

Pritch spoke up. "Julian." His dark eyes were steady as he addressed the boy, as an equal, Audrey thought. "So much is unknown right now. So much could happen. All I want, all *we* want," he gestured from himself toward Audrey and Yvonne, "is what's best for you. That's why we're all here, you see?"

Audrey shook her head, her eyes now brimming with tears as the shock of James's betrayal and the proposal she'd prevented threatened to overwhelm her. "I've made so many mistakes, Julian," she said, struggling for control, "but if you believe you're simply something to worry about, then I've really failed."

In that moment, all she could see was her nephew's face, her nephew's face with her sister's eyes, eyes that now filled with the tears of an anxious young boy.

She took a deep breath. "It's funny," she finally said, forcing a weak smile. She wanted to reach out to him, but held back, still unsure how he'd react. "You've decided you might want to move just as I've realized I can't sell your mother's house."

Chapter Twenty-four

Surrounded by fresh December snow and blue winter shadows, under a night sky of breathtaking depth and clarity, Audrey decreed shoveling an art.

She pushed along, clearing the driveway and adding to the growing snow banks at its edge. The muffled sounds she created echoed in the crisp air—the smooth scrape of her shovel on the pavement, the beat of silence as she raised a new mound, the satisfying thump of snow added to snow.

She smiled, perfectly aware of the reasons behind the peace she'd made with the winter's coming. Her mother's money had indeed helped ease her way to this moment, to the newly paved driveway, the new car a few feet away, the new coat and boots she wore. But she understood, too, that her recent decisions—to stay in her sister's house, break up with James, and accept a job that had already brought her so much satisfaction—had led her here, too.

She straightened, watched the broad vapor cloud she created as she sighed, and thought of James. While she hadn't seen him since his mother's party, Audrey had heard plenty about him from Pam.

"I feel so bad, Audrey," Pam had wailed over the phone a few days after Margaret's party. "How could he do this to you? Oh, that Bridgit! If only I'd been there. I swear I would have—"

"What," Audrey had laughed, "wrestled her to the ground? You keep forgetting you're pregnant."

"All the more of me to keep in line!" Pam moaned. "Really, though, I feel terrible."

"So you reunited me with James for a while, Pam. Why feel so bad because things didn't work out?"

"Because I'm Catholic, I don't know! Because I'm

wracked with guilt over the silliest things. Because . . ."

Audrey sensed in her friend's pause that Pam was trying to decide how to deliver awkward news. "Spit it out, kiddo," she said. "What's the word around town? I know you've heard something."

"It's just . . . my friend Lindy, the travel agent, you know? She works in the same office with a friend of Bridgit's, and it turns out Bridgit's been bragging all over the place about getting back together with 'her old love.' She's even told her boss she can't leave the country with her beloved still recuperating from having his Beemer stolen and being mugged and all that crap. Plus—"

"Can we wrap this up, please?"

"It gets worse, Audrey. Lindy said Bridgit insists she 'saved' James that night, that she took care of him, nursed him back to consciousness when he passed out in her kitchen, even . . . oh! That wench! She slept with him, Audrey. That night, the night he was mugged, or maybe the next morning, I don't know, but he spent the night at her place, and you know what that means! No man could ever escape a snare like that."

Audrey had squeezed her eyes shut at this news, wondering how soon after her own night with James all this had happened. "He never made any sort of commitment to me, Pammy," she murmured. "Nothing was ever . . . promised, I mean."

"He's bought a ticket for Paris, Audrey," her friend had added. "I'm so sorry."

James had called the next weekend. Audrey told him she'd interviewed for the new job and expected an offer, he mentioned how much he missed her. She said she'd decided to keep the house and contacted the historical society, he reported the buyer had changed his mind, anyway.

"You were right," he said, finally, "to stop me, at Mom's party. I was so sure, though, until that moment. So sure we were supposed to be together, that we could make it work, despite my mother."

Audrey paused, determined to remain clear-headed and calm. "Maybe we could have," she answered. "If things were different." She enjoyed talking with him, enjoyed hearing the sound of his voice, and admitted she missed seeing him. But she trusted her original instinct that told her James belonged in her past.

Her mother had been a surprising ally in her struggle to convince herself she'd done the right thing. The evening of

Margaret's party, Yvonne sought out her daughter in her room, saying she'd been thinking of Audrey's father and the effect he must have had on Pritch to prompt him to leave Laura. "Your father could be intimidating, you know." She sat beside Audrey on her bed. "And over-protective, of all of us, at times." Yvonne described how concerned he'd been when James called Audrey when she was only sixteen. "Daddy asked me to stop you from getting 'too involved.' He was afraid you'd get hurt, that's all," she insisted, "but when I spoke with Mrs. Sullivan on the phone—"

She paused at Audrey's shocked expression. "Yes, Margaret and I spoke, back then," she said, "but never met until today. She had reservations about you two dating, too, said it was 'inappropriate,' that sort of thing. She had more on her mind than your age, I'm afraid." Yvonne glanced at her daughter. "After what happened today, I thought you should know."

Audrey had recalled her mother's words as she listened to James apologize over the phone. He admitted he'd been to see Bridgit the day of the mugging, but failed to mention he'd spent the night with her. Audrey was hardly surprised. Some people, she decided, would always gloss things over, pretend certain wrongs were all right, diminish their guilt by wishing away their mistakes rather than owning up to them. Some people, she knew, were not trustworthy. Maybe that's what her father had tried to teach her, all those years ago. Audrey smiled sadly. He should've known I'd have to learn the hard way, she mused.

"Bridgit and I have talked a lot, this past week," James had added.

She'd shut her eyes and rubbed her temple, the sound of his voice reaching her as though through a long tunnel, his words anticipated before they were spoken.

"Suddenly my mother doesn't care if we sell the house," he continued, "and she's doing all right on her new medications, so . . ." His voice trailed off.

"Enjoy Paris, Jimmy," she said.

"Audrey." He paused. "I'll always wonder—"

"So will I."

Returned to her shoveling, she wished a long, dreary winter on the city of Paris as she reveled in the clear December night. The Rochester area had thawed quickly after the early November storm, and enjoyed a few weeks of unusual temperatures that rarely neared freezing. Audrey slid the shovel along, thankful now her mother had insisted they take advantage of the weather and pave the driveway right away.

"It's a pet peeve of mine," Yvonne had argued, winking at her grandson. "That popping sound of driving on gravel makes me certain one of the tires is about to pop, too."

Her mother's attention to the house—and Julian—had allowed Audrey to concentrate on her interview and subsequent start to her new job. Her interview had been a formality, with the head of Human Resources at the Moon Resort already convinced she was the perfect candidate. He cited not only her experience, but her performance in the previous interview and the polite way she'd stayed in touch after being turned down for another position.

"Your perseverance and professionalism precede you," she'd been told.

Audrey had spent the past four weeks acclimating herself to her new job, while her mother had set into motion a dozen projects around the house. As soon as the inspection was done and with Pritch's help in hiring contractors, critical concerns such as the furnace and roof were addressed right away. Repainting, wallpapering, and floor repairs were scheduled for after the holidays, with more external repairs slated for the spring.

Pritch had been right when he'd reported the foundation sound and the frame sturdy. Only a few beams had to be replaced and bracing installed in some areas. Though the chimney remained in need of repairs—and a good cleaning—it did not have to be rebuilt. Audrey had breathed a sigh of relief with each piece of good news, despite the fact her mother's financial support and enthusiasm seemed limitless.

Yvonne also seemed to have set aside any lingering concerns regarding Pritch as contractors were scheduled and the first jobs progressed. When he suggested an old coworker who could give them a good deal, she elbowed him good-naturedly. "No cutting corners, now," she chided. "Let's get the best man for the job, eh?"

Pritch had bristled. "Would you care to take over, Mrs. Conarroe?" he'd asked. "I could leave for Philadelphia early then, be out of the way altogether."

Audrey had glanced at her mother, who simply waved away Pritch's defensive question. "Of course not," Yvonne replied. "You've been a terrific help around here, Harrison, with the house and . . . otherwise." She signaled toward the ceiling in the direction of Julian's room, where her grandson had gone to finish homework. "You're going to be greatly missed."

Yvonne had confessed to Audrey that she still did not fully trust Pritch, despite his efforts and help with the house, and his obvious love for Julian. "I keep waiting for him to show his true colors," she admitted, "but perhaps he already has."

Both Pritch and Yvonne had been instrumental in getting so much work scheduled so quickly. Pritch had found many contractors eager to take on their projects during the off-season, with some curious about the old farmhouse, apparently intrigued by its age and history.

Audrey hesitated as a shovel-full of snow landed in a bank, realizing she hadn't dreamed of the female fugitive since her last night in Nashville. She had read through the entire diary, however, and come across a disturbing passage describing a female slave who showed up one bitter night, an infant, dead from exposure, clutched in her arms.

"We had received no word to expect a visitor," Nell Morris wrote. "Indeed, she appeared at the front entrance, blind to the dangers of such a brazen act, while Warren worked in the barn, tending our ill mare. She fell into my arms, wild with grief, hysterical with the many miseries of her desperate existence. Truly, she is the sister I was never given, and I shall treat her as such as long as she'll remain. She requires considerable nursing, which I alone shall provide, at the ready to defend her mightily against all threats of capture.

"Her own still child she would not surrender; indeed, she slept that night with her burden held dear to her heart. Only in the morn's light could we reason with her, assure her Warren would lay her son to proper rest. Only then did she allow us to relieve her, her eyes—fevered by madness mere hours before—now dried, dulled, empty of all but frank despair."

Shortly after, Warren and Nell Morris were warned to discontinue their work on the Railroad. "It appears we are under watch," Nell Morris wrote, "and no longer serve as a safe refuge. How we shall miss our role as God's agents on this long, anguished road."

Audrey scanned the porch, imagining the best spot for the plaque the local historical society planned to place there when exterior repairs and painting were complete. The plaque would designate the house as a stop on the Underground

Railroad, establishing it as a historical site thanks to the proof provided by the diary.

She glanced at the front door of her home and the wreath that hung there, then at the windows where she'd placed white candles for the holidays. How inviting the old house must have been to escaped slaves, she mused, their bodies yearning for Southern warmth while their hearts compelled them to venture farther and farther north. How devastating it must have been to be torn from one's family, forced to leave the only people who loved you so completely, who needed you as much as you needed them, simply because you were their own.

She shook her head to stop the eerie tingle that ran up her spine, recalling the day her sister had asked her to move in and help with her newborn nephew, the day she'd turned her back on her family. Never again, she promised the broad night. Never again.

Audrey pulled off her left glove to admire Laura's resized diamond ring as it reflected the crystalline snow and the sequined sky. Then she tucked her chin inside the collar of her coat, inhaling the lingering scent of Laura's favorite perfume, which she'd begun to wear, too.

She continued to shovel, thinking of the new neighbor who'd stopped with her baby to talk one Saturday while Audrey was raking, after the snow had melted and the ground had dried a bit. The woman introduced herself as Mindy Steinman and said she heard from Mr. Benton that the farmhouse was going to be preserved. She added she was an artist and would like to paint a portrait of the house, when she had some spare time. "Of course, I don't have much of that these days," she said with a laugh, gesturing toward her sleeping daughter. "But I'm sure that'll change."

Audrey mentioned that her friend, Pam, recently had a baby girl, and she was going to be the child's godmother.

Mindy suggested they all get together some time. "I love to meet other young families," she said. "This neighborhood isn't exactly full of them." She asked if Audrey had any children.

"Only one," Audrey answered, wondering at her racing heartbeat. "He's my nephew, actually, and we're not all that young, I guess. He'll be fourteen in January."

"Perfect!" Mindy exclaimed. "He'll make a great baby-sitter next year." She promised to exchange phone numbers, thanking Audrey again for taking the initiative to preserve her historic home.

Audrey sent another shovel-full of snow flying. She thought of Laura, the house's original savior, and caught her breath as the front door opened just as she imagined her sister emerging from its shadows.

Julian stepped out onto the lit porch and zipped up his new parka, smoothing the front of it and pulling the hood over his head. Audrey recalled how proud he'd been the first time he showed her the coat after a shopping trip with his grandmother. She still thought it made him appear larger than ever, certainly no longer a small boy. She mused at how much he'd seemed to grow, and mature, in just the past few weeks.

Julian waved to his aunt. "Dad called," he shouted, his excitement evident in his voice, the sound of which boomed in the night air despite the snow's muffling effect.

As her nephew approached, Audrey could tell he was trying to suppress a grin by the way he forced the corners of his mouth in, forming endearing dimples in his round cheeks. Julian had been grinning a lot, lately, and Audrey was fairly certain of the reason. She was barraged by a litany of details regarding Tina, his date, when she picked him up from the school dance, and since then he'd talked with "his girl" on the phone nearly every night. His newly animated personality, quick laughter, and boundless energy reminded her of the way Laura had always described her young son—boisterous but sweet, intensely affected by every emotion he felt and everything he experienced. Audrey suspected he might be using Tina as an excuse, actually, to stop brooding and get on with the life he wanted to lead. She understood well the way a relationship, however brief, can draw one's focus away from one's self, providing a new perspective and a chance to redirect misguided energy.

"Dad said he'll be here by Christmas Eve," Julian announced.

Audrey leaned on her shovel as her nephew rambled on regarding his father's plans. She recalled the overcast morning they'd stood in the same spot, waving good-bye to Pritch as his truck disappeared around the corner. Julian had said he couldn't wait for Christmas and liked knowing his dad would only be a state away. Then he'd squinted at the house, his voice strained when he spoke again.

"He asked if I wanted to go with him," he said.

Audrey had known this, had heard this from Pritch. She

also knew the boy's father encouraged him to stay with her, at least for now, in the town he shared with his friends, in his mother's house. And she knew her nephew had confessed his relief when the decision was finally made, admitting he loved the old house and his aunt. Pritch had told her all this, and thanked her, before leaving.

"I came here alone, and I leave with a family," he'd said, adding his belief Audrey had been right to break up with James. "Questions of color aside," he explained, "I remain convinced you deserve better."

"He said I was welcome to go," Julian had continued. "But . . ." He'd crossed his arms and bowed his head, pinching the bridge of his nose, his arms soon dropping in defeat as the tears finally came.

Audrey had reached for her nephew, surprised by the strength of his embrace and the sudden force of his sobbing. He wept angrily, his body rigid, gripping his aunt as though he'd fall away if he released her. "I know Dad had to go," the boy wailed, "but Mom, she was supposed to stay. She was supposed to stay!"

She held him and rocked him, then, held him and rocked him, consoling her sister's son before leading him back inside their home.

Now, shovel in hand, she glanced at her beaming nephew, then past him toward their wide, white yard. "I never realized how beautiful winter can be," she murmured.

Julian scooped up a snowball and threatened her with it, then tossed it aside with a grin. "Maybe you were too busy hating it." He sank into a snow bank, sending clumps of snow tumbling to the driveway.

"Hey," Audrey chided. "Go play somewhere else, would you?"

Julian tightened his hood before flipping backward into the yard, laughing as he tossed more light snowballs toward his aunt.

"Hey!" She dropped her shovel, grabbing fistfuls of snow to throw back at him. He laughed and ran, prompting her to climb over the snow bank, her boots sinking into soft drifts.

"That'll teach you," she yelled, throwing her last.

Julian scoffed as he sat and then lay back in the middle of the yard. "Me? You started it." He stared upward for a moment. "The Big Dipper," he said, pointing.

Audrey followed his gaze to the sky. "The Drinking

Gourd."

"Huh?"

She explained she'd checked out some library books about the Underground Railroad. "It's from a song the slaves sang, to teach others to follow the North Star to freedom. They called the Big Dipper the Drinking Gourd."

Julian said it, too, as though tasting the term for the first time.

Audrey looked again to the winter sky, then back to her nephew as she heard a rustling sound. She grinned while he made an angel in the snow.

He continued to stare upward, his limbs spread. "Didn't they talk a lot about flying, too?"

As he pressed the snow into shape with his moving arms and legs, Audrey noted again how much he'd grown, as though the confidence he'd gained since meeting his father had sparked his body to take the next, needed steps toward manhood.

"Yes," she finally said, suddenly aware she'd been nodding mutely.

He leaned out of the angel, pushed himself up to stand next to it, and proudly surveyed his work as he brushed snow off his parka.

Audrey wished Laura could see him. She strained to feel her sister's presence in the closeness of the snow, the vastness of the winter sky, the shock of crisp air that filled her lungs. Again she watched the heady vapors that escaped her—proof that she breathed constantly, that she lived.

"They said if you closed your eyes and wished with your heart, you could fly anywhere you wanted."

She watched Julian tilt his chin toward the stars, then lower his gaze to meet hers, his face illuminated not by the heavens or the snow or the brisk winter air, but by the well of joy and possibilities he now seemed to harbor. As easily as she recognized his mother's wisdom in his next words, Audrey saw her own reflection in her nephew's wide, slow smile.

"Isn't it something, though," he said, his face lifted to the sky once again, "when you realize you can fly, but there's nowhere else you'd rather go?"